*She wasn't ber̶a̶t̶i̶n̶g̶ ̶h̶i̶m̶ ̶f̶o̶r̶ tearing her heart out, nor was she throwing herself on his broad chest in joy that he'd come home safely. Her hands weren't even shaking. Those twenty-three months had taught her something besides arithmetic, after all.*

*How kind the years had been to her, Gray was thinking. He'd aged, a century it felt like, with scars and weathered wrinkle lines, but Daphne had ripened. Only her unruly blond curls remained of the hoyden who used to tag at his heels, but now the vibrant gold locks were cropped into a short fashionable do, with a ribbon threaded through to keep the curls off her perfect face. She looked like a wood nymph, innocent and seductive both.*

*When it came to fools, he'd take every prize. . . .*

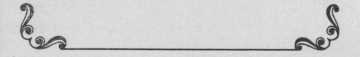

# LADY WHILTON'S WEDDING

## Barbara Metzger

FAWCETT CREST • NEW YORK

A Fawcett Crest Book
Published by Ballantine Books
Copyright © 1995 by Barbara Metzger

All rights reserved under International and Pan-American Copyright Conventions. Published in the United States of America by Ballantine Books, a division of Random House, Inc., New York, and simultaneously in Canada by Random House of Canada Limited, Toronto.

Library of Congress Catalog Card Number: 94-90870

ISBN 0-449-22351-5

Manufactured in the United States of America

First Edition: May 1995

10  9  8  7  6  5  4  3  2  1

to Ramona the Donor
and all the other givers of this world

# *Chapter One*

*It* was an arranged marriage. Unlike most such marriages of convenience, this one was arranged by the bride-to-be herself. Miss Daphne Whilton of Woodhill Manor, Hampshire, left the crowded lawn of her birthday party and approached Lord Graydon Howell, heir to the Earl of Hollister, where he stood apart from the other guests under a shading elm tree. She kicked him on the shin to get his attention and said, "All of the other boys are toads. You'll have to marry me, Gray."

Lord Graydon rubbed his leg and looked back toward the others. The boys were tearing around, trying to lift the girls' skirts. The girls were shrieking or giggling or crying for their mamas, who were inside taking tea with Lady Whilton. At least Daffy never carried on like that. And she could bait her own hook. He nodded. "I s'pose," he said, and they shook hands to seal the contract.

Their parents were delighted to join two ancient lineages and fortunes so pleasantly. Their children would be out of the reach of fortune hunters and adventurers and misalliances. Besides, the couples were lifelong friends and neighbors. The Hollisters preferred the politics and parties of London to the rural pleasures of their Hampshire seat, whereas the Whiltons chose to spend their days close to the land on their Woodhill barony, but the two families spent summers and the Christmas holidays in nearest and most welcome proximity. Their off-spring had played together since they were in leading strings. Each being an only child in the house, and the only children of nobility in the region, they were natural playmates.

Since he was the elder by three years, and a boy besides, with the run of the neighborhood, young Lord Graydon ran tame at Woodhill Manor. He often stayed there overnight when his parents accepted a house party invitation elsewhere, rather than remaining in solitary, servant-surrounded splendor at Howell Hall. It was Graydon who taught Daphne to ride, albeit not in a style conducive to her mother's mental ease, had Lady Whilton known. And 'twas the handsome lad who taught Lady Whilton's curly-haired blond cherub to climb trees, catch fish, and carry the hunting bag without complaining. Miss Whilton, on the other hand, caused her young Lancelot to learn how to repair dolls, how to sit through countless imaginary teas, and, most important, how to be gentle with small, fragile things.

Daphne thought the sun rose and set with Graydon's company; Graydon supposed he liked Daphne better than his spaniel, who sometimes didn't come when he called. Daffy always did.

If not made in Heaven or Almack's sacred precincts, the proposed marriage still gladdened the hearts of the readers of both *Debrett's Peerage* and purple-covered romance novels, and the couples' fond parents. No announcement was made, of course, due to the tender ages of the pair, nor papers drawn, since neither father wanted to force his child's hand if preferences changed with time. No formal notice would be taken, the earl and the baron decided, for ten years, until Miss Whilton turned eighteen and had a London Season. But the understanding was accepted, acknowledged, and toasted with champagne. And watered wine for the children.

Succeeding years did bring changes, as time usually does. First, the death of Daphne's aunt Lillian brought her two new boys to dote upon, the little brothers she never had. Torrence and Eldart were just five and six when their mother took her own life, rather than suffer their father's profligate ways. At twelve Daphne was too young to understand the servants' gossip about Spanish whores, French pox, and Greek love, but she knew they didn't mean Uncle Albert was well traveled. Her father's brother was a mean-spirited, angry-tempered man who kicked dogs, shouted at children, and had hair growing out of his ears and nose. Daphne didn't blame Aunt Lillian a bit, despite the scandal. She vowed to be even kinder to the quiet, timid little boys her father fetched home from London, rather than leave to Albert's untender mercies. So she passed on Graydon's teachings while he was away at school, the riding and fishing, skating and sledding. Her letters to him were full of her cousins' achievements, how Dart could climb Gray's favorite elm tree, how Torry loved the rope swing Gray had built for her.

If Graydon felt the merest twinge of jealousy when he read his old playmate's letters, it was more for her carefree days than for the affection she was showering on her little cousins. Why, Daffy spent a scant few hours a day with her governess, then some minutes practicing her scales and perfecting her needlework, while Graydon was hard at work at his studies and his sports. He hardly had time to learn the ways of the world, which, for a teenaged boy, meant women, wine, and wagering. Those happened, in fact, to be the vices Daphne believed Uncle Albert indulged in, and which she therefore, for her cousins' sakes, deplored.

Uncle Albert couldn't have cared less about the opinion of his brother's girl-child. He could hardly remember the chit's name. Nor was he jealous of her attention to his sons either, no more than Graydon. Albert was only glad someone had relieved him of the burden of the brats' upkeep. For certain he was not about to offer his brother any recompense for taking in the motherless boys.

Then Daphne's father died in a hunting accident and Uncle Albert became baron. He got so castaway, celebrating his succession to the title and estates, that he missed the funeral altogether, to no one's regret.

Graydon stood by Daphne's side during the service, while his parents supported her mother. He didn't complain when Daffy's tears made his neckcloth go limp, although it was the first creditable Waterfall he'd managed to tie, nor that she wadded up his monogrammed handkerchief and stuffed it in her pocket. She was his to comfort and protect, especially now that she had no father. She was his even if, at fifteen, she was as graceful as a broomstick, with a figure to match. His father nodded approvingly.

Graydon returned to his books and burgeoning manhood. Daphne washed and ironed his handkerchief and slept with it under her pillow. With foresight, Graydon's parents stayed on in Hampshire to assist Lady Whilton. Despite having more funds at his disposal than he ever hoped or dreamed of, Uncle Albert would have tossed all of his relatives, his own sons included, out on their ears and sold off the property to finance his gambling, if not for the entail. Even then he would have emptied the coffers and beggared the estate, except for the power and influence of Lord Hollister, who was watching out for his friend's widow's interest. The earl threatened to take Albert to court if he mishandled Dart's inheritance; he threatened to see him blackballed from every club and gaming den in London if he misused the widow or the children.

Lady Whilton could have taken her handsome jointure and her well-dowered daughter and set up a comfortable household of her own, but she stayed on at Woodhill Manor for the sake of the boys and the tenants. The new Lord Whilton stayed away for the most part, except when he came to see what monies he could bleed from the Manor acres, what costly repairs he could refuse to make, which servant he could dismiss to save the price of his wages. But Lady Whilton stood firm, the bailiff and her loyal butler beside her. Daphne was always nearby, too, which only served to infuriate her raddled uncle further, since he believed the earl would have kept his long nose out of Whilton business if the chit weren't to be Lord John Hollister's future daughter-in-law.

"And a good thing you made a cradle-match, too," Uncle Albert sniped at his ungainly young niece whose unruly curls refused to stay in ribbons or braids, whose skirts were muddied from playing with the barn cat, and whose face tended to break out in spots. "For you'd never snabble such an eligible *parti* as Hollister's whelp on your own, no matter how large your dowry."

Daphne stuck her tongue out at him from behind her mother's back. If Graydon were here, she told herself, he'd call the old mawworm out. But Graydon wasn't there. He was at university, practicing profligacy, or in London being introduced to his parents' world, which amounted to the same thing. Veering between the *ton*'s debs and the demimondaines, he might have agreed with Uncle Albert's assessment of the betrothal, if he thought of it at all. Marriage and the future and Hampshire seemed an eternity away.

Barely a year later, Graydon's mother contracted an inflammation of the lungs at a boating party and passed on between the ball at Devonshire House and one of Catalani's solo performances. Her last comment was that she'd be sorry to miss the fireworks at Vauxhall.

Distraught, Lord Hollister could not bear being alone at Howell Hall in the country with so much extra time on his hands, since even the local assemblies and card parties were denied his mourning state. The earl leased the Hall to an India-trade nabob and returned to his life in London, throwing himself deeper into politics and errands for the Foreign Office. He did maintain a warm correspondence with Lady Whilton, and he did make sure Albert knew he kept his interest there. Lord

Hollister's presence in London kept in check Albert's greed, if not his gambling and affinity for low company.

Daphne and Graydon met occasionally when his father sent him to Hampshire to confer with the Hall's steward. He came between university terms and house parties and walking tours and hunts in Scotland. They still roamed the countryside together, Daphne sopping up the tales of his experiences, expurgated, of course, like a thirsty seedling. And like a tender flower, she turned to his warmth as to the sun. Like the sun, he smiled down, accepting her worship as his due.

He taught her to shoot and to use a bow and arrow, and to retrieve his practice cricket shots. He also instructed her in what ladies of fashion were wearing and reading and thinking. In turn Daphne taught him not to laugh at a girl's first attempts to bat her eyelashes or flutter her fan. His knuckles were raw from that lesson, but he learned, the same as she learned the latest dance steps. They were the best of friends. She still thought he was Romeo and Adonis and the hero of every one of Maria Edgeworth's novels combined; he thought she was all right, for a dab of a chick.

Then the little boy cousins went away to school, Daphne and her mother agreeing they required more than petticoat governance. After all, Eldart was going to be baron one day, and not that far off either, if the wages of sin took their usual toll. Dart needed a broader education and a stable male influence to offset his father's reprehensible example.

Lady Whilton also felt that her daughter should get a shade of town bronze before being thrust into the London whirl next year. Daphne was too much the hoyden still, with her open, countrified ways, to find acceptance among the *haute monde*. She was too innocent and trusting to survive there, besides. So Lady Whilton took a house in Brighton for the boys' summer vacation, where Lord Hollister happened to be in attendance on the prince.

Daphne adored the sea bathing in the morning with her cousins, then visiting the shops and the tearooms in the afternoons with the crowds of young people her own age. There were picnics and dancing parties and amateur theatrics, just for those too young to take part in the doings among Prinny's crowd. Daphne didn't even mind being left alone evenings with her books and the fashion magazines while her mother went about to the concerts and fetes and banquets at the Regent's oniondomed pleasure palace, escorted by Lord Hollister. Daphne played at jackstraws and speculation with the boys. Then she played piquet with her mother's cousin Harriet, an impoverished, opinionated spinster who was thrilled to act as companion to Lady Whilton and occasional chaperone to Daphne, especially since Dart and Torry had a tutor of their own. Not even schoolboys were exempt from Cousin Harriet's dislike of the male species. In Lady Whilton's eyes, this made Harriet the perfect chaperone for Daphne on those afternoons when the baroness was preparing for the night's festivities ahead or resting after an early morning return from the previous evening's entertainment. Lord Hollister was insisting she deserved such gaiety, after being buried in the country so long. Cleo Whilton was finding that she agreed with him.

Daphne thrived. She grew an inch and gained a few pounds—some even in the right places—and her complexion cleared, to her mother's relief. She made friends, and her bow to royalty, and she even made her way through the snakepit of petty jealousies among adolescent females. She didn't need to compete with the other well-born daughters for the lordlings' regard; she had Gray. Her calm and composure won her approval among the hostesses, and her unthreatening friendliness made her a favorite among the boys, when Cousin Harriet let them approach at all. If Daphne wasn't quite blossoming, she was at least a bud ready to be unfurled. In London, for Graydon Howell.

## Chapter Two

*H*air up, hems down. Remember your governess's etiquette lessons, forget the stablehands' vocabularies. Curtsy at the drop of a title, but never run, laugh out loud, or dance with the same man more than twice, even if he is your almost-betrothed.

Daphne's head would have been spinning, if not for her early forays into society at Brighton. Lady Whilton congratulated herself that her daughter had done so well: She was well behaved, well informed, well dressed, and well endowed. Welcome to London, Miss Whilton.

Daphne was presented at the Queen's drawing room, then at a ball in her honor at Howell House, where she and her mother were staying, at the earl's insistence. They couldn't very well take up residence with Uncle Albert, not when he'd turned Whilton House into a sinkhole of depravity no respectable member of the *ton* would enter. Besides, he hadn't invited them. The earl had, citing the absurd expense of renting a suitable location for the

Season, and the acres of empty rooms at his Grosvenor Square mansion. It would do his heart good, he said, to see the ballroom in use again, to hear the sounds of music and laughter. And there could be no hint of impropriety attached, not with the earl's widowed sister and the baroness's misanthropic spinster cousin in residence, and his son not. Graydon had bachelor quarters at the Albany, but he was there to lead Daphne out for the first dance at her come-out ball.

"I can see I'm going to have to look to my laurels," he told her as they took the lead spot for the cotillion.

Daphne was too lost in her own dreamworld to pay attention. Here she was, eighteen and finally Out, in the arms of the most attractive man in the ballroom, and he was her own dear Graydon. Soon their betrothal would be formally announced, then the wedding, and her life would be started at last. She floated on a cloud of joy, *his* hand in hers, *his* spicy cologne scenting the air, *his* flowers in her hair, *his* locket at her neck. His. Life was so intoxicating, she had no need for champagne.

"I say, success gone to your head already, that you don't even listen to another compliment?"

She looked up at him, into teasing brown eyes she knew so well. "Oh, I'm sorry, Gray. I was woolgathering, I suppose, just thinking how happy I am right now. The room looks so lovely, and everyone has been so kind. What were you saying?"

"I was trying to pour the butter-boat over your head, brat, by telling you what a success you'll be by morning. You'll have every beau in town at your feet by week's end, unless I miss my guess. They'll be writing poems to your eyebrows or your elbows,

*11*

or whatever poppycock is in fashion this sennight. Just see that your head doesn't get turned by all the praise."

"Gammon," she said with a laugh, flashing her dimples at him. Trust Gray to try to make her feel comfortable when all eyes in the room were on them, as if she cared what anyone else thought of her. He'd already complimented her with a wide grin before the family supper earlier. His father had said she was almost as pretty as her mother at that age, high praise indeed, but Gray had whispered, "Fustian, no one can hold a candle to my Daffy."

It wasn't just Spanish coin he was handing her either, Graydon reflected. His little tagalong chum had improved no end. She almost reached his shoulder now, for one thing, especially if you counted the blond curls piled high on top of her head. They were threaded through with blue ribbons that matched her eyes, and the white roses he'd sent, on his aunt's advice. Daphne was dressed all in white, of course, but with a gauzy overskirt embroidered with tiny blue flowers that made her seem a fairy sprite. That fall of lace at the neckline was a clever touch, too—Lady Whilton's fine hand, no doubt—adding a hint of mystery where he knew very well there wasn't much of a secret, or anything else. Still, she was the comeliest deb of this season, he thought with pride, but perhaps too comely. Those dimples were deuced appealing.

Gray frowned over Daphne's head at the young bucks on the sidelines who were ogling his partner as if she were a tempting morsel. "You're no lobster patty," he fumed out loud, causing her to miss a step.

She giggled. "If that's a sample of the handsome compliments I can expect to receive, you needn't worry my head will swell."

"Not what I meant at all, brat, and you know it. I just don't like the way those chaps are looking at you, like cats about to pounce. Stop showing those dimples, blast it!"

She laughed the harder. Dear, dear Gray.

"I'm serious, Daffy, you have to be careful. You'll be all the crack, a regular Toast. Add a dowry rich enough to set the poorest makebait up on Easy Street, and they'll be after you like flies on honey. And those whose dibs are already in tune are looking for a pretty, well-born chit to be mother to their sons. Deuce take it, you're the daughter of a baron, with an earl sponsoring you."

"Do you think that's enough to make people forget about Uncle Albert?"

The current baron had arrived that evening at Howell House, uninvited. Luckily he came before most of the invited guests, for he stood in the entryway ranting that Daphne was way too young and gauche to be presented, much less engaged. She wasn't betrothed, not formally, but Uncle Albert never asked, too concerned with losing the interest on her dowry. He was also too castaway to put up much of a fuss when Graydon and two footmen bundled him into a hackney and sent him home before he could ruin Daphne's big night.

Remembering how the man stank of stale whiskey and staler linen, Graydon brightened. "Right, no one would want that dirty dish in the family. I cannot imagine how he and your father came from the same parents."

"Neither could Papa. He used to call him Awful

13

Albie, you know, and wondered if Grandmother had played her husband false."

"Nice talk, Daffy. Don't let the old tabbies hear you or they'll label you fast. You'll never get vouchers to Almack's."

"Sally Jersey already promised them. So did Princess Lieven, I'll have you know."

"Lud, when you show up at the Marriage Mart, every basket-scrambler in Town will be sniffing at your skirts."

"If you're so worried about other men paying their addresses," Daphne told him in what she thought was a reasonable tone, instead of the breathless yearning she really felt, "why don't we announce the betrothal tonight?"

Graydon had to reach up to loosen a neckcloth that was suddenly too tight. "Tonight? No, no, there's no reason to rush the blast—ah, blessed thing. I only meant you shouldn't go putting on airs like every other belle who makes a splash."

Daphne looked away and bit her lip. Graydon misinterpreted her disappointment. "I'm not saying you will, Daff, just that it'll be hard to resist all the lures cast your way. But then that's what this Season is for, isn't it? To give you time to meet other chaps, to know your own mind."

To know her own mind? She'd known what she wanted since she was six! She wasn't about to change it now. But that was just like Gray to be so fair and considerate. Of course, the thought of her falling top over tail for another man was too silly to mention, so she just danced on happily.

Graydon wondered at her silence and the knowing smile that softly curled at the edges of her mouth. Deuce take it, when had little Daphne turned into such a charmer? And why, for heaven's sake? He looked around to see if anyone else noticed that beguiling grin. "Everyone who's anyone is here tonight," he said, caught between pride and chagrin.

"Everyone who matters to me was here for dinner."

Since they'd dined *en famille*, Graydon's chest swelled and he relaxed. She was still his sweet little Daffy. This first dance together should put his mark on her for anyone unaware of the understanding between them. A few words here and there should refresh a few other memories, so he really didn't have to worry about the hordes of admirers waiting next to Lady Whilton hoping to sign Daphne's dance card. He couldn't have another set with her until the end of the evening, he knew, but would have to do his duty by every wallflower in the room, under his aunt's gimlet stare. He kissed Daphne's hand when he left, purposely lingering over her fingers so everyone noticed, and said, "Enjoy yourself, brat, but don't forget about me."

Forget about him? Forget to breathe, more like. Smiling, Daphne fingered the gold locket he'd given her. She was the luckiest girl alive! Graydon was the kindest, most handsome man in the world—and he was jealous!

Daphne was the success Graydon had predicted. Word of their almost-betrothal was circulated all over, but that simply made her more appealing to the bucks who liked a challenge, or the Tulips who liked to worship at some goddess's shrine without paying the ultimate sacrifice, marriage. She was a safe flirtation, and she was delighted to play this new game.

There were Venetian breakfasts and balloon ascensions, rides to Richmond and ridottos. Sightseeing and being seen in Hyde Park at the fashionable hour. Musicales, masquerades, and military parades. Morning calls, afternoon at-homes, three balls a night. Sometimes Graydon escorted the ladies; more often Lord Hollister did when the entertainments were too tame for his son. Daphne understood: Gray was letting her spread her wings. She was soaring.

Then came the night at the opera when she looked across the vast concert hall to see him, her almost-fiancé, Graydon Howell, in a private box with a lady no lady would recognize. Thud. Her plummeting spirits fell so hard, she was surprised the sound didn't drown out the tenor.

"Ignore it," Cousin Harriet hissed in her ear. "It's the way of the world."

"Not my world," Daphne protested.

"Of course not, you ninny. It's a man's world, and they're all alike." Cousin Harriet had never married, and had never met the man who could make her regret that fact. She pointed out Lord Oglethorpe with his hands all over Lady Armbruster, while Lady Oglethorpe was being ogled by Sir Gervase Ashton. Lord Armbruster, across the aisle, had his arm across some demirep's shoulder, and on and on.

But not Gray. Those old court-cards, that reckless here-and-thereian, but not her idol, her Lochinvar, her best friend.

Her knight's shining armor took a severe dent when Graydon nibbled on the woman's ear, and a bad case of tarnish when one of Daphne's new "friends" was quick to inform her at the first intermission that Lord Howell's "friend" was an actress from Drury Lane. It seemed that friendship meant something different here in London.

"Mama, I have the headache. May we go home early?"

"That was not well done of you," the Earl of Hollister lectured his son the next morning, having called at the Albany for the express purpose of ruining Gray's day, since Lord John's own pleasant evening had been cut short with weeping and recriminations. Four women—Daphne, her mother, that man-hating cousin, and his own sister Sondra, b'gad—could get up a deal of caterwauling.

Graydon didn't require anything else to make him miserable; his aching head already took its toll. After dinner with Fancine at the Pulteney, and dessert, to put it nicely, at her place, Gray had gone on to White's. Everyone there had wanted to know if his deliberate insult to Miss Whilton meant the understanding was off. Was the fair lady fair game? He might be able to whistle her fortune down the wind, but other chaps weren't so fortunate. That's when he'd heard his Daffy had left the Opera House near tears. Bets were running high against the odds of his winning the Toast's hand. He had to cover the wagers, of course—his pride demanded no less—and drink to each entry in the betting book. Then he had to stay and drink to show he wasn't really worried. Then he had a few more brandies at home, because he *was* really worried. He wasn't concerned Daffy'd take up with one of those fops who followed her around, but he was deuced sorry he'd hurt her feelings.

His head was pounding and his position was indefensible, yet he answered his father's sermon with: "Dash it, Daphne knows I'm not a monk."

"She's a sweet young thing, still new to the social rounds. It's her innocence that makes her so appealing, and at the same time so vulnerable. Who knows what she thinks? You could have shown a little discretion, however."

"Blister it, I have enough trouble keeping track of my own social calendar. Am I supposed to memorize hers, too?"

The earl studied his fingertips. "Perhaps it might be a good idea to move the wedding forward, to relieve her worries."

"The wedding? We're not even formally engaged! I'm not ready for leg shackles yet. By Jupiter, I've barely reached my majority. Most chaps wait till they're thirty or so to set up their nurseries."

"If you're having second thoughts about Miss Whilton, you'd do better to bring them out now, when she can make another choice. I'd hate to see it, naturally."

Graydon dragged his fingers through his already tousled hair. "Lud, that's not it. I know my duty to the name and all. You've told me often enough that there are no other Howells to succeed me, and Daffy's just what I'd want in a wife, if I wanted a wife now. Daffy's a right 'un. She'll understand. After all, she sat next to that Fanshaw fop all night and I'm not complaining."

"But she didn't sit in his lap. And Fanshaw's a viscount. He'd never go beyond the line."

"And I would, you think?"

"I think you could break her heart."

"Gammon, Daffy's too downy for that. She knows it's all in fun."

"Fun? Seeing my promised husband making a cake of himself over a . . . a lightskirt in front of half the *ton*? No, I do not consider that fun, Lord Howell."

"Cut line, Daffy, we aren't even engaged yet, and it's just your pride that's hurt. I said I'm sorry, and I swear I won't embarrass you that way again."

"You won't embarrass me by taking your fancy piece out in public, or you won't take her out at all?" she wanted to know. "There is a big difference, my lord."

They were dancing at Almack's, not the most propitious place for such a conversation, but Daphne hadn't been home the afternoon after the opera, not to Graydon, at any rate, and then he'd gone out of town to a mill planned ages ago. Almack's was his first opportunity to smooth the waters, and her stormy look told him he'd better paddle hard and fast. His apology hadn't worked, though. Daphne wanted her pound of flesh, too.

"You're asking me if I'll give up my, ah, outside interests before we're even betrothed?"

"I'm asking if you intend to be faithful to your vows or not, Graydon Ambrose Hastings Howell, and you very well know it."

He missed his step, causing the next couple in line to fumble. "The devil! We haven't taken any vows, Daffy!"

"We've been pledged for ages, haven't we?"

"That's different. After we're married, of course . . ."

"Oh, then I can take lovers now?"

19

He stopped dancing altogether, earning them frowns and mutters from the rest of the set. Gray pulled his partner to the side. "Don't be a widgeon. It's altogether different."

Daphne stood her ground. "Why? If you don't consider yourself promised, why should I?"

"It's different, that's why. Promised or not, you are supposed to stay pure and chaste for me—for your husband. It's the man who needs the experience."

Daphne stamped her foot, oblivious to the stares from those around them. "The deuce it is! Do you think I want a man like Uncle Albert? Is he experienced enough?"

Now Graydon was starting to lose his temper, too. "Blast it, are you comparing me to that old reprobate?"

"Why not? Everyone's been quick to keep me informed about your drinking and your reckless wagers and the low company you're keeping. What's so different there?"

He wanted to shake her, and would have, if not for Lady Drummond-Burrell's throat-clearing. "I am not like your uncle Albert," he ground out. "And you're making a mountain out of a molehill, brat. It's not like I'm even keeping a mistress or anything, just having a little fling here and there. It means nothing, Daffy."

"Obviously it's my feelings that mean nothing to you! You can't even give me your word!"

"After we're married, I swear!"

"After? If you loved me, you'd never look at another woman, before, during, or after!"

The music had stopped. Now everyone was staring at them, still on the sidelines of the dance area.

He tried to tug her farther out of the way, but she dug her feet in. He couldn't very well pick her up and toss her over his shoulder the way he used to. Instead he turned his back, trying to shield them from prying eyes. "What the devil does love have to do with anything, Daffy?"

"If you don't know that, Graydon Howell, then I don't want to know you!" she shouted. So much for a bit of circumspection. When he was sure they had every eye in the place on them, Daphne ripped the locket off her neck, threw it to the floor, and stamped on it twice for good measure. "That's what you've done to our understanding, you dastard!"

Now there was nothing for it but for Graydon to grab her arm and pull her after him, willy-nilly, into the refreshment room. He shoved a glass of punch into her hands. "For heaven's sake, Daffy, calm down. You're making a scene."

"I'll make more than a scene if you don't unhand me, sirrah. And stop calling me Daffy. I'm not that little girl who used to follow you around, happy just to be in your shadow. I'm a woman now, even if you haven't noticed, with a woman's feelings."

"Then act like one and drink your punch instead of looking daggers at me for everyone to see. And what am I supposed to call you? Miss Whilton? After wiping your nose for you a hundred times? Listen, things will look different in the morning. We'll go for a ride, talk this out."

"We have nothing more to say. Good evening, Lord Howell."

She made to leave him, but he grabbed her arm again and spun her around. "Dash it, Daffy, don't make this any worse. You can't stir up a bumble-broth at Almack's."

"Why not? Why can't I complain about my fiancé's lack of fidelity here, of all places? After all, everyone does it, they tell me. The best people, the highest sticklers, every one of them seems to cheat on their husbands and wives, if you listen to enough gossip. Why, even Sally Jersey is said to be having an affair with—"

He clamped his hand over her mouth, so she kicked him in the shin. Then she poured the contents of her punch glass over his head. "I don't care if they never let me back in this dreadful place, and I don't care if I never see you again either. I wouldn't marry you, Graydon Howell, if you were the last man on earth."

# Chapter Three

$\mathcal{A}$s far as public notices went, Daphne's went far indeed. And fast. By morning, everyone in London knew that her informal betrothal was infamously ended. What Rumor didn't spread, the gossip columns did. Daphne couldn't have put her nose outside even if she wanted to, even if it weren't all red from weeping. What she wanted was to get out of this wicked city of shattered illusions, out of his father's house of painful reminders. She wanted to go home to the country. The air was cleaner, the people were more honest, and one didn't have to work so hard at having a good time. Besides, after that outré outburst, she might be invited to another London party in a year or two, if she was lucky.

Lady Whilton and Cousin Harriet were even now making travel arrangements and overseeing the packing, when they weren't trading recriminations over the incident. Lady Whilton blamed her cousin for Daphne's intractability; Cousin Harriet blamed Mama for raising her daughter with blinders on.

While her relations bickered, Daphne took care of some housecleaning. A bundle of letters, a box of fairings, a monogrammed handkerchief, and a recently pressed white rose all joined the broken locket in the dustbin. With them went the last of her childhood.

So many years, so many dreams. So very, very stupid. Gray didn't love her and never had, except in an offhand, brotherly fashion. He was used to her, perhaps even fond of her, but he never loved her. He was prepared to do his duty by his family name and social standing eventually, that was all. He'd be comfortable married to his childhood pal. Daphne'd be miserable, even more miserable than she was now, if that were possible. She shredded those letters into bits so small, they could have been grains of rice, at a wedding that never took place.

Lady Whilton had a few broken dreams of her own, but she set them aside for her daughter's sake and took up the loose threads of her country life again. She was a mother first, she told herself as she visited tenant farms instead of the theatre, and sat in on church-lady committees instead of literary salons. She could catch up on her resting, reading, and needlework, fiend seize them all—and that wretched, wretched boy.

Cousin Harriet felt vindicated. She'd always said the only thing between a man's ears was a hatrack, that what they used for brains was between their legs. She'd just been proved right again, damn them all, especially that Howell fellow for making such a mingle-mangle of the whole thing. Harriet never wanted little Daphne to fall into a decline, and she never wanted her to dwindle into an old maid. Men did have their places, after all—in bed making children, and at the bank making money. If there was a way to do without them, Harriet certainly hadn't found it, loving her cousin's child and living on her cousin's largesse. That wasn't what she wanted for Daphne. Neither was a lying, cheating, womanizing, silver-tongued devil of a handsome man for a husband.

The lying, cheating, etc., non-husband-to-be was still in London, but not for long. He was a laughingstock among his friends, and a great deal poorer after paying off those exorbitant wagers at White's on his chances of turning Daphne up sweet. Sweet? She'd rather suck a lemon than read one of his letters, it seemed. They were all returned unopened. He paid up; the betrothal was off.

Graydon should have felt like a free man. He didn't. He shouldn't feel guilty for doing what every other man in London did, engaged, married, or otherwise. But he did. Damn and blast! He wasn't ready for parson's mousetrap, but he wasn't prepared to be the target for every matchmaking mama in town either. Two young ladies had already tripped outside his rooms, and one fell off her horse in front of him at the park. Peagooses all. If he wasn't ready to wed Daffy, he surely wasn't going to drop the handkerchief to some conniving miss who had designs on his fortune and title, and who couldn't ride. Why would a man marry someone he couldn't trust? A tiny voice that sounded remarkably like Daphne's echoed in his conscience: Why would a woman?

Deuce take it, the worst thing was, he couldn't even confide his confusion to his best friend. If she wouldn't answer his letters, she sure as Hades wasn't going to welcome him at Woodhill Manor. If the impossible brat weren't so damn honest and open . . . he wouldn't like her half so well.

Maybe it was for the best. Maybe she'd find a man worthy of the adoration he'd accepted as his due for all those years. Maybe she'd find a man to love her to distraction, like those heroes in the novels she was always reading. And maybe Gray would tear the dastard's heart out. With his teeth.

Did he love her? She was just Daffy, his fishing companion. She wasn't the most beautiful chit in the world, though not far behind, nor the most even-tempered or seductive. She wasn't even the brightest female of his acquaintance or the most talented. Then why did he feel that a vital part of him had gone missing, an arm or something? If he'd just taken her for granted, always there, always ready for anything, then why was he lost without a road map for his life? What was he going to do if he wasn't going to marry Daphne Whilton? The endless rounds of parties and sporting events didn't hold much appeal, nor did women who put a price tag on their charms. Daffy'd been his for the asking.

"You're asking me for advice? Now?" His father was no help. "How did I ever raise such a fool? You had what every man wants: the love of an honest woman who's an heiress to boot. And you toss it away for a bit of slap and tickle. Faugh! I wash my hands of you, you gudgeon. Besides, if you weren't my own son, I'd call you out. The gel's like a daughter to me and you insulted her, made it hard for her to show her face in town, dash it."

As upset as Lord Hollister was for Daphne's sake, he was more irate for his own loss. "And that means her mother won't put a foot out of Hampshire either, blast you. Deuced comfortable woman, Cleo Whilton."

Graydon put his glass down and sat up. "Meaning . . . ?"

"Meaning nothing yet, you cawker. And likely nothing ever, thanks to you. How can I go courting a woman whose daughter hates the sight of my son?"

Courting? His father and Daphne's mother? Now that he thought of it, they were perfect together. Lady Whilton had thrown herself into the earl's busy political schedule with pleasure, and she was the first woman the earl had squired about since the death of Graydon's mother.

"For all I know," his father was going on, "they hold me to blame for your sins. That Cousin Harriet's got us both tarred with the same brush anyway. Slammed the door in my face when they left. My own door, too." The earl stared morosely into his brandy glass.

Lud, now he had to feel guilty for blighting his father's chance for happiness, too, Gray thought, as he downed his own drink. The governor needed a hostess and social partner, and deserved a warm companion as much as anyone. There was no one Gray would rather see in his mother's place than Lady Whilton. She was already one of the family. Or had been. His father was right: She'd never take up with Gray or his family now.

27

"Deuced shame, too," the earl mumbled. "One of the finest females a fellow is like to come across."

"Lady Whilton?"

"Her, too. But I meant little Daphne. Sweetest gel *you'll* ever find. Too bad she thought you were some kind of god, a regular hero. The silly twit."

There was nothing for it but for Graydon to leave town. No, the country. If he was gone, perhaps Lady Whilton and the earl could get together without upsetting Daffy, who'd never had a selfish bone in her body. She wouldn't curse his father if he wasn't around to embarrass them all. So he'd leave. To hell with the empty London life, and to hell with the succession and his father's dreams of a government career for him. Graydon emptied his purse and bought himself a commission. She wanted a hero, he'd damned well be a hero.

Graydon was right, the older couple did manage to settle their differences eventually, without his presence as a source of conflict. They shared his letters from the Peninsula, glowed with pride when his name was mentioned in the dispatches, and worried together over rumored battles. What they didn't do was plan his homecoming.

Daphne never asked about him or showed any interest in his posted valor. Her mother was careful never to mention his name, in return for Daphne's agreeing to reenter society. Since it was either that or see her mother mope around the house all day, Daphne attended a few local assemblies. The men she danced with were mostly old friends like Squire Pomeroy's son Miles, too delighted Howell was out of her life and out of the country to ask awkward questions. The new young curate, a visiting scholar,

28

someone's nephew down from university, were all pleasant partners, undemanding and unexciting.

Lady Whilton got her to Brighton for the summer by pleading her cousins needed the holiday. Torrence had had the measles that spring at school and was still recuperating. Eldart was growing so fast that, at thirteen, he was almost as tall as Daphne. Lady Whilton insisted she couldn't manage them on her own, when Daphne tried to stay behind in Hampshire, and the boys added their persuasive voices. No one was more fun at the beach than Daphne, no one could ride better than their favorite cousin. How could she refuse? They were turning into fine lads, with no remnants of that nervous timidity they'd shown at first. Any father would have been proud, except Uncle Albert, who ignored his sons' existence altogether. Daphne believed this was a mixed blessing, for the rakehell's influence could only have been for the worse, but his cold disregard had to hurt the boys' feelings. Daphne had to supply what sense of security and family feeling she could, even if it meant going to Brighton.

There were some stares and titters at first, until Lady Minton ran off with her head groom. Daphne's broken troth was old hat, after all, and the scandalmongers had other bones to gnaw. Besides, Daphne spent the majority of her time with her cousins, letting her mother accept Lord Hollister's invitations with a clear conscience.

Daphne held out against London in the fall, but her mother was so disappointed and restless, she surrendered by the spring Season. She refused to stay at Howell House, though, no matter what arguments were brought to bear. If the expense of renting a house was too dear, they needn't go at all. If her mother was insecure without a male's presence, let them take their trusted butler, Ohlman. Daphne would not stay at *his* house under any conditions, even if he was on another continent. It wouldn't be proper, she said; it would lead to more gossip. It would hurt.

They took a small house in Half Moon Street, Mama, Cousin Harriet, Daphne, and Ohlman. It was nicely furnished, large enough for modest entertainments, and had its own stable mews, so Daphne could keep her own horses in Town and ride in the park mornings before the rest of society was out of bed. She found most of her pleasure there on horseback, or playing three-handed whist with Ohlman and Cousin Harriet when Mama was out with the earl, rather than at the grand balls and extravagant displays of wealth and social standing.

Miss Whilton was still popular at the parties she did attend, but not as outgoing as before. Now she had to look at each dance partner for ulterior motives. Was Lord This only interested in her fortune? Was Lord That only interested in seduction? Cousin Harriet's warnings stuck in her mind, that men were deceivers ever. Or was that Shakespeare? No matter, trust betrayed is a trust not easily bestowed again. She danced, she flirted, and she kept her distance from all the eligible men who would have paid her court. Daphne's gaiety became so forced, her mother reluctantly permitted her to return to the country she preferred over town life, to Lady Whilton's bemusement. Ruralizing was all well and good, but hadn't they had enough of that for all those years?

Lady Whilton had commitments that would keep her in Town, however, a dinner she was throwing for Lord Hollister's party members, a reception for one of the foreign delegations she was helping him plan.

So Daphne went home, along with Cousin Harriet and Ohlman, and Mama gave up the little house and moved in with the earl and his widowed sister. Why pay rent for one person when she was at Howell House most days anyway, conferring with his chef and housekeeper?

Lady Whilton begged Daphne to accompany her—and the earl—to a round of house parties that July and August, but Daphne didn't want to leave the boys with servants when they were home on vacation. Besides, it was time Dart learned about the land he would inherit someday—and in the not too distant future, either, if the rumors of Uncle Albert's continued dissipation were true.

In the fall there was the harvest and repairs to some of the tenant farms. Daphne had to stay in Hampshire to make sure Uncle Albert didn't come and divert the monies. And there was the Sunday school class she volunteered to teach. The roads were in disrepair from the fall rains, and the boys would be home soon for the holidays, anyway. Daphne stayed in the country; Mama stayed in London, or wherever Lord Hollister went. At least someone's courtship proceeded apace, to the point that Lord Hollister stayed with them over Christmas, and came to ask Daphne's permission to wed her mother in the spring.

"I know it's not the regular thing to do, asking a young chit like you, but your mother couldn't be happy if we were to cause you any discomfort.

There'll be family gatherings, you know, and the wedding itself, where you'll have to see my son. He is selling out after that last injury, finally. I begged him to, the succession, don't you know, and I can't lie to you and say I'm sorry he's coming home, because he's my son, for all his faults, and I've missed him."

"Of course you have, and I'd never want you to—"

"But he has his own rooms, so you won't have to see him night and day when you come stay with us in Grosvenor Square. I mean to say, you'll always have a home with us where you can be comfortable, even if I have to banish the nodcock to the Jamaican properties."

"No, no, that won't be necessary, my lord. We're adults. I'm sure we can rub along well enough." Daphne tried to swallow her panic, lest she let her own fears stand in the way of her mother's happiness. He did keep separate rooms, and he did have a different circle of acquaintances. And she hardly went to London anymore. She'd go less, after the wedding. "We were always friends," she said with more enthusiasm than she felt. "We should find no difficulty as relatives by marriage. It's been nearly two years, after all." She could have said how many days, hours, and minutes, but didn't.

Lord Hollister was smiling, relieved. "I knew you were a reasonable chit. Told your mother you were too sweet to hold a grudge so long."

Nineteen months, eight days, and seventeen hours since she'd seen the dastard. Nineteen awful months of hating him and missing him and worrying to death over his horrifying heroics. Daphne vowed to stay in the country until she put down roots like a turnip, rather than batten on the newlyweds—or have to worry about confronting Gray at every social gathering. She supposed it would get easier in time, except for the occasions when she had to look across the theatre at him every night, wondering if the woman in his box was a new bird of paradise or a prospective bride. No, Daphne rather thought she'd prefer to set up housekeeping somewhere with Cousin Harriet and raise pug dogs and roses. She hated pug dogs. And roses made her sneeze.

# Chapter Four

*J*ust when you think things cannot get any worse, they usually do. Lady Whilton decided to hold the wedding in the country. Not only would Daphne have to come face-to-face with Graydon at the ceremony, she'd have to entertain him at her own home! Howell Hall next door was still under lease to Mr. Foggarty of the India trade, so the earl and his family would stay at Woodhill.

"Don't you think they should put up at the inn?" Daphne tried. "It's bad luck for a bridegroom to see the bride before the wedding, and all that."

"Rubbish," Lady Whilton replied. "That's just for the day of the wedding, and I'll be so busy dressing and such, I won't get a chance to visit with John, anyway. Besides, can you really imagine the Earl of Hollister putting up at the Golden Crown?"

No, but she could well visualize his son there, drinking with the local farmers and flirting with the barmaids. And good riddance to him, too.

"But a tiny chapel wedding, Mama? Wouldn't you

rather have a lavish gala in London, with all of Lord Hollister's grand connections? Perhaps the prince might even come."

"He'd most definitely come, which is why John and I decided we'd rather have a quiet, private ceremony instead of some absurd public spectacle. That's for the young people. We're too old for all that folderol, and we've each been through it once, anyway. Now we want a simple country wedding, with only those closest to us."

Too close. Daphne was getting desperate. "Then why not one of those lovely little churches in Richmond? Or you could even hold the ceremony at the earl's house in Grosvenor Square."

"What, and have everyone thinking there was some hugger-mugger we were trying to hide? Never. There will be talk enough as is. Let it come after the fact, I say, after a perfectly respectable wedding in the church where I've worshiped for half my life. You have to admit our own St. Ethelred's is quaint and dear, especially when it's filled with flowers. Besides, your father lies in the graveyard there. I'd like to think of him at the wedding. He never wanted me to stay a widow, you know. I think he'd be pleased I'm marrying his friend John."

"Yes, Mama, I'm sure he'd rest easy knowing you were so well and happily circumstanced. But . . . but what about Graydon?"

Mama willfully misinterpreted. "Oh, he's pleased as punch, too. He wrote back immediately after his father sent the news. The dear boy wants to know if he should call me Mother when he gets back. What do you think?"

Daphne thought the dear boy should drown on his way home from Portugal.

Her mother was going on. "And that's another reason not to plan a complicated affair: We're not entirely sure when dear Graydon will arrive, or how well his leg will have healed. His father does want him to stand up as best man. You'll be my attendant, of course."

Of course, so she'd only have to stand next to him for the wedding, the rehearsal, the receiving line, the breakfast after. Good grief! If her mother weren't so much in alt, Daphne'd accuse her and the earl of planning this whole thing just to throw the two of them together. No one got married just to see their children made miserable, though, not even Lady Whilton. "How delightful, Mama. I'd be thrilled." She'd rather be boiled in oil.

Lady Whilton might want a small, simple wedding, but she had to have her bride clothes made by her favorite London modiste and the refreshments ordered from Gunter's.

Daphne refused to accompany her again, this time citing the need to ready Woodhill Manor for the occasion. Under Uncle Albert's decree, no funds had been spent on the house for ages, other than standard upkeep. Now Lady Whilton would use her own substantial income to refurbish the parlor and a few of the guest rooms. Someone had to remain behind to oversee the workers, Daphne claimed, and it could not be Cousin Harriet, who'd have them all tossing down their paintbrushes and hammers in a day and a half. Besides, someone should turn out the closets, inspect the linen, and inventory the china if they were having company. And someone should not have to face her former sweetheart's homecoming.

Daphne decided it would be better to meet here, perhaps with just the family as witnesses, rather than under the eager eyes of the upper ten thousand. She could be mature about this, she told herself, nod graciously, welcome him home, inquire for his health. And Gray could be trusted to be dutifully polite back, she supposed. After almost two years, he couldn't still be angry over her public humiliation of him. Just because she blamed herself for sending him into army-exile, endangering his very life, was no reason to believe he outright hated her. He never cared that much anyway, so why would he feel awkward now?

She practiced upstairs to match his supposed *savoir faire*, to get it right without trembling. Welcome home, Lord Howell? Major? Graydon? Rats, she couldn't even think what to call him, other than a word Torry had his mouth washed out with soap for using. Perhaps she should try calling him brother, Daphne thought, half-humorously, half-hysterically. Lud, those were going to be a difficult few days.

She mightn't go to London to welcome the prodigal son, but Daphne heard all about him. Mama's letters were full of how handsome he looked in his uniform, how well received he was in his hero's homecoming. No party was a success without his presence, Mama reported, and his company was sought for six events a day. Women were throwing themselves at him, Lady Whilton added in her crossed lines. He caught a few, too, Daphne read in the society columns she swore never to look at. The gossip pages enumerated every woman the newest Nonpareil sat out with—his leg being not entirely healed—and who shared his box at the opera. A dashing young widow seemed to be in the forefront of the pack for the Hollister heir stakes.

Daphne recalled Lady Bowles well from her time in London, although Seline was a woman with no time for lady friends. She spent her days striking attitudes as the lunar goddess her name denoted, wearing silvery gray gowns that looked spectacular next to her pale skin and ebony hair. At night she donned spangled gauze as the other moon deity, Diana the Huntress. She'd once commented in Daphne's hearing that a rich old husband was the best kind.

Daphne supposed even the Moon Goddess, as Seline was termed in the clubs and scandal sheets—where her name was mentioned with shocking frequency—could make an exception for a rich young man if he was the most eligible bachelor in town. Perhaps his injury was bad enough that Seline could envision herself becoming an even wealthier young widow. Or maybe Gray's practiced charm could melt the harpy's mercenary heart, and her dampened muslins could rouse his ardor. Maybe they'd fall madly, passionately in love and fly off to Gretna Green to sanctify their vows. Before Mama's wedding. And maybe pigs would fly.

Ah, well, Daphne thought, it was only for a few days. She'd survive seeing him, the same way she'd survived the last twenty-three months, twenty-one days, and seven hours of not seeing him. Miserably.

* * *

A few days, she could manage, but weeks? Miserable did not begin to describe how her mama's next letter made Daphne feel. They were all returning to Hampshire shortly, Lady Whilton wrote. Graydon's doctors thought he'd recover better in the country, away from all the hustle and bustle of his busy social life. He was staying at the Grosvenor Square mansion, having given up his third-floor bachelor quarters on account of his injury. Lady Whilton was able to report that it was no wonder the leg was still bothersome. Dear Graydon was seldom in his bed before dawn, if at all.

She and the earl, therefore, had suggested Graydon accompany them to Hampshire next week for the first reading of the banns. The wedding could take place three weeks hence, if Daphne thought all the arrangements could be made in time.

Well, no, she didn't think she could book passage to the Antipodes so soon.

The first meeting did not go so badly, for a hanging. In the first flurry of welcoming Lady Whilton home, greeting the earl and his sister, Cousin Harriet grumbling as footmen and maids scurried about with baggage, no one heard the beating of Daphne's heart. Ohlman the butler was taking wraps and asking for preferences of refreshment as he escorted the company into the parlor, and Mama wanted to know if the invitations had arrived from the printer, whether the boys would need new suits of clothes again, which flowers they could expect to be in bloom. Daphne answered her mother's chatter, then busied herself pouring the tea.

The blasted man couldn't take wine, like his father, from the decanter Ohlman was pouring. No, he had to stand next to Daphne, waiting for his cup of tea. And she, like a ninny, fixed it just the way he always preferred, without asking. His mouth quirked in a smile, but he did not comment on her blushes.

His first words, in fact, eased her mind somewhat. "You must be wishing me at Jericho. I offered to put up at the inn, but your mother wouldn't hear of it. I can make some excuse to leave until the wedding if you want, if you'll be too uncomfortable."

Daphne had to face him now, had to look right up into his warm brown eyes. He was even more handsome than she remembered, more muscular, too. The cane he carried added distinction, with the limp barely noticeable. She wondered if Mama had made up the whole faradiddle about his needing to recuperate, to explain his presence here, but why would he want to come so early? Gray wouldn't have left the gay life of London just to cut up her peace. He was doing a fine job of it, though, waiting for her answer, gazing straight through her eyes to her very soul. She wanted to tell him, yes, put up at an inn, on the moon preferably, and stop tearing her life apart, but she couldn't.

She handed over his tea and said, "The inn? No, of course not. The sheets aren't even aired properly."

"After Portugal, any sheets at all are a luxury. Truly, I wouldn't mind if you'd rather," he offered nobly, still standing as though poised to leave.

"Nonsense, unless *you'd* rather," she countered.

He shook his head quickly and finally sat down.

*40*

"Not at all. And the notion of more traveling about doesn't appeal either. Thank you."

"For what? You've always been welcome here. That is, Mama's always treated you like part of the family. I've prepared your usual room, unless you'd rather one on the ground level." Daphne wasn't sure it was polite to refer to his injury, but she didn't want him maiming himself for life on the stairs. She had enough on her conscience. "I could make the switch in an instant."

Graydon seemed relieved at her hospitality, but embarrassed to be reminded of his wound. "That's not necessary at all, but thank you. The leg is almost healed, the sawbones say, so the exercise should be good for it. In fact, I'm looking forward to some long tromps through the countryside," he mentioned, leaving room for her offer to accompany him, as she always had.

If he needed exercise, why hadn't he stayed in London with all its attractions? He could have strolled down Bond Street with the other town beaux, or danced all night at Vauxhall. He'd be bored with the tame rural pastimes within a day. Tromping through the countryside, indeed! Hadn't the papers claimed he'd cut a wide swath through City life since his return? Instead of expressing her doubts and distrust, she replied, "Then you'll enjoy the pleasant weather we're having. The roadside wildflowers are in color, and the formal gardens are beginning to look lovely. Mama won't have to worry about the church being decorated properly."

Daphne couldn't believe this conversation they were having. If anyone had said she'd be discussing spring blooms with Gray Howell, she'd have

41

laughed. The empty phrases made her want to cry, though, all the while she was congratulating herself on how well she was handling an awkward situation. She wasn't berating him for tearing her heart out, nor was she throwing herself on his broad chest in joy that he'd come home safely. Her hands weren't even shaking. Those twenty-three months, etc., had taught her something besides arithmetic, after all.

How kind the years had been to her, Gray was thinking as he stared at Daphne over the rim of his teacup. He'd aged, a century it felt like, with scars and weathered wrinkle lines, but Daphne had ripened. She had been an adorable child and a pretty girl after that awkward stage, but now she was a beautiful woman, poised and elegant. She could have been a duchess sitting at the tea table, in her Nile green silk gown that shimmered with every graceful motion. No demure debutante white for Miss Howell anymore, and no fall of lace at her bosom to hide her lack of assets, either. His old playmate had assets aplenty.

Only her unruly blond curls remained of the hoyden who used to tag at his heels, but now the vibrant gold locks were cropped into a short fashionable do, with a ribbon threaded through to keep the curls off her perfect face. She looked like a wood nymph, innocent and seductive both.

God, she was everything he remembered, and more. And less, for this time she wasn't promised to anyone, himself included. The gentlemen hereabouts must all be dicked in the nob or in their dotage, or dimwits of the tenth degree. Of course, when it came to fools, he'd take every prize. Still, she was going to let him stay at the house. There was hope ... unless she'd just pasted on a polite veneer like all the other stone-cold London Diamonds. Not his Daffy, please.

# Chapter Five

Things weren't going badly, for a disaster. Daphne even managed to find a few bits of silver lining in the cloud that hung over her head. It wasn't pouring rain, for one thing, and no virulent epidemics were ranging the countryside, so Graydon was getting the exercise he wanted—and getting out of Daphne's way. At least she was managing to avoid his company most of the time. With Mama in such a dither over the wedding plans, changing her mind over the guests, the refreshments, and the decorations, it was easy. There was so much to do that Daphne found it simple to make excuses for missing lunch or tea. She took breakfast in her bedroom, the better to consult her lists, she said, and she planned her busy day by watching the front door for his departure. Other times she left by the kitchen door, if he was still around at the front of the house. She often stayed away on her errands and commissions— with a novel, a blanket, and a packed lunch—until late in the afternoon, returning the same back way to avert any chance encounters.

Graydon was keeping busy, too, it seemed, refamiliarizing himself with the neighborhood and conferring with the bailiff at Howell Hall. His father had never taken the same interest in the land, so there was a great deal to be done after Gray's absence. He'd also studied some new farming methods while he was recuperating, and was anxious to implement the latest advances. Or so Daphne gathered from the conversations at the inevitable times when she could not escape her mother's machinations, mostly at dinner and the hours after. No amount of cautious maneuvering could politely excuse her from taking supper with the guests, Lady Whilton insisted. Lord Hollister and his sister would start to think she was avoiding them. How many headaches could she claim?

Instead, Daphne took to inviting company: old Squire Pomeroy when he was well enough to leave his sickbed, and his family, including Squire's married daughter Sally and her husband, and Squire's son Miles, of course; the Hartley sisters and old Admiral Benbow, who was mostly deaf; the vicar who would perform Mama's wedding ceremony, his wife and young curate; even Mr. Foggarty, Lord Hollister's tenant, who, while a bit rough around the satin and lace edges, had wonderful stories of his India days.

The guests reciprocated with invitations of their own, so that meant a few less evenings Daphne had to spend in Graydon's company. She made sure she was never alone with him even then, nor available for private conversation. Daphne thought she'd scream if he tried to get up a flirtation with her, since he'd be missing his London lightskirts. Instead she conferred with Mama about the wedding, or practiced the pianoforte, concentrating fiercely, or she got up whist games with his aunt and Cousin Harriet while Lord Hollister and Mama cooed in the corner. And she was always the first to scurry off to bed, claiming another early morning. At least she was getting a lot of reading done.

No, things were not going too badly at all, Daphne congratulated herself, and almost a whole week had gone by.

Almost a whole week of his visit was gone, without one comfortable tête-à-tête, Graydon fumed. He was as close to recapturing their old friendship as he'd been in Portugal. He'd been hoping for companionship at the very least. Instead she wanted to know if his room was to his liking, if there was a horse up to his weight in the stables, if he preferred macaroons to poppyseed cake with his tea. She was being a blasted hostess, when he wanted his playmate back! The woods were indeed full of wildflowers, and the streams were full of fish. He wanted to share them with her, the way they used to. He wanted to discuss his plans for Howell Hall, to see if she was interested. She was too busy interviewing musicians. He never even managed to get her alone long enough to ask her forgiveness, an apology he'd been carrying around for nigh onto two years.

This wedding nonsense was taking all of Daffy's time, dash it. The poor puss was being run off her feet. Why, she never had an afternoon free to just sit and chat, and she was yawning over her teacup every night right after dinner. Her eyes weren't their usually wondrous clear blue, he noticed, but looked tired, as if she'd been poring over her mother's endless lists too long. As for Lady Whilton, she was practically useless, giggling like a schoolgirl with her first beau. Graydon was delighted to see her so enamored of his father, of course, but couldn't help resenting the absurd juxtaposition of the older woman's giddiness while her daughter drudged to make the perfect wedding.

The situation was deplorable. Graydon vowed to be what assistance he could, to lift some of the burden from Daphne's slender but alluring shoulders. He made a note to ask Foggarty if he'd mind denuding Howell Hall's gardens and forcing houses for the occasion. The older man was pleasant enough, accommodating Graydon's wishes to inspect the house and grounds, even though Foggarty knew it meant the end of his stay in the neighborhood. Gray thought he'd miss the nabob's tales and exotic dinners when Foggarty's lease was up, but of course, the chap had to go if Graydon was going to reclaim his own home. The governor didn't care for the Hall, but Graydon did. He was tired of rented lodgings, army bivouacs. He wanted something permanent, even if it meant dislodging his amiable, well-heeled tenant.

Maybe Foggarty would make an offer on Pomeroy's place. With the old squire ailing, perhaps the Pomeroys would rent a house in Bath. Lud knew Graydon would be happy to see Miles Pomeroy out of the neighborhood, the way he was looking at Daffy. According to Lady Whilton, Pomeroy had been hanging around, biding his time. Miles was older than himself by a few years, and firmly entrenched in the neighborhood, acting as magistrate since his father took ill. From all Graydon heard or remembered, there'd never been a more upright and honest man. Or a duller one.

Miles Pomeroy took his job as magistrate seriously. For that matter, he took life seriously. But crime was no laughing matter, so when he heard of an attempted robbery in his precinct, he was quick to make an investigation. When he realized the victim of the attack was none other than a relation of Miss Whilton's, on the way to Woodhill Manor for the wedding, he hurried to offer his assistance. Thus it was that Miles, hoping to find favor with Miss Whilton, dropped into the midst of an already awkward house party the one person in the world Daphne would less like to have stay at Woodhill Manor than Graydon Howell.

"You're the ninnyhammer who brought Uncle Albert here?" she shrieked at the unfortunate Mr. Pomeroy in the Manor's now-deserted hallway. Ohlman the butler was assisting the foulmouthed and foul-breathed Uncle Albert up the stairs—to the master suite. Mama was having hysterics in the parlor, being comforted by Lord Hollister, of course, while Cousin Harriet was threatening to start packing, swearing she'd not spend one night under the same roof with such a fiend. Meantime Harriet was administering smelling salts to Lord Hollister's sister in the morning room. Daphne neither knew nor cared where Graydon was, but she could only assume he was having a grand laugh at her predicament. "Whyever did you have to bring him here, of all places?" she wailed at poor Miles.

"Well, he is Baron Woodhill. Naturally I assumed . . . I mean, this is his home and all."

"His home is a gaming hell in London's slums. That loose screw has only come to make trouble, I know it!"

"But I couldn't have left him at that tumbledown hedge tavern with his valet injured and his carriage missing a wheel."

"Why not? I assure you Uncle Albert is quite at home in the lowest dive. He must have crawled out from under a rock to get here."

"Please, Miss Whilton, you're merely overset at the unexpected arrival of an additional guest. He's your relative, an older gentleman. You must strive for a little respect."

Daphne was striving not to beat her slow-top suitor over the head with an umbrella from the nearby stand.

"You do not understand, Miles. My uncle is not in the least respectable. He'll insult the other guests with his gutter language, or try to cheat them at cards if he doesn't cast up his accounts on their shoes or molest their servants. The old rakehell will ruin Mama's beautiful wedding."

Miles Pomeroy refused to listen to gossip and never read the latest crim. con. stories in the London papers, so he truly did not know the worst of Albert's reputation, only that he preferred city life to the country. "Nonsense," he said now. "You've hardly seen your uncle in years. And what should a young miss like you know about rakehells and loose screws? Nothing, I'm sure, but the tattle-mongers' tripe. Come, he is the head of your family. In fact, I was delighted to be of service to him. Perhaps he'll look more kindly on my request for a private word about a certain matter."

Lud, it needed only that. "Miles, Uncle Albert is

hardly ever sober enough for a rational conversation, and the only family he's head of is the lizard family. He wouldn't recognize his own sons if he passed them on the street, and I do not recognize him as taking my father's place in anything but title." There, that should cure Mr. Pomeroy of his latest notion. Nothing, she feared, would cure him of his pomposity.

He merely patted her hand and said, "Tut, tut. I can see you're still overset."

Daphne jumped on that excuse to see Miles on his way. "Yes, I'm sorry I cannot invite you to stay for supper, but, as you say, we are all at sixes and sevens." She stepped closer to the door, forcing him to head in that direction, too.

"I'll just be off then to pursue my investigation." He reluctantly took up the gloves and hat she handed him. "I'm sure the miscreants are long gone, although Lord Woodhill did think he wounded one of them. I'll call tomorrow to see how you get on, and to report to Lord Woodhill on my findings. Nothing was taken, at any rate."

He most likely didn't have anything the thieves wanted, Daphne thought. Uncle Albert's pockets were perennially to let. She was positive now that her uncle had come, not to disrupt the wedding, which was still two weeks away, but to threaten to do so. Lord Hollister was certain to buy him off, or Mama would. Daphne'd hand over her own pin money to see the miserable muckworm out of the county. For now it was enough to see Miles out the door. She leaned against it when he was gone, her eyes closed. Then someone put a glass of sherry in her hand. Her eyes snapped open.

"Here, you can use this." Graydon was smiling

down at her. "I'm afraid we'll all need some Dutch courage before the night is over. I cannot promise to slay your dragons for you," he added with a nod toward the door, "but at least I won't desert you."

"Miles didn't—" she began, but Ohlman returned down the stairs then, holding on to the banister. For once the implacable butler's composure was shaken. Daphne shoved the glass of wine into her loyal retainer's hand. "You need this more than I do," she said. "Was he in a rant?"

Ohlman drank the wine down in a gulp, said, "Thank you, Miss Daphne," and mopped his brow. "It wasn't so much what he said, as what he threw. I'm too old for all that ducking. I'll make sure to send two of the quickest footmen up with his dinner tray. Then I'll say my prayers that his valet recovers enough to get here tomorrow. If I have to shave the man, I refuse to answer for the consequences." Ohlman straightened up, bowed to Daphne and Lord Howell, and resumed his stately tread to the small butler's pantry where he likely kept a stronger restorative than sherry.

Daphne took one look at Gray's twitching lips and had to clap her hands over her mouth. One tiny giggle escaped before she remembered where she was—and with whom. "It's not funny, Major." She'd decided on Major as being the middle ground of names and titles, not as formal as Lord Howell, not as familiar as Graydon. "I'm afraid that man"— she jerked her head upward—"means to cause trouble."

"Oh, I'm certain of that. We'll just have to make sure he doesn't, won't we?" And he grinned at her, emphasizing the "we." He would have taken her hand, perhaps to kiss it, but Ohlman returned then to announce that dinner was served.

No one ate much of Cook's fine meal except for Graydon, who was delighted with the turn of events. Being partners in adversity was better than not being partners at all.

# Chapter Six

*If* dinner was dismal, the gathering afterward was ghastly. Everyone was on tenterhooks, hoping the tea cart—and an excuse to retire—arrived before Albert. They didn't.

The baron hobbled into the parlor supported by a heavy bone-handled cane, looking more raddled and rheumy-eyed than ever, aged well beyond his years. Lord Hollister's sister gasped when he brushed past her, and held a lace-edged handkerchief to her nose.

"Niminy-piminy female," Albert wheezed, sinking into the most comfortable chair in the room, the one Daphne's mother had just vacated to flee to Lord Hollister's side on the sofa. From his place near the fire, Uncle Albert took out his quizzing glass and surveyed the company, his gaze lingering longest on Daphne. He licked his lips. Lord Hollister's sister drew in another quick breath of air, which in turn drew the most ignoble nobleman's attention.

"What, trying to fix m'interest, are you? Too bad your husband left you as poor as a church mouse, else I'd offer you a tumble, even if you are as shriveled as a prune."

The lady ran from the room, weeping. Her brother, the earl, said, "Here now, Baron, there's no call to be insulting the ladies."

Albert laughed, or wheezed—it was hard to tell which. "Thought I was payin' a compliment. Don't expect the old bat gets many offers these days." Before Lord Hollister could decide on an appropriate response, feeling that planting the decrepit man a facer was beneath his dignity, Albert turned to Graydon. "You, boy. Get me a drink."

"I'll just go see what's keeping the tea tray, shall I?" Lady Whilton hopped up again.

"Sit down, sister. I ain't about to maudle my insides with that catlap. I said I want a drink." He pounded his cane into the floor next to his chair, making the china shepherdesses on the nearby étagère shake, along with Lady Whilton.

Not Cousin Harriet. She headed for the bellpull. "I'll tell Ohlman to bring coffee. That's what you need, you old sot, not any more Blue Ruin."

Albert sneered at her through his looking glass as if she were a cockroach. "What's that Friday-faced old sapphist doing here? Get out, woman. It's my house and I'll drink what I want. Get out, I say."

Harriet stormed to the door. "Don't worry, sirrah, I wouldn't stay under the same roof as you. One of your so-called social diseases might be catching."

"In your dreams, woman, in your dreams."

Cousin Harriet left in a huff as Ohlman entered with the tea cart. Daphne didn't know whether to go after her or stay to comfort her mother, who was sniffling into Lord Hollister's handkerchief. She poured a cup of tea for Mama first.

"Where's my drink, damn it?" Uncle Albert thundered, slamming his cane down again.

Daphne started to ask how he liked his tea, but Graydon, who'd been standing near the mantel, reached for a decanter and poured out a glass. He handed it to the older man, saying, "Here, Baron, some fine brandy. No need to disturb the house." Then he came to stand behind Daphne's chair.

"Why did you give him brandy?" Daphne whispered. "Anyone can see he's had more than enough to drink."

"Yes, but this way he's liable to pass out. Otherwise he'll just get meaner. Trust me, I've seen enough drunks in my day."

Well, she certainly hadn't, so Daphne held her peace while Uncle Albert sloshed down his drink, then rapped the glass on the chair arm for more. To distract him, Daphne said, "Mr. Pomeroy wasn't clear on the details of the robbery. It was a whole band of cutthroats that attacked you and your valet?"

"Aye, a murderous band of road pirates." He turned to growl at Lord Hollister. "And if you blue bloods did your job and took better care of the highways, none of it would have happened, by Jupiter."

No one cared to mention that Albert's blood, what wasn't turned to vinegar, was as blue as anyone's, and as a major landholder, he was equally responsible for seeing to the roads. Daphne just thought to keep him talking until he lost consciousness, as Gray had promised. "I thought Mr. Pomeroy said the attack took place at a low tavern."

"Which I'd never have patronized, missy, if my blasted carriage hadn't lost a wheel to the bloody ruts. So there we were, Terwent and I, stranded at some dingy pub while a grubby urchin went to fetch a blacksmith. Most likely took my coins and left the neighborhood," he muttered, staring at his glass. "Still empty, blister it!"

Graydon poured out another round. Daphne frowned, but he winked at her as he took his position behind her chair with the cup of tea she had prepared for him. "And then?" he prompted. "You and, er, Terwent found yourself at a hedge tavern, you say?"

"Thieves' ken, more like. They must have pegged us for nobs right off."

If the highwaymen figured the two were rich swells, Daphne thought, looking at Uncle Albert's rumpled clothes, spotted linen, and scraggly, unkempt hair, then Terwent must cut quite a dash. He surely wasn't much of a gentleman's gentleman, judging from his master.

Albert was going on: "I had my purse out to pay. Blasted innkeep wanted to see my money before serving the swill he called supper. That's when the band of robbers made their move. Set a big dog on me, they did."

"A dog?" Lady Whilton asked in faint tones. "You were robbed by a dog?"

"No, by George, I foiled their plans. That big ugly hound lunged for my wallet on the table. I was wise to that ploy. Not born yesterday, don't you know. Dog steals a man's purse and runs off, but no one claims the cur, so they get away. Takes a real organized band of felons, I figure. But I stopped 'em dead in their tracks, I did." Albert lifted his glass and toasted his own genius. "I knew which crafty devils had been feeding the beast: an old gaffer who must have been the mastermind, and his two apprentice thieves, one big, the other real small. So when the dog grabbed my lamb chop—"

"A lamb chop? I thought it went for your purse."

"Didn't anyone teach you not to interrupt, gel? Of course, I wasn't going to let any mangy mutt get my blunt. I had that back in my pocket before the landlord could put the dishes down. So the dog grabbed the dinner instead. I demanded my money back, right off, then started laying into that brute of a dog with my cane." He waved the heavy-handled instrument around, in illustration. Graydon hurried to move the oil lamp from the table next to the baron's chair.

"And I was right, for didn't the old codger jump up to defend the flea-hound? So I hit him a good one right across the brain-box. He went down, but then his accomplices waded in, the big one screaming and the little one whining. So I laid into them, too. Left. Right." He waved the cane over his head, left, right, and snagged the lace doily on the back of the chair. It sailed across the room and into the fireplace, where it sizzled into threads in seconds. "Got Terwent a good one, too, sad to say. He should be right as a trivet tomorrow, as soon as the carriage is ready."

"But what about the thieves, Uncle Albert?" Daphne doubted the band of footpads was anything but an innocent party of poor travelers and their hungry dog.

"Got away, of course. Your magistrate didn't show up for hours, either. Couldn't find a trace of 'em, then he tried to say they didn't get away with anything anyway. Surprised the gudgeon can find his way home at night."

Daphne felt she had to defend Miles, perhaps because she could hear Graydon chuckling behind her. How the beast could find anything funny in this situation was beyond her. "Mr. Pomeroy is very conscientious about his position as justice of the peace. He works quite hard at it, as a result of which we have very little crime in the neighborhood."

"Very little of anything else in the neighborhood, either. Deuce take it what you turnips find to do in the country."

Lord Hollister tended to agree with him, but only said, "If you find the rural life so tedious, I wonder why you've left the city at all."

Uncle Albert started wheezing again. Or laughing. No, Daphne thought as the sound went on and on, he was definitely wheezing. She poured him a cup of tea, which he batted out of the way. She sat down again with the cup. She could use it, if he couldn't. When he caught his breath Albert gasped, "The wedding, you gabby. I've come as head of the family to stop the wedding."

Mama cried, "I knew it!" but the earl patted her shoulders.

"Don't be a peagoose, Cleo," he said. "You're of age and need no one's permission. Whilton cannot stop the marriage."

"He cannot even stop a dog from stealing his supper," Graydon murmured into Daphne's ear, which riffled the curls there and tickled. She shifted farther away in the seat, fussing with the pastries on the tray.

"But I can point out you're blighting your children's chances of making a good match, I can. You almost ruined it already, raising 'em up like brother and sister. Took all the spice out of it, if you know what I mean. Of course, there's Byron and his sister. . . . Any road, making 'em brother and sister in fact likely makes it illegal for them to marry anyway."

Suddenly Graydon did not find the situation quite as humorous. "Gammon, we're hardly relations. Besides, with enough money, one can get a dispensation for anything." He bit down on the lemon tart in his hand.

"Mama and Lord Hollister must think of their own happiness, Uncle," Daphne put in, ignoring Gray's rebuttal as mere argumentation. "I am thinking of making a match elsewhere, if it is any of your business."

The rest of Graydon's lemon tart fell to the floor.

"What, that prosy stick who hinted he had an interest here? You'd do better with Hollister's cub, gel. He'll be an earl someday, no matter how wild he is now."

"Wild?" Graydon sputtered on the crumbs in his mouth.

"He's a good, reliable, steady man, for your information, Uncle Albert."

Graydon cleared his throat, but both Albert and Lord Hollister exclaimed, "Howell?"

While the major glared at his father, Daphne answered, "No, Miles Pomeroy, of course."

"Faugh, with a husband like that, you'd be taking lovers in a month."

It was Daphne's turn to glare, at her uncle and at the choking sounds behind her.

"No," Uncle Albert was going on, "you'd do a parcel better with Howell." He ogled her from under his bushy eyebrows, looking her up and down—and inside and out, it felt. "Didn't turn out half bad, for a filly from a weak stable. Too bad you're so prim and proper; you'd make some man a cozy armful. As it is, you'd send him"—with a nod toward Graydon—"back to his mistresses afore the cat can scratch her ear. That little protégée of Harry Wilson's as good as she looked?" he asked the younger man. "Or are you saving your shot for that Bowles widow, like a regular mooncalf?" He slapped his thigh at the witticism, and almost knocked himself out of his seat. "She'll be more expensive in the long run, mark me, boy. And if she does get her claws into you for the gold band, that's the last you'll see of her panting to get between your sheets."

Mama gasped, and Lord Hollister said, "I must protest this frightful conversation, Baron."

"Protest all you want, from the other side of the door. You don't like it here, get out. It's my house, remember. Besides, where the boy makes his bed wouldn't matter if you weren't marrying an old biddy like my sister-in-law, Hollister. Man like you ought to be getting himself a young wife who can give him more sons. The one whelp you've got's bound to get his head blown off; did you think of that? Then where'll you be? Even I've got two boys, the heir and a spare."

"Enough, Baron," Graydon said with enough force to rattle the teacups in their saucers. "We've heard enough of your filth. Now, what did you really come here for? You must have known you couldn't stop the wedding, and I doubt you want to give the happy couple your blessings."

Lord Whilton took a piece of crumpled paper out of his pocket and tossed it on the table in front of him. "This is what I want, my brother's widow's signature. It's a waiver of her widow's benefits, is all."

Daphne and Graydon looked at each other. "But Mama's annuity will cease when she remarries, of course."

"Oh, but m'brother had a crackbrained notion of seeing her married again. She's to get twenty thousand pounds."

"Is that true, Mama?"

"Yes, John didn't want me to stay a widow, and he wanted me to be able to marry a man of modest means, if I wished, without having to live in a cottage."

Uncle Albert grunted. "That's so sweet, I could puke. But you ain't marrying a poor man. You're marrying a regular Golden Ball, so you don't need the blunt. I do, and I aim to have it. I'll sit right here, in m'own parlor, until you sign the thing."

"That's outrageous," Lord Hollister fumed as he waved a vinaigrette under his fiancée's nose. "It's blackmail."

"But you can't do a thing about it, can you? Can't throw a chap out of his own house, Earl."

Graydon was clenching his fists as if he wanted to, very much.

"Try it and I'll gather up those two brats of mine you females dote on and I'll sell them to a chimney sweep. Then you'll have no excuse to be here with your noses in my business."

Daphne spoke up, horrified: "They're your own flesh and blood! Besides, they're too big for sweeps. That's how much attention you've paid them, you awful man, not even to know how big they've grown."

"Awful, eh, missy? Then mayhaps you'd rather I sent them to a flash house. Do you know what they pay for clean young boys, gel, do you? It's not a bad idea, now I think on it. The brats disappear, there's no entail. I get rid of you harpies and I can unload this millstone. Not a bad idea at all."

"Why, you despicable—" Daphne felt a firm hand on her shoulder.

"I'm sure Lady Whilton will think about your suggestions, Baron," Graydon said in a reasonable tone, quite at odds with the grim look on his face. "Why don't you retire after your adventurous day and let her and my father discuss things in private?" He opened the door to find the efficient butler waiting on the other side with two footmen for just such a call. "The baron is going to bed, Ohlman. He might need some assistance up the stairs."

Then again, if he fell and broke his scrawny neck, no one would mind.

# *Chapter Seven*

"*O*h, why did that dreadful man have to come here now?" Mama wept in Lord Hollister's arms. Daphne hovered nearby with fresh tea, sherry, and the smelling salts, but the earl seemed to be managing. Daphne looked at the tea, then drank the sherry. Graydon nodded approvingly. He was pouring himself a glass of cognac from the new decanter Ohlman had brought, Uncle Albert having taken the other one with him.

Lady Whilton sat up and dabbed at her eyes. "I cannot imagine how he found out so soon, with the banns just being read last Sunday and no notice in the newspapers yet. I made sure none of my particular friends would gossip, not that they travel in the same circles as Albert." She shuddered to think of those noisome circles, one of whose denizens was right this moment upstairs in the bedchamber adjoining hers. She'd make sure Ohlman checked the locks before she put one foot inside her room. Otherwise she'd sleep with Daphne, or Lord Hollister—

and propriety be damned! "Oh, why did he have to find out before the wedding?" she lamented anew.

The earl cleared his throat. "I'm, ah, afraid I told him, my dear. I called on him at Whilton House before we left. The place is like a stable, Cleo. You'd be embarrassed to own it."

"Well, I don't own it, so the wretch can use the Chippendales for kindling for all I care, as long as he stays away from Hampshire and the boys. But, John, why the dev—uh, whyever did you call on Albert in the first place?"

"Yes, Father," Graydon put in. "Why the deuce did you have to give him notice of the nuptials?"

Lord Hollister wasn't pleased to be the recipient of three sets of condemning stares. "My duty, don't you know," he blustered. The stares did not abate one whit. "I didn't want him thinking we were doing anything havey-cavey. He *is* head of your family, Cleo."

Daphne groaned. Here was another misguided male whose sense of honor outweighed his sense. Couldn't they see that Uncle Albert was a headache, not head of anything?

"Furthermore," Lord Hollister continued, "I wanted to discuss the settlements with him."

"What was there to discuss?" Mama asked. "My widow's pension ends, and I get the twenty thousand pounds dear Whilton set aside for me. He was thinking of my happiness."

"Yes, well, so was I. I felt it wouldn't be right to take your first husband's money along to your second. You wouldn't be comfortable."

"I? I'd be perfectly comfortable taking what's mine, and keeping every shilling I could away from that old goat. He'd only gamble it away, or spend it on other evils too depraved to mention. Why, the monies I've spent on his children and his home alone entitle me to my bequest."

"Well then, *I* wouldn't be comfortable. Dash it, Cleo, a man wants to support his own wife. And I told Whilton that."

"You what? You discussed my income with that gallows-bait, without talking to me first?" Lady Whilton was rigid now, not the limp, weepy female who not a minute before was clinging to the earl for support. "How dare you? That money was not yours to dispose of!"

"Now, now, Cleo," the earl tried to soothe, "you know that a wife's assets become her husband's on marriage anyway. And it's not as if you cannot have anything you want. All of my wealth is at your fingertips."

"Yes, for you to dole out in pin money or paid bills. What if I wanted to do something special with my own money?"

"Like what, dearest? Name it and it's yours."

Lady Whilton was not mollified. "Like give it to Daphne, for one thing."

"But Daphne already has a handsome dowry. It's all in trust where Albert cannot touch it."

"But her husband can. He can gamble or invest unwisely; he can even spend it on his mistresses." She fixed a basilisk eye on Graydon, who was trying to fade into the upholstery, wondering how he got dragged into this domestic quarrel.

"Mama, you know I wouldn't marry a man like that," Daphne put in. "If I wouldn't have Gray . . ."

"Oh, for Heaven's sake," that gentleman started, only to be interrupted by Lady Whilton again.

"No, but you might marry Miles Pomeroy, and

65

the money would be handy so you didn't have to live with Squire and play nursemaid to him all the time, under his wife's high-handed direction. The woman is a shrew," she said of one of her oldest friends.

"Daffy is not going to marry that prig Pomeroy!" Graydon exploded.

To which Daphne shouted back, "I'll marry whomever I please, Graydon Howell. And Miles is not a prig! He is a fine, upstanding man who doesn't consort with fallen women or fast widows."

"He's a pompous windbag, and you know it! Wasn't it you who dared me to put glue on his seat at church?"

"I was seven years old!"

"And he was fifteen going on forty-five!"

"And you were ten, and a hellion even then. Reckless and foolish and—"

"Children!" Lord Hollister shouted, to be heard above the bickering. "You are acting like infants. Daphne, you may marry where you choose, of course, although I had hoped . . . At any rate, you have a fine enough dowry that you can pick for yourself, without needing your mama's twenty thousand."

Daphne had her arms crossed over her chest. "Perhaps I'll choose not to marry anyone at all. I cannot see where there's much joy in it for a woman. Perhaps I'd do better to set up housekeeping in a cottage and take care of Dart and Torry, to keep them out of Uncle Albert's way."

"You see?" Lady Whilton cried. "Now she's talking of never getting wed! And without the marriage, she cannot touch the dowry, no matter how fine it is sitting in the bank. You can be sure Albert will never release it to her even when she turns thirty. Thirty!" she wailed. "My precious girl will dwindle into a down-at-heels old spinster because you gave away my twenty thousand!"

"Gammon, she'll be snapped up within a year, if that prig, ah, Pomeroy doesn't come up to scratch. Besides, she'll always have a home with us, you know, and I'll always support her."

Mama wasn't listening. "My baby will end up on the shelf, and I'll never have grandchildren, all because your wretched son broke her heart!"

"Mama, he didn't!" Daphne shrieked in mortification while Graydon had another glass of wine.

"Balderdash!" Lord Hollister exclaimed. "If Daphne wasn't such a stubborn little prude, they'd be married by now and starting their nursery, and my son wouldn't be off trying to get himself killed."

Mama was sobbing hysterically. She paused to howl, "That's right, tell her she's welcome in your home one minute and call her names the next! Why would Daphne want to live with me, her own mother, when you'll be counting out her allowance and inviting disreputable characters like Albert into our house? Cousin Harriet is right: Men have too much power. That's not what I want for my darling girl, and it's not what I want for me! I don't want to live in your stuffy old house either, so you and your rakehell son can have all the orgies you want!"

While Lord Hollister was shouting that he'd never let Albert cross his doorstep, that he'd always loved Daphne like a daughter, Lady Whilton struggled to pry his engagement ring off her finger.

"No, Mama," Daphne cried, and Lord Hollister yelled, "Don't be a fool, Cleo," at her.

"Fool, is it? You're right! I was a fool to be so blind. Daphne saw it years ago. I was a fool to trust a Howell." The ring was so thick with diamonds and emeralds, she couldn't get a good grip on it. "Even your blasted ring is trying to choke me."

She finally got the ring off and threw it at the earl. Then she grabbed Daphne's arm and dragged her from the room, where Lady Whilton collapsed into Ohlman's waiting arms, to be led upstairs.

Graydon handed the earl a glass of wine. "Orgies, Father? What orgies?"

Graydon proceeded to help his father get drunk. There was not much else to do. Not only hadn't Graydon killed any dragons for Daphne, he'd managed to let slime get all over everyone. Blast his reputation! His case was worse than ever.

"Think she'll see things differently in the morning?" his father asked, staring at the ring in his hand.

Why should she? Her daughter hadn't, not in the morning, not two years later. "Strong-minded woman," was all he could offer.

"Aren't they all?" the powerful Earl of Hollister humbly noted, and his son drank to that.

Graydon wished he could offer his father a smidgen of hope. Oh, how he wished it, both for the governor's sake and his. Deuce take it, Daffy'd never forgive him for contributing to the jeopardy to her mother's happiness. Somehow she'd fix all the blame on him, he just knew it. Besides, if the wedding were off, he and his father would have to leave Woodhill. In fact, he wouldn't be surprised if Ohlman scratched on the door any minute to announce that their bags were packed and their carriage was waiting outside. Daffy must have mellowed some after all, or else she was too busy calming her mother to worry about ejecting the rejected, dejected suitors in the parlor.

If they did have to leave, though, Graydon believed he'd never have another chance. He'd be leaving the pigheaded chit at the mercy of that Pomeroy flat. With Uncle Albert making threatening noises, Daphne might think she needed to marry for protection, for her and her mother and those young cousins. She never listened to reason before; he doubted she'd start now. He could only pray her mother wasn't cut from the same bolt.

"Perhaps an apology is in order?" Graydon suggested.

"Even though I still think I was right, if I thought she'd see me, I'd beg her forgiveness. Me, the Earl of Hollister. Can you believe it?"

"Easily. I've seen stranger things in the name of love. And you did insult her pride and her intelligence, don't you know, by negotiating away her portion without a by-your-leave. If I were you, I'd grovel."

"That's if she agrees to see me. I cannot very well barge into the bedroom of a respectable female and demand she hear me out."

Graydon had seen stranger things than that, too. In fact, he'd been considering undertaking such a maneuver soon, if he couldn't have a private talk with Daffy. Now a private talk was the last thing he wanted, if he had to pay for his father's sins as well as his own recently resurrected failings. What he had to do, and do fast before anyone questioned his presence here, was get this hobble with Albert resolved so his father and Lady Whilton could reach an understanding.

Graydon saw nothing for it but to cut a deal. Having recently come from the battlefront, he was a great proponent of negotiation. What they had to do, as he saw it, was get the old sot to hand over Lady Whilton's twenty thousand pounds. The loose screw would do it, Graydon figured, for a like sum from the earl, under the table, of course. In effect his father would be paying his own bride's dowry, but as long as she didn't know it, she'd be satisfied at having got her money and her own way. The governor might have to up the ante some to win assurances from the bastard baron that there would be no future demands or threats on the boys, but he could afford it. Any price was worth it to see the last of that curst rum touch.

"But that's dishonest," the earl protested after Graydon explained his plan. "It's lying to Cleo, and letting her keep her addlepated notions besides. Women's independence and all that rot. I'm not sure I want to live under the cat's paw."

Graydon picked up the engagement ring from the table in front of his father. "Do you want to live alone the rest of your life?"

After seeing her mother put to bed with a dose of laudanum, Daphne didn't know what to do. She wasn't tired, but she didn't want to face the earl—or his son—again this night. She was sure her mama would reconsider her hasty and impassioned decision in the morning. She just had to, Daphne swore, for Lady Whilton and the earl were meant for each other. Daphne didn't dare go offer Lord Hollister her reassurances, however.

Gracious, she couldn't let difficulties between herself and Gray get between the older couple again. But how to convince her mother of that? By convincing Mama that Graydon hadn't broken her heart, not by half. She'd been disappointed in his character, that was all. With all the recent gossip being confirmed and amplified by Uncle Albert— and not denied by Major Howell, Daphne noted— her assessment had been correct: Graydon was a libertine. Her heart wasn't involved one jot in the decision to jilt him, she told herself firmly, rehearsing what she'd tell her mother in the morning. Not one iota.

Miles would make a much better husband. He'd teach her cousins and her future sons about the land and about honor. Yes, she'd do well to accept Miles's steadfast loyalty. For sure Daphne could never go live with Mama and the earl, not after this upset, not if her presence was going to remind them of their children's brangling. She'd pay them visits, of course, when she knew Graydon was else-where. Daphne knew she couldn't stay on here in her childhood home, either, not when awful Uncle Albert was liable to pop in. That left Miles, worthy Miles, who was most likely too high-minded to out-smart that low-blow bounder.

Mama had to marry Lord Hollister, if only to pro-tect the boys from Uncle Albert. She and Cousin Harriet were right: Men did have all the power, and they needed every bit of it to keep her cousins from falling into their father's evil clutches. Daphne didn't think Uncle Albert would go through with his threats to see his sons sold into slavery or whatever, but the threats were bad enough.

She'd have to go to him herself, Daphne decided,

and tell him she didn't want the cursed twenty thousand pounds, that she'd convince Mama to sign the paper if he'd just leave them alone. It would be Daphne's decision and her mother's, not Lord Hollister's. That should please Mama, even if losing the money didn't. One couldn't ask for everything.

# Chapter Eight

As she walked from her mother's room to hers, Daphne heard noises coming from Papa's—now Uncle Albert's—bedchamber. The mutters and mumbled curses she would have ignored, but the thumps and thuds sounded ominous. If she called for a footman, she'd likely wake the rest of the house, Cousin Harriet and the earl's sister included, so Daphne decided to investigate herself.

She scratched on the door and softly called: "Uncle Albert, it is I, Daphne. Do you need anything?"

What she heard could have been "Get in here." It also could have been "Get out," but she chose the former, cautiously opening the door a crack, prepared to duck flying missiles. When no boots or books came her way, she edged into the room, leaving the door ajar behind her, just in case.

Uncle Albert was lurching about, his cane neglected, as he tried to open the brandy decanter. His hands were shaking so badly, he could not remove the stopper, and his face was empurpled with his rage and frustration. His breath was coming in short, gasping inhales and long, rasping exhales. He did not look well, even for Uncle Albert.

"Uncle, are you ill? Should I send for the doctor?"

"What, some bloody rustic leech? Wouldn't trust one of your quacks," he panted out. "Terwent'll be here in the morning with my potions and stuff. Not that they do much good anymore." He stumbled closer and thrust the bottle at her. "May as well be of some use, now you're here. Open the blasted thing."

Daphne was undecided, until the baron started waving his arms around, saliva dribbling out of the side of his mouth. Maybe Graydon would prove right after all, Daphne thought, and Uncle would collapse, unconscious, once he'd drunk his fill. For sure he was working himself into an apoplexy this way. She pulled the stopper away from the neck of the crystal decanter and looked around for a glass.

"Here, give me that," the baron snarled, grabbing the bottle and lifting it to his mouth. Daphne could hear his every gulp, and watch his bony Adam's apple bob up and down. He finally lowered the decanter and wiped his lips with the back of his coat sleeve, and belched. "Better," he grunted, and indeed his breathing was more even and his coloring more restored to its usual splotchy flush. He clumped over to the bed and threw himself down, still holding a firm grip on the bottle.

"Should I ring for Ohlman to help you undress, Uncle? You'll be more comfortable without your boots on, I'm sure."

"Wouldn't let that bugger touch me. Or my boots. Terwent'll be here in the morning," he repeated, with another long swig from the bottle.

"Then perhaps a blanket?" He was lying on all of his. The last thing Daphne wanted was for the soused baron to take a chill and have to be nursed here at the Manor. She found a quilt over the back of a chair and brought it closer, hesitating.

"What's the matter, gel? I won't bite. Not enough teeth left, heh-heh." And he began that half laugh, half wheeze again, necessitating another hard swallow of brandy.

Daphne tossed the blanket over him and stepped back quickly, hoping that if the baron was going to fall into oblivion, he'd do it soon, before the brandy was gone and he threw another fit. His eyes seemed to be drifting shut, so she backed away cautiously. Unfortunately her foot hit his dropped cane on the floor, and she squealed as she tried to regain her balance.

Albert's eyes snapped open, and he stared at her wildly, trying to recall her identity. He must have figured it out, for he growled, "What are you doing here anyway, gel? Young chits ain't supposed to be in a man's bedchamber. Didn't your ma teach you that? She sure as hell didn't teach you good sense, whistling a fortune down the wind when you tossed Howell out on his ear. No gel of mine'd be given the choice, I can tell you that. At least m'sister-in-law had the brains to hook the big fish, even if she let the minnow get away. Hollister's as rich as Croesus," he rambled on, eyes going unfocused again. "Doesn't need my blunt. Shouldn't get it. Ain't right."

Daphne decided to take the chance on a rational conversation with her uncle now that he was somewhat subdued. She didn't think he'd be any more open to reasonable discourse tomorrow, when he finally awoke. "That's what I came to discuss, Uncle Albert, Mama's twenty thousand. You know it would cost you less in the long run to give it to her now, than if you had to keep paying out her widow's pension if she never remarried."

"What's a female know about finance? You ain't figuring the interest on the twenty thousand, interest I get to keep. And you ain't figuring that my long run is getting shorter every day. I could have one more good ride on all that brass afore I cash in my chips."

"Yes, well, that's actually what I wanted to talk to you about. And to see to your comfort, of course."

"Of course," he mimicked. "You always cared so much for your dear uncle's well-being, you used to run and hide when I came around. Still would, I warrant, if you didn't want something. What is it, gel? Spit it out, I can't stand mealymouthed chits."

Talking so much made him wheeze again. The level in the bottle was getting dangerously low, so Daphne hurried into speech. "You're right: Mama doesn't need the money, and Lord Hollister feels he'd rather support her himself. She only wanted it for me, it seems, so I wouldn't have to worry about marrying for money. I think I can convince Mama I don't need it."

"What, going to have young Howell after all?"

"No, definitely not."

He pounded the bottle down on the bed, spilling a few drops. "What are you using for brains, girl, pigeon droppings? Fellow's rich and handsome. So what if he's a rake? You look the other way a bit like every other female, and in return you can have anything you want, even get to be a countess one day. Who knows but the jackstraw'll come down heavy for your own dear uncle."

"So that's why you think I should wed Graydon, so you can bleed him dry? Well, think again. I won't."

Albert laughed, which turned into a long gasp for air. When he could speak again, after another swallow, he said, "So it's to be that countrified chowderhead, is it? You'll be sorry, mark my words."

Daphne stood firm. "Your opinion is irrelevant, Uncle. If I marry Miles, my dowry will be sufficient, and he'll still see that I want for nothing."

"Nothing except a little rum-diddly-dum," he said with a snicker. "What you ought to do is bed both of 'em. Then you'd see."

"That's a horrid suggestion, Uncle! As if I ever would do, you know, before marriage!"

"I know, all right. It's that prunes-and-prisms Pomeroy that mightn't." He thought this was so funny, he slapped his knee, unfortunately with the bottle. He doubled over, choking again between cackles. The sniggers came less frequent as the wheezes and ragged inhalations took longer. He did rattle, "Try 'em both, you'll take the rake every time."

To which Daphne replied, "Never!"

Albert fell back on the pillows, the bottle tilted up, but he was gasping too hard to swallow. "Famous . . . last . . . words," he managed to whisper, which turned out to be his. Last words, that is.

"But will you leave if Mama signs the paper relinquishing the money?" Daphne persisted.

Uncle Albert had already left.

"Uncle? Baron? Should I send for the doctor?" In her heart Daphne knew the doctor would be too late, by years. She tried to convince herself, though, that the baron had simply passed out finally. But his chest wasn't rising, wasn't falling, no matter how closely she watched. The hairs in his nose weren't fluttering with every breath. There was no breath, period. Daphne tiptoed closer and lifted the bottle away from Albert's hand, to stop it from dripping on the bed. He let her take it. He must be dead.

"God have mercy," Daphne whispered, her hand to her mouth.

Not on this sinner, He wouldn't. Uncle Albert was dead. He was going to stay dead, and he was going to get deader, if possible, soon, unless Daphne did something, but what? It was too late to send for the vicar, not that a few last-ditch prayers could have gotten this heathen into Heaven.

Mama. Daphne'd go ask her mother—no, Mama was fast asleep and liable to stay that way through half of tomorrow, after taking the laudanum tonight. Besides, she'd only go off into hysterics again.

Ohlman would know what had to be done. Their devoted and organized butler was capable of meeting any challenge. He'd send for the vicar, the undertaker, the lawyer—goodness, little Eldart was baron now!—and the heir. Efficient Ohlman would see to notices in the papers, hatchments for over the doors, refreshments for the funeral guests.

Guests. Wedding guests. "Oh no!" Daphne moaned. The wedding would have to be canceled, whether Mama and Lord Hollister became reconciled or not. The Whiltons would be in mourning, and even if they chose not to wear black for the blackguard, they couldn't very well hold a festive celebration in his own house, with him fresh in the grave. A year, they'd have to wait. Six months at the minimum. The wretched marplot had managed to disrupt the wedding after all, for all the good it did him. The cad couldn't even die without making things difficult for his relations.

If they let him. Perhaps it was reaction to the death, or the wine she'd had during the last crisis downstairs, or just all the tension of the past weeks, but Daphne wasn't ready to concede. There just had to be a way to cheat Uncle Albert of this final victory. Heaven knew he'd cheated often enough in life. With a little time and thought, she'd figure a way to queer his game. And Ohlman must be asleep by now anyway. There was no reason to wake the man—he wasn't getting any younger—or to rouse the whole household, which would be inevitable. No, Uncle Albert would still be dead in the morning. Unless Daphne could come up with a plan.

Somewhere in the back of Daphne's mind was the idea that if she could just get rid of Uncle Albert before anyone found out, and just for the two weeks till the wedding, then the marriage could take place. Mama would be happy, Lord Hollister would be named guardian for Dart and Torry, and Uncle Albert wouldn't be laughing at all of them from the depths of hell.

She'd need help, of course. She couldn't ask the servants to take part in anything so improper, though, no matter how loyal and trustworthy they were, not even Ohlman. That wouldn't be honorable. Pretending Uncle Albert was still alive was. At least it was in a good cause.

The name that kept popping into her thoughts, a

name that, indeed, was rarely out of her thoughts, she refused to consider as a co-conspirator. She would *not* go running to Gray to get her out of a scrape the way she used to do when they were children. This was not like being caught in Farmer Melford's orchard with a pinafore full of apples. Graydon was no relative, not much of a real friend except in her memory. She couldn't even trust his loyalty the way she did her butler's. Ohlman didn't share his devotion and his talents among every other family in the county, not for all the years he'd been employed at Woodhill Manor. He never did; he never would.

Graydon was reckless and daring enough for such a hey-go-mad scheme, that was for sure, but Daphne couldn't ask him. She didn't want to be beholden to him, she told herself. She didn't want to involve him in another possible scandalbroth, and she didn't want him to think her attics were to let. Mostly she didn't want to be alone with him, to ask.

His father was much too much the gentleman for such a venture. Besides, the earl would be too busy mending his fences with Mama. Daphne refused to consider that the wedding plans might be terminated anyway, regardless of Uncle Albert's terminal condition. Cousin Harriet was too outspoken for subterfuge, if she hadn't already packed and left. Which left . . . Miles.

Miles was the justice of the peace. He'd have to be involved one way or the other in his official capacity. The question was, could Daphne ask upright Miles to bend the rules for her? Then again, if she did ask, would he agree? He would if he loved her. He'd see that she wasn't looking to hurt anyone or cheat anyone out of anything, just help her mother find happiness. He doted on his own ailing father, after all. Of course, pushing the man's Bath chair wasn't quite the same as stashing a body and sidestepping statutes, but he was bound to understand, Daphne tried to convince herself. And if he didn't . . .

She wasn't about to take Uncle Albert's outrageous advice about taking Miles and Gray to her bed. That was beyond consideration. On the other hand, a comparison, a test of faithfulness, perhaps, was not a bad idea. She had always insisted she wanted a man she could trust, one whose first loyalty was to her and no other. Graydon had already failed the test. He'd ride *ventre à terre* to her rescue, she knew in her heart, grinning the whole way, but she couldn't trust him. Miles was the most trustworthy soul of her acquaintance, but if he wouldn't stand by her, no matter what, then it didn't matter, not a whit. It wasn't as if she were asking him to put love above honor, not precisely. And it wasn't as if there were any grand passion on either side, either. There had to be some strong foundation for a decent marriage, though, and she thought steadfastness was a good place to start.

Through all her cogitations, Daphne had been straightening the room. She picked up Uncle Albert's cane and put it and his portmanteau on the mattress next to him, then she drew the velvet hangings closed around the bed. Anyone looking into the chamber would think the baron was sleeping, not to be disturbed. They'd think he liked fresh air, too, for Daphne opened the windows and banked the fire. For certain it wouldn't do to let the room get overwarm. She blew out the candles, except for her own, and closed the door firmly behind her.

The house was dark and quiet. The only one who appeared to be stirring was Daphne's maid, quietly mending while she waited to put her mistress to bed. Daphne quickly dismissed her, chiding the woman for thinking she couldn't undress herself, and then asked her to spread the word belowstairs that Baron Whilton was ill and possibly contagious. The doctor would be called in the morning if he did not improve. Meantime, Daphne would see to his needs since she was already exposed. Most important, Daphne emphasized, none of the servants should enter his room until the baron rang. Which would be a long, long time.

*Chapter Nine*

$\mathcal{O}$nly one footman remained on duty late at night at Woodhill Manor. It was his office to make sure the candles were all doused, the fires all extinguished, the windows and doors all locked after the last guest retired. He also got the job of aiding Major Howell in helping the earl up to his room. While he assisted Graydon in supporting Lord Hollister's substantial, stuporous body up the stairs, the servant passed on the information that Lord Whilton was ailing.

"Gammon, castaway is more like it."

"No, milord, Miss Daphne told her maid to inform the staff to stay away in case it's the influenza."

"Bosh, the man is just disguised. Worse than the governor here, I'll warrant."

"Begging your pardon, milord, but Miss Daphne did say as how no one is to go into the baron's room but herself." As if anyone wanted to.

"Devil take it, she already has enough on her

shoulders without worrying about some cad in his cups."

The footman nodded his agreement with that assessment, Miss Daphne being a favorite with the staff, Baron Whilton being the bane of their existence. "Mayhaps it's as you say and his lordship is just above himself. Miss Daphne did say as how the doctor wasn't to be called until tomorrow, if then."

"Then he cannot be that sick. Good."

He couldn't be too sick for a visit, Graydon decided after he put the earl into his valet's competent hands. It wasn't all that late by London standards, and if the baron was suffering from his overindulgence, perhaps Graydon could fetch him a restorative or something. If he did require a doctor, the servants would be only too happy to ignore his bell after Daphne's warning, and wake her up instead. She needed her sleep.

The major didn't fear being struck by anything more than a tossed boot. He'd gone through two years of the army without succumbing to any vile diseases; he wasn't going to get one now. And if Awful Albert wasn't really sick, then Graydon could discuss how much blunt was required to see him gone.

It was extortion, pure and simple. And it had to be paid if Gray's father and Lady Whilton were to make a match. They deserved their chance for happiness, and he, Graydon, deserved two more weeks to try to change Daphne's opinion of himself.

He stood outside the baron's room, listening. Lady Whilton's chambers were next door; he could hear snores from there. Daphne slept a few doors down, but that was too tantalizing a thought for this time of night.

There were no sounds from Albert's room, so Graydon rapped softly at the baron's door. When he still heard nothing, he quietly entered, shielding his candle.

No noises came from the bed, but tarnation, it was no wonder if the man took a chill if he liked to sleep in so cold a room.

The bed-curtains were all drawn, but Graydon decided that since he'd come this far, he had better make sure the old man was all right. He could ride for the doctor himself if necessary, and not disturb Daffy at all.

So he pulled the curtains a bit, thinking that if the tosspot had passed out, there'd be no worry over waking him. In the pale circle of his candle's light, he studied the recumbent figure.

"Lord Whilton? Baron?" Yes, he was passed out, sleeping like the dead. That was too bad, for now conversation and negotiations would have to wait for the morrow. Nothing could be resolved between the governor and his bride.

Just to make sure it was the drink and not a disease that had Albert laid so low, Graydon put a hand to the man's forehead to feel for temperature. The baron had none whatsoever. He was as cold as a stone, and Graydon didn't think it was because the windows were open. He brought his candle closer. Bloody hell, the baron was dead. The major had seen enough death in the war to recognize it.

Gray took a minute to consider the implications. "Thunder and turf," he cursed out loud, knowing there was no chance of waking this sleeper. The implications did not please him. Oh, there'd be no question of Lady Whilton getting her money from the estate now, but there'd be no question of holding the wedding now either. And complications, there'd be a blizzard of them: naming a guardian for the boys, the funeral arrangements, the legal rigmarole. No doubt Daphne would take up the reins as she usually did. She adored her cousins and was devoted to her mother, who had no head for details, as charming and delightful as she was.

And Graydon couldn't even help. Since he was no relation, he couldn't stay on, battening on a house of mourning. Which meant he couldn't show Daphne he was not such a frippery fellow as she thought. But maybe he could do something to help. . . .

He could get Albert out of here and back to London, for his valet to find. Considering the time it might take for the valet to get here, then there, then send a message back here, to which a message would have to be sent back there saying to send the baron back here for burial, perhaps they could hold the wedding after all. Especially if Albert weren't found dead on his back here in the house.

Graydon could say that Lord Whilton had a change of heart and realized his sister-in-law was entitled to the money after all. No one would believe it, or that Albert had a heart to change, but the old rip wouldn't be there to refute anything.

There was no big problem with making a run to London, but not in the middle of the night, and not without telling anyone. They'd have the whole county looking for him, and a fine hobble that would be, getting caught with Albert's corpse. No, Graydon decided he'd have to wait for tomorrow night. He'd have all day to make up excuses for the baron's departure and his own, and to figure a way to get the dead man into his carriage. Meantime, he couldn't just leave him here. Poor Daffy'd come in in the morning and find the blighter. Not a pretty sight. The girl had bottom, but she was a delicate female for all that. She shouldn't be exposed to such dire experiences. Besides, she'd raise a ruckus so there'd be no hiding the facts. Graydon had to hide Albert instead.

It wasn't going to be a pleasant job, but Graydon had done worse in the army. He kept telling himself that he was doing this for Daffy, as he wrapped the baron in the quilt on the bed and slung him over one shoulder. Thank goodness Albert was not a big man. The major needed his other hand for the candle, so he had to leave the man's satchel and cane, and his own cane. He'd manage.

Graydon staggered his way down the endless flight of marble steps, praying that last footman had gone about his rounds, then gone to his bed, and wondering if he'd do better to roll the bastard down. Then he could just dump him in some London back alley. The authorities would assume he'd been beaten and robbed at one of his usual low gaming hells—when they managed to identify him, hopefully after the wedding. No, even Gray's larceny knew some limits. He trudged on. At the bottom he propped the shrouded body against the carved newel post at the foot of the stairs, to rest.

"Couldn't even have the grace to cock up his toes on the ground floor," Graydon mused, then took up his burden again. He lurched down the long corridor to the back of the house, bashing his elbows on the narrower walls while Albert's booted feet kept banging into his legs, especially the wounded thigh, which was throbbing at every step. He put the body down again, to mop his brow, but none too gently this time. The dastard's false teeth fell out. Oh, how Daphne had better appreciate what he was doing for her, Graydon swore as he gingerly picked the ivory chompers up in his handkerchief and stuffed them into Awful Albert's coat pocket.

He slung him over his shoulder again and bent down for the candle. The teeth bit into his collar-bone. He grunted and proceeded through the kitchen and down another flight of even more narrow, twistier stairs to the wine cellar.

His leg protesting vehemently, Graydon found Albert a nice, cool resting place behind the well-stocked shelves. "You like it cold?" he asked the corpse, his voice echoing in the silence. "Better enjoy it now, old man, because it's hot where you're going."

Graydon wanted to wipe his sweating forehead and his hands, but his handkerchief was irretrievable. Thank goodness it did not have his monogram. He used his coat sleeve.

Albert would keep until tomorrow, but Graydon still had to go back up all the stairs to bring down the man's satchel and his cane. No one would believe he left without them.

By the time the major was finished, his leg almost buckled under him, even when he used his own cane. It was a marvel that no one in the house, upstairs or down, thought burglars had attacked. He collapsed onto his bed.

He needed a hot soak, but that would mean waking too many servants or carrying cans of water himself. Not tonight. Sleep was a long time coming, though, with that continuous ache. His last thought before he finally drifted off was that not even Daphne was worth this.

No one was having a good night. Of course, no one was having quite as bad a time of it as Uncle Albert, but *bad* was a relative term. Jake of the recently named Lamb Chop Thieves was having a lot of problems with his relatives, too.

The baron's wayside-tavern assailants were formerly called Sal's Fleas, Sal being the ugliest dog in the kingdom, and the smartest. The big tan hound would grab a purse, a parasol, or a parcel, anything of value, although her favorite was lunch pails. The bitch could prig fancy laundry off a line before the maids finished pegging the sheets. She could make off with small merchandise if the shop counters weren't too high, and she could drag away a haunch of beef while the butcher was wrapping Jake's measly sausage. Sal was so smart, and so well known to Bow Street, the Watch, and the shopkeepers, that Jake and his nephews had to leave London for a while.

Jake's nephews were so stupid that when Jake dyed the dog's fur to disguise her, Sailor and Handy were the only ones who couldn't recognize the four-legged felon. They were so inept, they couldn't keep a decrepit old man and his prissy valet from battering Jake's skull with a cane.

Now Jake had a bad headache. He also had no money, no place to sleep, and nothing in his belly. Sal was too smart to share the lamb chop. He also had two fools with nothing in their brain boxes. They were city boys who couldn't start a fire in the woods, couldn't snare a rabbit or tickle a trout. Nor could they be trusted out of Jake's sight without getting lost, since Sailor couldn't remember in which direction the sun rose and set, and Handy couldn't figure out why north wasn't up. It always was on the maps Jake tried to show them. Sal had more brains than the two of them combined.

Jake had always wanted a gang of his own. Some youngsters dream of having a fancy carriage, a yacht, a big house. Jake wanted a gang, a band of cutpurses, pickpockets, highwaymen, all under the command of his master thievery. That's why he took in his sister's two half-grown brats when she ran off with that cardsharp, the bailiffs at their heels. He didn't blame her for leaving; it was a step up for the girl. But Jake should have known she'd have taken the brats with her if they'd been worth tuppence. They weren't.

She'd named her sons after their respective fathers: Hey, Sailor, and Hi, Handsome. Sailor was too big and clumsy to be a pickpocket, and Handy was too weak to run fast enough. Sailor couldn't load a pistol correctly, and Handy was too squeamish to handle a knife. They were just as bad at cutting off ladies' reticules as they were at rolling drunks. Thank goodness for Sal, except that Jake resented being dubbed one of her parasites. It was supposed to be his band of rogues, not a blasted dog's. He'd have hated being part of the Lamb Chop Gang, if he knew that's what the denizens of that rural thieves' den were calling him and the boys. But he'd love the lamb chop.

After the old toff made the barkeep send for the magistrate, there was nothing for it but to take to the woods, Sailor and Handy supporting Jake between them. They were lucky to find an abandoned cottage. Hell, Jake was lucky the boys didn't drop him in a stream to drown. They had to lie low for a while, at least till his head cleared from that knock. He sent Sal out to see if she'd bring back a rabbit or something, or a chicken if they were near a farm. If his luck held, she wouldn't eat the whole thing.

While Jake nursed his broken head in the broken shack, he was plotting, as a clever ringleader was supposed to do. The old codger'd been talking of a wedding hereabouts soon, with earls and baronesses. That meant money. Lots of money. Rich guests would be arriving from London, and so would fancy foodstuffs to serve them and gifts for the newlyweds. With all that coming and going, a downy cove ought to be able to turn this setback into a golden opportunity.

Jake's plan was diabolically clever: it had two parts. One was to get his nevvies hired on as temporary help at that Woodhill Manor where the wedding was to take place. Jake still had a copy of those glowing references from Sir Winfred Prustock, that set him back a bundle from Frankie the Forger. Once inside the house, the lads could wait till nightfall and then hand him out any number of forks and spoons, silver teapots and gold plates, whatever they could carry off and fence. The rig almost worked twice in London, but the first time the incompetent gudgeons were dismissed in an hour. The next time they were put to washing windows, outside. They did manage to steal the rags and buckets.

The wedding wasn't for two weeks, from what Jake picked up at that tavern. Those swells wouldn't be desperate for hired help yet. Meantime, Jake was ready with the second part of his masterstroke: they'd take to the high toby. Jake and the Boys,

Highwaymen. It had a ring to it. And watches, stick-pins, purses.

Jake had a bad headache, and a really bad idea.

While Daphne was discovering the dead baron, Jake and his nephews were back on the main road not too far away from Woodhill Manor, lying in wait. Sailor was sleeping in wait, having been lying so long. Jake kicked him. A coach was coming.

Highwaymen usually had horses and guns. That was the accepted *modus operandi*. Jake was doing it the hard way, on foot, with one battered old pistol between the three of them. Sal stayed in the woods hunting rabbits. The dog was too smart to get involved.

While Graydon was struggling to convey the corpse to the wine cellar, a carriage was nearing the narrow part of the road Jake had selected. They could see by the lanterns on its sides that the coach was big and shiny and prosperous-looking. Jake gave the signal, a whistle. Then he whistled again. Finally he shouted, "Now, you dunderheads!"

"Stand and deliver," boomed Sailor from one side of the roadway.

"Or we'll shoot," squeaked Handy from the other, while Jake stood in the center of the road in front of the oncoming vehicle, brandishing his pistol. Jake let his eyes follow the movements of his nevvies. They were right in position, so the driver would think he was surrounded by highwaymen. A regular band of bridle culls, Jake thought proudly, except that Sailor had forgotten to raise his kerchief over his round, red-haired, baby face, and Handy was waving a tree branch, leaves and all, instead of the short oak limb that was supposed to look like a pistol. The coach kept coming. The driver whipped up his team. The guard on the seat next to him raised his blunderbuss.

Jake fired his pistol to show he meant business, hitting the coach dead on, taking a big chunk out of the polished woodwork. "Good shootin', Uncle Jake," Sailor yelled when the splinters stopped flying. Now the coachmen knew who they were, and knew Jake's gun was empty. They kept coming.

At the last minute Jake panicked and jumped aside, yelling, "Run, boys," as he dove into the woods. The coach didn't hit him, the wheels didn't run over him, the iron-shod hooves didn't come close, and he rolled down a sudden incline so fast that the blunderbuss missed him by a foot.

Then he struck a rock with his head, which wasn't made out of steel any more than were his nerves.

Now they were wanted in a whole nother county, and Jake had a lot worse headache.

# Chapter Ten

𝒯here was no rest for the weary, not at Woodhill Manor, and no avoiding old flames over the kippers and eggs, not for Daphne. She had a hundred things to do this morning, all of them problematical. Having breakfast with Gray was not high on her list of things to worry about. Making sure none of the servants went in to light Uncle Albert's fire or bring him hot water was.

She'd hardly slept all night, hearing noises that couldn't possibly be there. Her exhausted mind was merely playing tricks on her, she told herself. Uncle Albert was *not* coming back to haunt her; he had *not* been walking the manor house corridors and moaning on the stairs because he hadn't received proper burial. It was too soon.

Daphne didn't bother calling for her maid, but scrambled into an easily fastened dimity round gown and pulled a comb through her curls. No amount of primping by her abigail was going to erase the shadows under her eyes or put color back in Daphne's complexion, and there wasn't time.

Before rushing downstairs, Daphne popped her head into Mama's room. The bed-curtains were still drawn; Mama was still asleep. Next she peeked into Uncle Albert's room, after making sure the hallway was empty. The bed-curtains there were still drawn, too; Uncle Albert was still dead.

Then she had to spend time begging Cousin Harriet to stop her packing and come down to breakfast. Daphne told the older woman that the baron was too sick to be a bother to anyone, and Mama needed her support at such a time. Furthermore, Daphne needed her as a chaperone downstairs in the morning room. She shouldn't be alone with the two male guests. Thus appealed to, Cousin Harriet relented. In truth she didn't have anywhere else to go, Lady Whilton and Daphne being her only relatives, so she didn't need that much persuasion to stay. Her niece's wan face most likely would have been enough, after a hasty review of her own bank statements.

While Cousin Harriet changed out of her traveling costume, Daphne raced down the back stairs to the kitchen, scandalizing Cook and the other servants gathered at the table there by asking for a tray for Uncle Albert. No, she'd carry it herself, Daphne insisted, in case his illness was catching. She'd already been exposed. And no, she did not think a doctor should be sent for yet, but perhaps soon.

Cook fixed a tray of dry toast, thin porridge, and weak tea. Daphne decided her uncle would be too ill to eat much. The toast she could crumble into crumbs for the birds outside the open window, and the tea she could pour onto the lawn, but the gruel had to be returned to the kitchen unless she was to eat it herself. How could she think of eating anything, much less that mush, when her nerves were already gnawing at her insides? Besides, she still had to face breakfast with Graydon and his father.

First she scribbled off a note to Miles Pomeroy, begging him to come at his earliest convenience. The footman she handed it to said he'd get it to the stables instantly. A groom would set out within minutes. Daphne could breathe again. If Miles didn't come, didn't help, didn't have a plan . . . Oh dear, and she was supposed to make polite conversation?

No one at the table had much to say. Lord Hollister looked as bad as Uncle Albert, and his son looked worse. They must have stayed up half the night imbibing, like typical males trying to drown their sorrows instead of doing anything about them. At least the earl had an excuse for holding his head in his hands; his son never seemed to need an excuse for overindulging. Now Graydon's fine brown eyes were bloodshot, his complexion was pasty, and his usually laughing mouth was drawn down in a grimace. He even took his time standing when she entered the morning room. Good. She hoped he was suffering for his sins, of which he had many. She had made a good decision, Daphne told herself, to choose Miles—for help with Uncle Albert, that is.

As Daphne pushed some eggs around her plate, she wondered how soon she could expect him, and how soon she could expect Uncle Albert to make his presence, and present condition, known now that the sun was up on a lovely spring day. Even with the windows open and the drapes pulled, the room would grow warm.

No one else made a good meal of it either, except for Cousin Harriet, who ate as if this were her last breakfast. If that old buzzard left his sickbed, she might have to leave the manor. Daphne could not reassure her, not under the present circumstances. She just sent Ohlman out to refill the serving platters.

The butler returned with a fresh pot of coffee, since the gentlemen were making inroads there, at least, and a footman bearing a tray with additional portions of steak and kidneys. He also brought Miles Pomeroy, who was a frequent and welcome enough visitor that strict formality needn't be observed.

"I took the liberty, Miss Daphne—" Ohlman began, only to be interrupted by Daphne's scraping her chair back and leaping to her feet.

"Miles! You came even sooner than I hoped! Thank goodness."

Politeness dictated that Graydon and his father also stand up. Lord Hollister didn't bother. He just groaned and whispered, "Don't shout, girl." The major struggled erect, frowning mightily, both for the aggravation to his leg and the effusive greeting Daffy'd given her local swain.

Daphne recalled herself, and the company, and said, "But we can speak later. Won't you join us for breakfast?"

"Only for a moment, Miss Whilton. Shire business, don't you know." He took a seat next to Daphne, Graydon noticed with annoyance, and Ohlman poured him a cup of the fresh coffee while the footman filled his plate. If he ate all that, Graydon thought, the local pillar of virtue would turn into the local pillow of lard. The fellow was already leaning toward a paunch, Gray noted with satisfaction, as he sucked in his own firm abdomen. Besides, if Pomeroy's errand was so urgent, why was he wasting time, his and Daffy's?

"What is this official business, Pomeroy?" he prompted, hoping to get rid of the fellow with a reminder of his duty. It usually worked with those conscientious blokes.

Miles did put down his fork, but only to drink some coffee. "Another attempted robbery, Major," he said after a moment.

"What, did some poor starving mutt swipe a leg of mutton this time?"

"No, no dog was seen, but a band of ruffians did try to hold up Mr. Foggarty's coach last night. We think it might be the same gang"—Jake's heart would have swelled—"for they were just as bumbling and incompetent." He would have cried.

"Did they get away with anything?" Graydon wanted to know, thinking of his own ride tonight.

"No, Foggarty's guard scared them off with his blunderbuss, and the driver kept on moving."

"How awful," Cousin Harriet declared, watching Miles finish the last rasher of bacon, "that a body is not safe on these country byways. What are you doing about it, young man?"

"I've got men out trying to follow the bandits' paths, but they scattered into the woods. They're most likely long gone by now, but I'm trying to gather descriptions for a wanted poster. Strangers aren't all that frequent in the neighborhood. Two of the men wore masks, but the driver can identify the third robber. I want to see if his description matches Lord Whilton's of those footpads at the tavern with the dog."

"You want to see Uncle Albert?" Daphne asked in a faint voice. She had to get him aside first. "That's, ah, too bad. He's ill. You can't—"

"What Miss Whilton means is that you cannot see the baron because he already left," Graydon interrupted.

Daphne dropped her spoon. "He did?"

"Yes, I was about to tell you before Mr. Pomeroy arrived. The baron felt a bit better, but wished to consult his own London physician. Rather than wait here for his valet, he decided to ride to meet him on the road back, saving time. He left before the household was fully awake and entrusted me with his good-byes."

"Dash it, I must have just missed him!" Miles tossed his napkin on the table.

"To . . . to London, you say?" Daphne asked. At Graydon's nod, she put her own cloth down and stood. "Will you gentlemen excuse me for just a minute? I, ah, forgot something upstairs."

The men could hear her soft slippers scampering down the hall. Miles frowned. Miss Whilton shouldn't be running in the house that way, although he'd naturally not mention it in front of her relatives. He'd take her aside later. A little whisper in her ear should do it, unless she was rushing to get back to his company. His brow cleared at the thought and he was able to take another helping of shirred eggs. With the baron gone, there was no need for him to rush off in an ill-mannered frenzy.

Daphne tore up the stairs and raced down the

corridor. The last thing she was worried over was being thought a hoyden. None of the servants were about, so she dove into Uncle Albert's room and pulled open the bedhangings. Uncle Albert was gone.

To London? Daphne sank back on the bed where the baron had recently expired, she thought. There wasn't even a crease on the cover. Could she have been wrong, or was it all just a bad dream? Perhaps the oysters she ate last night had gone off. No, he'd been there, gasping and wheezing, then neither wheezing nor gasping. He was dead. She knew it. Could God have wasted a miracle on such a sinner? She didn't think it was likely. But Uncle Albert was gone.

She went back to the breakfast room, a great deal slower. The men stood until she resumed her seat, Graydon scowling. Daphne didn't notice. Miles did and thought the major was going to scold Daphne for her manners. Frippery fellow had no business calling Miss Whilton to account, had no business being here at all, if anyone asked his opinion, which they hadn't. But then, the lady had seemed happy enough to welcome him this morning, even effusive. "Had you wanted to see me over anything particular, my dear?" he asked, preparing to leave.

"What's that? Oh, no, just a detail about the wedding or something." She waved him away, leaving the butler to walk him to the door.

Yes, Miss Whilton's manners were sadly lacking. Of course, Mama could take her in hand.

Graydon felt better, seeing Daphne's absent-minded dismissal of her stalwart suitor. Now, if he could just get rid of everyone else, he might have her to himself for the morning. He suggested his father go up and start trying to make his peace with Lady Whilton. "Now that the baron is gone, there is no problem about that money. She doesn't have to sign anything to get rid of the dirty dish. So go tell her the twenty thousand is as good as hers, for goodness' sake, to do with as she wants."

"I don't know . . ." the earl began.

"What, are you afraid she's going to take the blunt and run off with some stable hand after you're wed? You have to know she's devoted to you. Besides, the money means nothing to you, and means a great deal to her."

"No, I meant I didn't know if she'd see me. I decided last night to swallow my pride, but she won't talk to me. I tried again first thing this morning."

"What, in her bedroom?" gasped Cousin Harriet, who was already irritated that young Howell could so cavalierly dismiss a sum of money she'd never see in her lifetime.

The earl gave her a sour look. "Never fear, her maid wouldn't let me in." He vowed to dismiss the hatchet-faced abigail as soon as he could, and find someplace else for this sharp-tongued cousin to reside. Maybe Cleo would give *her* the blasted twenty thousand pounds so she could set up her own establishment—in Ireland.

Daphne had been ignoring the conversation, but now she explained: "Mama was sleeping. She took laudanum." Then she went back to concentrating on the muffin she was shredding.

"You see? She didn't slam the door in your face. She'll see you soon, I'm sure. And you can turn on the Howell charm so the banns can be called Sunday."

"That vaunted charm didn't work for you, you silver-tongued devil," Harriet sniped as she left the breakfast room to fetch her pug for its morning walk.

Daphne was still not paying attention. She didn't even hear Graydon say he had an urgent task in London, that he might leave later that afternoon, or early the next morning. He'd return in a day or so, if anyone had any errands for him.

"I say, Daffy, I asked if you had any commissions in London for me."

"Commissions? I thought you were resigning yours."

Graydon shook his head at her vagueness. She didn't show a great deal more interest in him than she did in the Pomeroy popinjay. Deuce take the female, she was supposed to be relieved now that Albert was out of her hair. Perversely, she was drifting out the door, her brow furrowed with worry, her linen napkin still clutched in one dainty hand.

The earl left to camp outside his lady's door. Graydon decided not to follow Daphne while she was in this humor. Whatever charm he did possess would be wasted. He went to the stables instead, to notify the grooms he'd be leaving soon, and to see how hard it would be to get Albert into his carriage. The short walk convinced him he'd better go back upstairs and rest his leg before facing that ordeal. He didn't want Daphne to think him a paltry, whiny milksop, so he snuck in the kitchen entrance and requested a hot bath. Then he hobbled up the back stairs. Lud knew he was familiar enough with the route by now.

Daphne went about her business mechanically. She consulted with the housekeeper about the menus, tallied wedding invitation acceptances with the master guest list, and counted the flower tubs in the conservatory, all in a daze.

There was only one answer her reeling mind could come up with, an answer so unlikely that a miracle had better odds. Now, of course, the infuriating officer couldn't be found. Daphne knew Gray had gone out to the stables, she'd seen him head that way, limping badly, the clunch. He must be off on a long ride instead of resting his leg, and then he was leaving for a time. She shook her head.

Ohlman the butler was also shaking his head. He knew what he knew, and what he didn't know, he could find out. That was a butler's job. He knew the baron's hat and gloves were still on a shelf in the cloakroom where he'd put them himself. He knew Lord Whilton's bed hadn't been slept in. Ohlman checked: No carriage had been called out, no horse was missing, no carter had come by that morning. It was a definite puzzlement.

Ohlman wouldn't put it past that scamp Howell to have abducted the baron and spirited him away. Master Graydon had been a naughty little boy, a brash young man, and now a decidedly quixotic gentleman. Ohlman had hoped he was settled down enough for Miss Daphne, but if the handsome devil was still getting up to these mad starts . . .

But what was the point to abducting the baron? The dastard was still head of the family, to Ohlman's continued disgust and dismay. He shook his head and continued his chores.

One of those butler's duties was counting the bottles of champagne in the wine cellar to see if more was needed for the wedding, if there was to be a wedding. Ohlman prayed so, for he dearly loved his mistress, who kept him from having Awful Albert as a master. He'd been here at Woodhill Manor since she came as a bride, and he'd do anything to see her happy, her and Miss Daphne, of course.

And of course he found the baron, satchel and all. So the blackguard really was leaving, without any assistance of Lord Howell's, it seemed. Albert was obviously trying to pilfer some bottles from his brother's stock before he went. He'd even brought a quilt with him to keep the bottles from clinking. He must have got cold, though, taking a spasm or something, for he had the quilt wrapped around his shoulders. The villain never had time to lift one bottle. He never called for a coach because he never made it up the stairs.

But the family believed he'd left. They believed it enough to proceed with the wedding, without Albert's wretched interference. Ohlman knew what he knew, and he knew what had to be done to see his ladies happy. That was a butler's job. The question was if he was strong enough, and if the baron could bend enough. The rotter never bent when he was alive.

An hour later, Ohlman sent two strong footmen down to the wine cellar to move a huge cask of ale into the icehouse. The brew mightn't stay good till the wedding otherwise, he explained. There were bucketfuls to be sampled, to test the quality, so the lads were happy enough to comply. Albert didn't complain either.

# Chapter Eleven

$\mathscr{G}$raydon knew his way around Woodhill Manor, thank goodness. Having run tame there forever, and having played innumerable games of hide-and-go-seek with Daffy on rainy days, he knew all of the old place's ins and outs. One of those ins, or outs, used to be a door between the wine cellar and the service drive outside.

After a hot soak and a rest, therefore, Graydon went downstairs to reconnoiter, wandering through the pantry to the indoor entrance to the cellars. He found himself explaining his presence there to Cook, two helpers, and the pot boy, all looking at him curiously.

"Just checking to see if there is any special vintage I can pick up in London for the wedding celebrations. Something they mightn't have, don't you know."

Cook and the others knew Ohlman had spent an hour down there this very morning, checking the stock for the coming occasion. She shrugged and ordered her minions back to work. Cook didn't know what deviltry Master Graydon was up to now; she didn't want to know. She banged a few pots and pans as he lit the candle at the head of the cellar steps.

If he remembered correctly, the stairs to the outside door were along the opposite wall to the one he was on, and halfway back. The doorway was installed so large deliveries or huge barrels didn't have to be carried through the kitchens and wrestled down the narrow stairs. Yes, there it was, bolted from the inside. His luck was in that there was no padlock or key. All he had to do was draw the bolt now, bring his carriage around after dark, load up his burden, and be off.

He decided to bring that burden closer to the door, to save time later. He wouldn't want to keep his horses standing unattended any longer than necessary. Too, his leg would be less troublesome if he did the carrying in shorter segments.

Graydon carefully unlocked the door, in case there was someone about on the other side. Trust Ohlman to have even this exit so well oiled there wasn't the slightest squeak. He could only pray Ohlman wouldn't be around to check the lock today. Next Graydon retraced his steps down the stairs and back to the racks where he'd stashed the baron. Then he retraced his steps again to the racks in the other direction. And back. He ran to the other steps, the ones that led up to the kitchens, to reorient himself. He'd gone straight back last night, then right. No, maybe he'd gone left. Then again, maybe carrying the baron made the distance seem longer. He checked every narrow aisle, behind, under, and alongside every rack.

Unless there was another wine cellar altogether, Awful Albert was altogether missing. And Graydon's leg was throbbing again from tromping around the cold, damp, dirt floors.

He sat himself down on an upturned barrel to think about this new twist.

Jake would have been happy for a barrel or anything else to keep him off the cold, damp, dirt floor of the old cottage. But they'd burned the last stick of furniture in the place yesterday, just to cook a rabbit Sal brought in. Jake had set some snares last evening, but Sailor couldn't find them, and Handy couldn't bring himself to dispatch the trapped game anyway.

His head wrapped in a dirty bandage, Jake started to explain his new plan. The boys liked the old one better, where they'd go get positions at the manor house. They'd have dry beds instead of a pile of straw on the floor, and hot meals instead of the dog's leavings. Jake tried again for the fourth time, which was all right, because he was seeing two of each of them.

They couldn't go up to a nob's house looking like they were living off the land, he told them. No one was going to hire a down-at-heels vagabond to polish the silver. The servants might give them a bowl of soup, looking the way they did, but that was all. That was enough for Sailor and Handy.

"Then what about tomorrow and the next day, you misbegotten moth-brains?"

There were other big houses, weren't there? Sailor and Handy saw nothing wrong with making a living asking for positions but accepting handouts. They didn't even have to do any work that way.

They also couldn't provide for their poor old uncle, who cuffed Sailor along the head. "My way, we won't have to work for a long time neither, not none of us. We'll be on easy street with one quick job."

All they needed before approaching Woodhill Manor for that wedding was a stake. Clean clothes, a wash, a shave for Sailor, a haircut for Handy. Then they could even rent horses to make their getaway, Jake elaborated, forgetting that neither of his nephews had ever been on a horse. They'd never been footmen before, either, he said, brushing off their complaints. They just wouldn't make as fast a getaway, he reassured the boys, knowing that once they'd handed the sacks of booty to him through a window, he didn't care if they escaped or not. He'd be too long gone to know. Blood might be thicker than water, but it sure as hell wasn't as thick as the gold from melted-down candlesticks.

His new plan involved the rusty old saw he'd spotted in the back of the cottage. They'd lop a tree down right at that narrow part of the road, so carriages would have to stop. None of this getting mowed down by a fast-moving coach. When the guard got down to move the obstruction, Jake would aim his pistol at him, while the boys relieved the passengers of their valuables.

The plan was so simple, it had to work, if Sailor and Handy weren't simpler. They couldn't find the narrow part of the road, then they couldn't find an appropriate tree. They finally found a half-dead birch leaning against some others that seemed to fit the bill. If they could just push it hard enough, it might topple far enough into the road that they could drag it the rest of the way or roll it.

While they were preparing, Jake came walking down the road to see what was keeping the bacon-brained idiots. Two carriages had gone by and there'd be another any time now.

"One . . ."

"What the deuce is taking you nodcocks so long?"

"Two . . ."

"It doesn't have to be a big—"

"Push!"

"—tree—eeyee."

The birch tree didn't hit Jake. He jumped out of its way just in time. He did catch his foot on a protruding root, though, twisting the ankle so badly that he fell over, into a growth of stinging nettles that went right through his clothes but didn't manage to cushion his fall enough to keep his head from contacting yet another rock.

The boys dragged Jake back to the cottage, once they found it.

The next coach did come by shortly, but it was no grand equipage, which would have made Jake's regrets less, if he were conscious to appreciate the fact. The carriage, in fact, did not even have a guard or groom. It merely had one dour driver and one prissy passenger, Terwent, the baron's valet.

The driver refused to leave his cattle, smelling a trap. Terwent refused to leave the carriage, scenting hard work. So they sat there arguing long enough for seven gangs of cutthroats to steal the baron's baggage. Luckily a farmer came by in his empty wagon first, anxious to get to the bank to deposit the earnings from his successful sale. He kicked the birch aside as if it were a twig, spat on the ground, flicked the reins over his mules, and patted the heavy purse tucked into his shirt. Poor Jake. He'd have gone after the wrong vehicle anyway.

A dank wine cellar wasn't a great place to rest a wounded leg, but it was a fine place to think of ghosts and ghouls and dead bodies coming to life to haunt their tormentors, if one were of a gothicy turn of mind. Graydon wasn't. Unlike Daphne, he never once considered the metaphysical, miracle or mirage. No, he immediately figured that someone—not one of the servants, who would have caused an uproar at finding a cadaver between the Chablis and the claret—had made off with the baron's corpse. For sure Albert hadn't gone to seek better accommodations on his own.

Graydon knew that plenty of people in the house might have wished to see the baron disappear; in fact, he couldn't think of a single person who would weep at the wastrel's funeral. He could, however, think of only one resident of Woodhill Manor with enough daring and drive to do something about it. He slapped his thigh, then winced. But she was still his Daffy. They hadn't drained the pluck out of her after all, in making her a perfect lady.

Then Graydon thought some more, and was less pleased with the results of his cogitations. She couldn't have done it alone, moved Albert out of here and up one set of stairs or the other, to wherever she had him hidden. She must have had help, but who? Deuce take it, that must have been why she was so eager to see that Pomeroy twit.

How dare she turn to someone else in time of need?

It was Graydon who'd fished her out of Ryder's pond that time before she drowned. (He chose to disremember that it was he who let her tag along on an illicit swimming trip.) And it was he who dragged her off the back of that stallion to safety when the horse took exception to a hare breaking cover. He did not forget that she was on a horse too strong for her to handle—his horse, in fact—because he'd given in to her teasing to let her ride the brute. He'd never forget the lesson, that Daffy had more bottom than brains sometimes, and had to be protected from danger, from distress, and from her own often disastrous impulses. He'd made a mull of things in the past, but he was trying now. It was his job, looking after her. Let Pomeroy watch out for the rest of the county.

Which Pomeroy was doing, Graydon was sure. Miles had left after breakfast without a private parley with Daffy, without even a fond farewell. The conscientious clod was out looking for a pack of sneak thieves, not a hidey-hole for a dead noble-man. He'd been on horseback besides; the baron wasn't riding pillion.

If not Pomeroy, then who had helped Daffy, and why, and what the hell was she planning on doing with Uncle Albert?

"I? What have *I* done with him? What have *you* done with him, rather."

They were alone in the conservatory, except for a gardener shuffling about at the potting table in the corner. This wasn't how Graydon had planned on being alone with Daphne for the first time, but now wasn't the time for what he had in mind anyway.

"What do you mean what have I done with him?" he asked now, watching her clip withered blooms off a rosebush. "You didn't move him?"

She stopped clipping to look over her shoulder to make sure the gardener was out of hearing range. "Move him where?"

"How the devil should I know where! He's not where I put him."

"Aha! I knew you must have had something to do with—" Then his words penetrated. "He's not . . . ?"

"He's not in the wine cellar. Where did you leave him?"

"In his bedchamber, where he wheezed himself to death making nasty remarks." She shuddered.

Graydon wanted to take her in his arms but couldn't, not with the gardener present. Besides, she still seemed as prickly as the rosebush. "Poor puss," was all he said. "I didn't know you knew he was dead when I moved him. I hoped to save you from that, at least."

"Well, thank you, I suppose, although I lost two years off my life when I discovered him gone. What did you intend to do with him anyway?"

"Take him to Whilton House in London for his valet to find. I thought it might take long enough that the wedding could take place before the funeral."

She nodded. "That was my hope, too."

"By leaving him in his bed?"

"Of course not. I'm not that much a peagoose, Major. I simply hadn't figured it out yet. I was waiting to ask Miles—"

"Blast it, Daffy, how could you turn to that pompous jackass when I'm right here?"

She was cutting furiously at the plant now, half-live blossoms as well as the faded ones. "How was I supposed to know you'd help me?"

"You should have known, by Jupiter! I have always pulled your chestnuts from the fire."

"That was ages ago. We're not the same people. I have no reason to trust you the same way now." And plenty of reasons not to, she implied, turning her back to him, attacking a different bush.

That hurt. And he had no answer except his word on it: "You can."

The discussion had grown too personal for Daphne's peace of mind. She wasn't ready for this. Changing the somber mood, she turned back and taunted, "Certainly I can, after you've gone and lost Uncle Albert. Highly trustworthy, sir."

Graydon smiled. "A hit, Daffy, a palpable hit. But I insist he's not lost, just temporarily misplaced. We have to assume Ohlman knows where."

Daphne nodded. "Ohlman knows everything. I'll go ask him before luncheon."

"*We*'ll go ask him. I'm in this, too, sweetheart. I have to prove my reliability, don't I?" He reached out to pick a rose, to tuck in her curls, but she must have guessed his intention, for she swatted his hand away from the bush.

"Don't, we need them for the wedding," she said, as if she hadn't been decapitating the flowers and buds.

"So you think there will be a wedding after all? If so, there must be hope that the Whilton ladies have some forgiveness in them."

"Mama will do what's right for Mama," Daphne

stated firmly. "But yes, I think there will be a wedding in two weeks' time. If we are not all arrested for body-snatching."

# Chapter Twelve

The noontime meal consisted of cold chicken, cold beef, and a cold shoulder from Lady Whilton. She had consented to join the family for luncheon; she had not yet forgiven the earl. She wasn't ready to forgive his toplofty treatment of her, despite his seeming sincerity. He hadn't groveled enough, in her estimation, to ensure there would be no repetition of such despotism in the future. She did thaw a bit when she realized he wasn't just trying to coax her out of the megrims by saying Albert wouldn't bother them anymore.

"You mean the baron has really gone back to London?" she asked the company at large. Cousin Harriet shrugged, but Daphne nodded vigorously.

It was Graydon who replied: "That was my understanding of his destination, ma'am, but perhaps his plans changed. Your estimable butler might have additional information. Have you anything to add, Ohlman?"

Daphne watched as Ohlman straightened from

serving the earl's sister some pigeon pie. She saw that Graydon had none too subtly laid his finger alongside his nose, signaling the butler of his comprehension and connivance.

Ohlman cleared his throat. "Such was my understanding, ma'am, that the, ah, master was feeling poorly. Quite ill, indeed, and in something of a rush to be gone. You might say he was dead set on leaving us."

Daphne hid her face behind a napkin. Graydon winked at her. Ohlman continued: "Of course, I have no way of knowing if he reached his final destination of London as of yet, but I doubt it. However, I can assure you, madam, that he is definitely no longer in the house."

Graydon nodded and Daphne smiled at Ohlman, who continued serving the meal and directing the footmen. The old butler could only wonder if at least and at last these two recalcitrant lovers had reconciled, so in harmony did they seem.

Ohlman found out to the contrary later, to his disappointment, when they met after luncheon in the small butler's pantry to make plans for the evening. Ohlman would see that the servants were all busy close to the house, if Miss Daphne would ensure none of the guests chose to take an evening stroll.

"But I'm coming with you," she declared.

To which Lord Howell replied, "Oh, no, you're not, brat. You are staying inside."

Daphne stamped her foot. "Don't start giving orders, Major. You are not in the army anymore."

"And I've never turned a raw recruit over my

knee, so don't tempt me. You're to keep as far away from the icehouse as possible, for your own good."

"Now you're sounding as patronizing as your father, thinking you know what's best for everyone else. Don't you Howell men ever learn?"

"And don't you Whilton women ever use the brains God gave a duck to see what's in your best interest?"

Ohlman cleared his throat.

Daphne took a deep breath. "Don't be a cake, Gray. You'll need help. You and Ohlman cannot manage Uncle Albert and the horses and the icehouse doors, and keep watch, too."

"I'll have my groom."

"What? You might as well publish Uncle's death in the newspapers!"

"Nonsense, the man knows better than to gossip. Besides, I'll just say I'm carrying a load of bad ale back to London to complain to the shippers. Doing Ohlman here a favor."

"No one will believe such a Banbury tale, the dashing Major Howell playing errand boy."

"Thank you for the 'dashing,' my dear, I think. But they're more liable to believe that than they'll believe you just innocently happened near the icehouse in the middle of the night! Be reasonable, Daff; your reputation will be in shreds."

Daphne knew he was right; the icehouse was nowhere near the gardens. "That's Miss Whilton to you, Major."

"And that bird won't fly, brat, so stubble it. Save your airs for Moral Miles. You can't be a lady and a grave robber both."

"And I can't be a grave robber, if that's what it is, sitting in the parlor with my embroidery."

They all knew she'd be at the icehouse after dark. Graydon should have saved his breath to convince the baron's valet.

Terwent arrived midafternoon, insulted over his treatment at the hands of the bumbling footpads, bovine farmers, and insolent coachmen. Nor did he think the bandage tied around his head, from where it had connected with the baron's flailing cane, did much for his appearance. He was wrong, it did; the wide swath of white cloth hid some of the pinch-faced valet's resemblance to a dyspeptic dachshund.

Terwent refused to believe that his master wasn't at Woodhill Manor. That was the ultimate indignity. He'd had to suffer some rustic quack's ministrations, then a night in a hedge tavern sleeping on unaired, and likely unwashed, sheets, and a morning in a rattling coach going nowhere fast. And he had it all to do again in reverse, to find his missing master.

"No, the baron would not have left without me," Terwent insisted. "He distinctly ordered me to arrive here as soon as possible before he drove off with that bumpkin."

"That bumpkin is Miss Whilton's devoted friend and hopeful suitor," Graydon interjected with a touch of deviltry that brought a charming blush to Daphne's cheeks and a splotch of something else altogether to the valet's pasty complexion. They were in the butler's pantry again, which was becoming more and more crowded. Ohlman had sent for the major when the valet refused to be dislodged, recalling Master Graydon's facile tongue and easy disregard for the truth. Daphne had naturally followed, scenting more intrigue. Graydon was paying her back for snooping.

"Pardon, I'm sure, miss," Terwent stammered. "But, but, I have his lordship's medicines. He'd never go on without them. Or me."

"But he didn't, old chap." Graydon placed his arm across the valet's chicken-narrow shoulders and started herding him toward the front door. "He just tried to get to you sooner, to save you part of a wasted journey."

"But how could I have missed him then?"

"Who knows? We're not precisely sure who took him up. Perhaps they took a back road, or were in a closed carriage."

The valet was confused. He hadn't seen any carriages at all, just the farmer's wagon.

"It's possible he stopped in the village first," Daphne suggested, seeing the indecision in Terwent's beady eyes. "The Golden Crown serves a tolerable punch, I've always heard. The baron did like his, ah, refreshments, you know."

Terwent knew all too well. He was afraid the baron was lying in some field right now, passed out among something unmentionable but common in uncivilized rural areas, something for Terwent to try to remove from his clothing tomorrow. The valet wrinkled his long, thin nose.

"No," Graydon reflected. "I think he went straight to that low tavern where you were accosted and forced to spend the night. He was that worried about your health."

That was pitching it too rum, Graydon realized. The baron's being concerned with anyone else's well-being or comfort was as likely as him traipsing cross-country through the cow chips, or staying at the village inn when he owned the whole of Woodhill Manor.

The valet's eyes narrowed—from beady to slits—as Daphne, Graydon, and Ohlman watched him cogitate. They could almost hear the wheels spin. Terwent didn't know what to think, except that the two nobs and the oldster in the wig were mighty eager to see him gone. There was some hugger-mugger afoot here, or his name wasn't Versey Terwent, which it wasn't, but he wasn't going to confess his forged references now.

So what game were they playing, and was the baron in on it? Terwent wouldn't put it past the old sot to shab off on him, owing his back salary and all. But Terwent had the luggage. The baron had to know Terwent would sell everything he could, and ditch all those potions and elixirs that were going to keep the dissipated drunkard virile, he thought. No, there was something deuced odd here. He was even more sure when Major Howell tossed him two golden boys, for expenses, until he found the baron.

In general, Terwent was not at all devoted to his employer, just to his salary, when he got it. Meantime, it was not an arduous job, since the baron didn't change his clothes that often, and there was hardly any bathwater to lug around. He paid well when the dibs were in tune, which wasn't often of late, but Terwent always managed to find the odd coin or two in the baron's pockets when the old man was in his cups. Besides, other positions were hard to come by. With the baron as referent, they'd be just about impossible. Then, too, Lord Whilton clearly had one foot in the grave, despite all the nostrums in the kingdom. Terwent would have helped him lift the other foot, if he thought the baron had made the changes in his will the old rip had promised.

Meantime he had to find him. It sure as hell didn't look like this bunch was going to join in the search. What did they care that the baron was wandering around the wilds of Hampshire somewhere, cold, lost, hungry—and holding Terwent's back salary?

No one thought to put a lock on the icehouse door. There was a heavy bolt to keep children out and away from danger, but who would steal ice?

Sailor and Handy, that's who. Of course, they did not know it was an icehouse when they found a low door set into a rock arch near a pool, toward the edge of the woods. They were looking for the traps Jake had set, while he lay back at the cottage, alternately moaning from the pain to his foot, cursing from the sting of the nettles, or unconscious from the new blow to his head. The boys thought he'd be happier if they could find something to eat besides the stale bread and rabbit stew. He'd be happier yet if they could find something worth stealing.

The brothers were astounded to find a door so far from any sign of habitation. Country folk were different, but this was passing strange.

They watched from the woods for a good long while, waiting to see if anyone came or went. No one did, so Sailor pushed Handy out from under the concealing bushes. "Go knock."

"Why me?"

" 'Cause I'm bigger." What he meant was that

he'd box his little brother's ears if Handy didn't do the dirty work.

Handy scampered over to the low wooden door, rapped twice, then scampered back to Sailor's side. "No one home."

So they looked around some more, and listened to birds singing and Sal splashing in the pond. Then they approached the door. Handy kept looking over his shoulder while Sailor took a minute to figure out the latch. The cold breath of air that hit his face had Handy back in the woods before the ghost could say "Boo." Sailor went in, seeming to be swallowed up by the hill of dirt. He came out and beckoned to his brother. "Not even a pat of butter keepin' cold. Nothin' but ice, slabs what must've come from the pond in winter. And this big barrel what smells like ale."

So they took the barrel. Sailor slung it over his back and hunched toward the woods. Handy stole the ice, or as much as he could get into his hat and Sailor's hat.

They returned to the crumpled cottage and packed the ice around the still-sleeping Jake, around his swollen ankle, under his broken head, and on the angry red welts from the nettles. Uncle Jake was going to feel a lot better when he woke up, they were positive. Uncle Jake was going to have pneumonia when he woke up, his clothes sopping wet, his whole body chilled. But that was later.

First the boys were going to sample the ale.

Oh, boy.

Handy keeled right over, right on top of Jake's good ankle, which wasn't going to be so good after this.

Some time later, they sat in the cottage again, shaking their heads over the strange country ways.

"D'you think they do all their dead 'uns this way, like pickles?"

Handy giggled. "An' put their gin in coffins?"

They had found the baron's ivory-topped cane and his satchel that held a clean shirt and fresh cravat, a nightshirt, and a silver flask of Blue Ruin. Uncle Jake needed the cane. He could use the neck-cloth to tie up his head, and the nightshirt in strips to bind his ankle. The silver flask he'd sell for food—but he wasn't getting the whiskey.

If Jake were awake, he'd recognize what a valuable commodity they had on their hands. A dead nobleman was worth something to someone, especially to those folks who were keeping him on ice instead of giving him a proper burial. But Jake wasn't awake, and his nephews weren't about to spend the night with a baron in a barrel.

"His spirit's comin' to haunt us already," Handy swore, hearing a nightjar call.

"Our blood'll be sucked dry by morning, you wait'n see." Sailor was already pale, his freckles standing out like ink spots, or blood spatters. "He must be a vampire. That's why he's not in a church graveyard or nothin'."

Handy shivered. "No, I say he comes back as a demon what steals our souls 'cause we stole his barrel. Or else he wanders forever, wailin' 'cause he ain't got a comfortable restin' place, all scrunched up in that keg."

"Think we got to bury him?"

"Not me. I ain't touchin' him. You're bigger."

They decided to take him back, to let whoever put him in the icehouse suffer the consequences.

They'd return him, barrel and all, as soon as the silver flask was empty. Maybe they better wait for Jake to wake up, or for dark.

# Chapter Thirteen

"*B*loody hell! Not again!"

They were out by the icehouse after dinner. Lady Whilton wouldn't hear of Graydon setting forth for London after dark, especially with highwaymen in the neighborhood, so she moved dinner forward an hour. The earl had taken his son aside and begged, "Not that you've ever heeded my words, boy, but this isn't the time to be kicking up a lark. I don't know why you think you have to go haring off to the city, but if it's to stir up any more scandalbroth, please wait till after the wedding."

Graydon was able to assure his father that such was not his intention.

"Good, because if Cleo gets wind of your tomcatting, she'll have my hide. Insult to the chit, don't you know, even if you have no intentions there. Staying at the house and all."

"Don't worry, Daphne knows exactly why I'm going to Town, and she approves heartily."

His father smiled knowingly and bobbed his

head. "A surprise for the wedding, eh? That's aces, then."

A kegful of corpse would certainly be a surprise. Getting Albert packed off to London was definitely something for the wedding, so Graydon saw no reason to disabuse the governor of his happy surmises.

"Glad to see you two on better terms," the earl continued. "Make things easier for me with the gel's mother. Speaking of Cleo, could you stop in at Rundell's for me and buy her a trinket? I've got diamonds for the wedding, but might be she'd come out of the boughs a little quicker with a gift. You'll know what kind of gewgaw, something sincere."

Graydon agreed, eager to be on his way before the governor thought of any other errands. He didn't want to be in London when Albert's body was found. But his father wasn't finished: "Wouldn't do yourself any harm to get Daphne some frippery or other either, but that's neither here nor there. You never did take my advice," he complained, still angry that his son and heir had joined the army against his wishes. "You could never do better than the chit."

"I just might listen this time," Graydon said as he saw his father take his place at the whist table with Lady Whilton, Cousin Harriet, and his aunt Sondra. "And you take my advice," he whispered in the earl's ear. "Let her win."

Then Graydon had gone out to the stables to collect his curricle and pair. He gave some excuse not to take his groom after all, for the barrel had to be tied on behind where the servant would have stood. Unless they decanted Uncle Albert and laid him along the floorboards, which was Daphne's suggestion. Buy her some folderol indeed! That chit wouldn't be happy with rubies. Nothing less than his arrest would do!

She was waiting out there with Ohlman when Graydon drove around to the icehouse, blankets and ropes in her hands. She put them down to go to his horses' heads, crooning softly to the well-mannered pair. At least she was a competent co-conspirator, his Daffy. And she looked adorable in some dark-colored cloak, the hood sliding back from her golden curls, like a fairy nymph in an ineffective disguise.

Ohlman was holding a lantern. While he unbolted the icehouse door he reported that the servants were all indoors celebrating the prenuptials with the ale that had been in the barrel, before the baron. They would be too busy in the next two weeks for much belowstairs festivities, the butler had explained to the staff, and no one had argued.

So the baron's pallbearers and hearse were ready. The baron wasn't.

Daphne laughed. There wasn't much else to do, and the look on Gray's handsome face was priceless. Ohlman frowned, relatched the icehouse door, bowed, and made his stately way back toward the house in search of something a bit more sustaining than the ale in the kitchen.

"Thunder and turf." Coming around to the horses' heads, Graydon cursed again. Daphne laughed again, and he had to join in, so absurd was the situation. "Where the devil do you think he's gone to now?" he asked when they stopped chuckling. Neither, of course, had any answer, so the major piled the ropes and stuff onto his curricle. When he lifted the old blankets, he couldn't resist asking: "Care for a picnic by moonlight, sweetheart?"

To which his ever-romantical darling replied: "Don't be a clunch." But he noticed that she did clamber up into his carriage quickly enough for the ride to the stables, rather than walking back to the house by herself. Graydon wanted to tell himself that it was his company she sought. He rather suspected it was Uncle Albert's she was avoiding.

Miles Pomeroy was waiting for Daphne when they returned to the drawing room. He was waiting none too patiently, judging from how he was swatting his gloves against his thigh, Ohlman not having been on duty by the door to relieve him of those articles. The two older ladies were rapt in a hand of piquet, and Lord Hollister had finally got Lady Whilton to grant him a private conversation on the sofa across the room. They were all ignoring Pomeroy's presence, having grown accustomed to his frequent after-dinner visits. Not so Major Howell.

"What, back again, Pomeroy?" Graydon asked as he escorted Daphne to a seat near the fireplace. "Crime wave over for the day?"

Miles looked on the major with equal disfavor, noting the highly polished boots, the intricate cravat, the well-starched shirt collars of the dandified Town rake. "They told me you were leaving for London."

Cousin Harriet raised her eyes from the cards. "Thought you left already on some urgent business. Daphne said she was going to see you out."

"Yes, but one of my horses came up lame. I decided to wait for morning after all."

The major lied with an ease that had Daphne impressed at his ready ingenuity, and horrified at his lack of conscience. The man must make a habit out of prevarication, so readily did rappers fall from his lips. Uttering the slightest falsehood always had Daphne nearly stuttering, as now, when she saw Miles observing her wet slippers and damp hem.

"I, ah, went with him to the stables to, ah, look at the horse, too." Knowing how conscientious Miles was with his own cattle, although they were nowhere near the high-steppers Graydon drove, she added, "The horse seemed to be fine." That at least was the truth.

If he wasn't satisfied with what these two had been doing together for so long, Miles did not get the chance to complain, for Ohlman brought the tea tray in then. Daphne invited Miles to stay, of course; he accepted, of course.

Deuce take it, Graydon thought, didn't the fellow ever eat at his own table? Then again, he looked like he ate two of every meal. Pomeroy would soon look like a turnip if he wasn't careful, besides acting like one. What could Daffy see in the gapeseed?

Daphne saw a comfortable country gentleman who didn't like subterfuge, who disdained pretense, and who wasn't so puffed up with his own conceit that he spent more time with his tailor than with his tenants. With simple sandy hair turning to gray and hazel eyes, he wasn't stunningly handsome like Gray, but he was attractive in a pleasant, friendly way. If he was perhaps more solemn than she could have wished, well, he took his responsibilities seriously, unlike others she could name who almost broke their fathers' hearts by hieing off to war.

Mostly what she saw, as she looked from Miles to Graydon and back again, was that they were glaring at each other like two dogs with one bone. As ridiculous as it seemed, Gray, who could never be happy with just one woman, was jealous. It was ridiculous, and delicious. Let him see what it was like to share someone's affections, she thought with satisfaction, and smiled.

Graydon saw that smile and thought it was for puff-belly Pomeroy. He took his tea, sweetened just the way he liked it, and moved over by his father. Graydon took the opportunity of Lady Whilton's passing cups and plates to whisper that, with the London jaunt off, the governor would have to do his own wooing, without counting on buying the lady's favor.

The earl jerked his head toward where Miles hovered over Daphne and the raspberry tarts. "And you'd better look to your own interests, son."

Graydon did love raspberry tarts, but he didn't think that was what the governor had in mind. Still, he casually strolled back toward Daphne and Pomeroy. The female relations had gone to bed, and the earl and the baroness were resuming their conversation at the other side of the room.

Graydon dragged his chair closer to Daphne's. "What brings you out so late, Pomeroy?" he asked, hinting at the other's ill manners in calling after dark.

"Oh, Miles knows he's always welcome," Daphne chirped, revenge being as sweet as one of Cook's tarts.

But Miles insisted he was here on duty. "Some of us don't get to lounge by the fireside all night," he sniped.

"And some of us earned the right to some peace, at Salamanca," Graydon shot right back.

Daphne intervened. "There are many ways to

serve one's country. But tell us, Miles, are you still looking for those footpads?"

"No. I mean yes, but that blasted—pardon, Miss Daphne—that valet of Lord Whilton's has been pestering me all day. The fellow was at the Golden Crown claiming the baron must have met with foul play, and demanding I make an investigation."

"And you listened to a valet?" the major asked.

"Deuce take it, the man showed me all the baron's pills and potions. He swore the baron couldn't live two days without them."

He couldn't live one day without them, it seemed, but Daphne wasn't going to tell Miles that. Gray was no help, suddenly finding great interest in selecting another pastry. "Did Terwent go back to that hedge tavern where he was staying? Uncle Albert might have returned there looking for him."

"Yes, and he looked all through town and everywhere between. He says no one's seen hide nor hair of the baron. You have to admit they'd recognize him hereabouts."

"And if they didn't, they'd remember him," she agreed. Uncle Albert certainly made an impression.

"Terwent claims no one here could tell him who drove the baron away or who saddled a horse for him. He even suggested the man might never have left the Manor."

"Oh, he left, all right." Graydon wiped a crumb from his breeches.

Daphne said, "You know what Uncle Albert was like. Why would we keep him?"

" 'Was'? What do you mean, 'was'?"

Graydon jumped in. "She means the day you

brought him here. He was castaway and in a snit. We were all of us glad to see him leave." Not as glad as Graydon'd be to see this parsonlike Pomeroy leave.

"Then who took him, and where?" Miles demanded.

"Oh dear." Daphne just couldn't do it. She couldn't weave a story out of whole cloth, not to poor Miles, who never swerved from the truth, no matter how unpalatable. "I think we have to talk."

"Devil take it, Miss Daphne, we are talking."

"No, I mean really talk."

Graydon was frowning and shaking his head. "It's not at all necessary."

But it was, to Daphne. She couldn't lie to the man she was thinking of marrying. "Excuse us a moment please, Miles." She pulled on the major's coat sleeve until he rose with her and walked over to the window alcove. "We have to tell him. He's going to be looking for Uncle Albert anyway. Now he'll help us find him."

"But then what? He'll blast his find from the church steps."

"No, he won't. Miles is loyal and trustworthy and helpful," she insisted.

"Devil a bit, Daffy, if that's what you want, get a dog, for goodness' sake! Don't get porridge-head Pomeroy involved in this."

"Don't call him names, don't call me Daffy, and don't tell me what to do! You haven't been a whole lot of help in this situation, Major Missing-bodies, and Miles is my friend."

"Then go ahead and tell him, and wait for your friend to clap us all in gaol."

While Graydon was still seething, Daphne did

just that; she told Miles about Uncle Albert. She didn't have long to wait.

"You did what?" Miles shouted.

Daphne tried to shush him, looking toward her mother, while Major Howell grinned. Pomeroy's face had gone all red, and his cheeks puffed out. "That's criminal," he screamed, but in a hoarse whisper. "It's against the law!"

"What law?" Graydon wanted to know.

"There must be a hundred statutes about reporting dead bodies! I'd have to check my books. Lud, people'd be burying their grandmothers in the backyard rather than pay funeral costs." He took a deep swallow of tea. "Tarnation, Daphne, Miss Whilton, how the deuce could you think to keep it a secret?"

"Graydon and I thought it was more important to hold the wedding, for our parents' sakes." She nodded again toward the older couple, sitting closer together than they had been.

Miles didn't like that partnership, not the earl and Lady Whilton, but that "Graydon and I." He didn't like to think of his future bride—for so he was wont to think of Daphne—intriguing with that hey-go-mad Howell. "Well, you can't do it," he therefore stated. "As an officer of the law, I insist you declare him legally dead. I can fill out the forms. Then you must see him properly buried."

"That's just the problem, Miles. We can't bury him. We can't even find him."

Miles spilled his tea. Graydon helpfully handed over his own napkin. "Yes, someone stole the corpse on us," he offered. "Likely for ransom."

Pomeroy ignored him and glared at Daphne. "You

see? Do you see what your interfering with the law has done? Lies only lead to more lies, crimes to more crimes." He angrily swiped at the damp patch in his lap. "And you never did say what the baron died of."

Daphne was taken aback. "What, do you think I killed him?"

Now Miles turned his ire on Graydon. "I honestly don't know what to think anymore. That you could be involved in such hugger-mugger . . . and an ex-soldier. Everyone knows how cheap they hold life."

"No, everyone knows how precious they consider it, having been so close to death," Graydon responded furiously, restrained from contradicting his own words only by the lack of his sword at his side. "And that old makebait died because his heart finally shriveled up out of meanness."

"No, Gray, he died because he couldn't breathe right. He was wheezing something terrible when I went to see him. I do think I may have killed him after all."

"Don't be a goose, Daffy. You heard how many powders and prescriptions he took. He stuck his spoon in the wall after fifty or sixty years of dissolution. And last night he was as drunk as a—"

"Lord?" Miles put in, from his position in the landed gentry, and from seeing this handsome titled devil rush to Miss Whilton's defense.

Daphne was oblivious to them both. "But he mightn't have died right then if I hadn't argued with him again about the twenty thousand pounds."

Pomeroy's ears perked up. "What twenty thousand pounds?"

"The money Papa set aside for my mother, in

case she married and her widow's annuity ended. Mama's dowry, I suppose. Lord Hollister didn't approve, but Mama wanted the money for me, it seems."

"For you?" That widow's wedding was growing more important to Pomeroy by the minute. The major groaned as he saw the light of greed shine in Pomeroy's eyes. Poor Daphne, and she thought the dastard loved her. At least maybe Pomeroy would be more cooperative about keeping Whilton's death quiet now.

"So what will you do?" Graydon asked, bringing Pomeroy's attention back to the present and away from a town house in London, a racing phaeton, a box at the opera, and a yacht.

"Do? Oh, yes. I'll have to look for the baron, of course, as that Terwent character requested." He tried to make light of his defection. "Can't leave a body littering the countryside, don't you know. I suppose I'll have to look for the extortionists, too, once you get a ransom notice. If I find him, the corpse, I mean, I'll have to make the death public. But if I don't, there's no one else to say if he's dead or alive, right?"

"Ohlman knows," Daphne told him, ever truthful. "But he won't tell anyone."

"Then it's a matter of *habeas corpus*. No body, no, ah, need for a death certificate and all that."

Daphne smiled. "Thank you, Miles; I knew I could count on you to understand."

Graydon almost choked on his tea. Love might be blind, but was Daffy so enamored that she was deaf and dumb besides? He couldn't believe she'd lost all her wits—to this puff-guts.

Then she reached over and patted Pomeroy's hand and put the last raspberry tart on his plate. Hell and damnation!

# *Chapter Fourteen*

*J*ake woke with a smile on his face. His pants were damp; his youth was coming back. No, he was just wet. He looked up through the holes in the cottage roof and saw stars. It wasn't even raining. He remembered a tree falling on him, or near enough as made no difference, the way he felt. Those nimwit nevvies of his must have dragged him through a streambed before taking him home, if the abandoned shack could be so called. It was a wonder he didn't catch his death from the dowsing, whatever the dunderheads had done to him. Then he sneezed, coughed, shivered, and stopped wondering.

One good thing about the country: when the furniture was gone, you could still find something to burn. Jake hobbled to the stack of kindling he'd made the boys find yesterday, and threw some on the crumbling stone hearth. The fireplace might give off more smoke than heat, but it was something. He hobbled back to his pile of wet blankets to drag them closer to the miserly flames. Damn if both his legs didn't feel broke. One was wrapped in something, the other wasn't, and his cloth-head kin were nowhere in sight. He coughed some more. The smoke was worse than usual.

When his eyes cleared, he spotted a bundle of something in the corner, so he lurched in that direction. His eyes filled with tears of joy—or smoke. The boys had managed to steal something after all. On their own, after years of his lessons and lectures, they'd made a haul. Not a big haul, true, and they might even now be rotting in gaol for their crimes, but they'd done just right: they'd brought the booty to Uncle Jake. They were finally as smart as the dog Sal.

The satchel was of good quality, he could tell even in the dim light. Leather, with brass catches. Someone would pay something for it. Next to it was a silver flask, engraved, but with no initials, thank goodness. It would fetch a handsome penny, too. Too bad it was empty. And too bad he wasn't in London.

The rotten thing about the country was, there was so much of it, with nothing in between. Jake knew he couldn't try fencing this stuff in the local village so close to the crime, even if there was a pawnshop, which he doubted, and the next town was a good five miles away. He couldn't just walk to the corner and hail a hackney, either. In London he'd have traded these items for a heavy wet, a hearty meal, and a bit of jingle that could keep him till the next opportunity. Now all he could do was try to inhale fumes from the flask and keep looking.

Behind the suitcase was a cane, one whose

carved bone handle Jake recognized well. He should. There was a matching indentation in his head. So his gang of geniuses had managed to lift that old bastard's poke. Well, well, well. Jake hoped they bashed his head in while they were doing it, but his confidence in Sailor and Handy was not quite that high.

Either way, that old bugger was a flash cove with a carriage of his own and a valet, so there must be a fortune in the bag. There wasn't. Jake dumped the contents on the floor. No wallet, no jewels, no bank books or important papers. Nothing but linen. His addlepated relatives had robbed a well-heeled toff, and come up with his underwear!

Unless, Jake mused, there had indeed been a roll of soft that the boys had made off with, abandoning him here. He knew that's what *he* would have done. Jake rubbed his sweaty brow, thinking. He thought that he was too cold to sweat. The fire wasn't that hot; he was feverish. If they didn't come back, he was like to die here. Then again, with their level of competence, he was like to die if they did come back, only quicker.

Meanwhile he pawed through the stuff from the satchel. Shirts, hose—and a white flannel night-shirt that was the softest thing he'd touched since that French whore when the dibs were in tune, a long, long time ago. He quickly shed his damp garments and put on the long, flowing gown, marveling at its warmth and clean smell and feel of luxury. He used the cane to limp closer to the fire, almost crying with the pleasure.

That's how the boys found him when they returned from restoring the barrel: a white-robed figure standing in the smoke, moaning and waving the dead man's cane around.

"He's back!" Handy shrieked. "I knew he'd come back to haunt us!" He fainted again, this time missing his uncle.

Sailor didn't, when he keeled over.

"He's back," Ohlman whispered into Graydon's ear as the butler poured his coffee at breakfast the following morning.

"Who, that nincompoop Pomeroy?"

"No, the baron."

Graydon took a quick swallow, burning his tongue. "Well," he said loudly enough for the others present, "it looks like I'll be off for London after all. The horses are fine."

Neither his father nor Lady Whilton was down for breakfast yet, although it was Sunday and the banns were to be read in church today unless Lady Whilton sent word to cancel them. Major Howell's announcement was received with disinterest from his aunt and Cousin Harriet, but Daphne sat up straighter. She looked tired, as though she hadn't slept well for worrying, but pleased now.

"Do you have to leave before church? I know you don't care about not traveling on a Sunday, but Mama would be happier."

"I thought I might wait until dusk again, since it bids to be a clear night." And since he'd rather not be seen with an ale keg instead of a tiger up behind him.

Ohlman cleared his throat. "If I might suggest an earlier departure, my lord. The, ah, barometer is falling. I'm afraid there will be some, ah, deterioration in the, ah, weather."

Agh. Graydon made a face at the butler's none too subtle hints about the baron's condition. He pushed his plate away, having lost all appetite.

Daphne was anxious enough to see him gone now that she understood. "Yes, the sooner you leave, the less traffic there will be. You'll make better time. Unfortunately you'll miss Mr. Pomeroy"—please, Lord—"for he usually takes luncheon with us on Sundays."

"And any other day," Cousin Harriet added, making Graydon smile again. He even took a bite of salmon.

Daphne was impatient with him to finish his breakfast and leave. "Miles will soon be out looking for—"

"His breakfast? I'm surprised the chap isn't here now, or are we not in good odor with him?" Graydon teased, knowing she'd understand how some of them were not in good odor at all. Devil a bit, if he was going to drive the hearse, he may as well get the pleasure of seeing Daffy's dimples one last time. And if he could make Pomeroy appear the glutton, so much the better.

Daphne was starting to give him a setdown when Cousin Harriet pokered up. "What's that? The Whiltons not good enough for a mere country squire?"

"No, no, Cousin, that's not what Major Howell meant to imply. It better not be," she muttered under her breath. If she weren't ages out of the schoolroom, she'd stick her tongue out at him, insufferable man, teasing at a time like this. And picking on poor Miles, who was only trying to do his job. "Miles is just busy these days. There seems to be a rash of crimes."

Cousin Harriet went back to her hearty meal. "That figures, with Awful Albert in the vicinity. Rashes, fluxes, the pox. I wouldn't be surprised if that man brought plagues and locusts to the neighborhood."

Flies, perhaps, Graydon thought. "Yes, well, I had better be going."

They met again at the icehouse for a hasty conference. Daphne felt somewhat like one of Macbeth's witches out in the mist plotting their spells, eye of newt, tongue of bat, potted peer. Graydon had to be on his way before the family left for church and before the sun was much higher in the sky, but they had to rethink their plans.

It was too chancy for Graydon to be smuggling Uncle Albert into the baron's own town house by the light of day, or even after dark if any neighbors were about. The major might have done it sooner, carried the baron home as though he'd found him drunk somewhere. No one would question such a common event in Uncle Albert's life. But not even Gray could get away with such a thing now, and even if he did, no one would believe the baron had died a natural death, finding him in a barrel. Or bent over double. Ohlman was of the opinion that Uncle Albert might not straighten out again for three or four days, if ever. The very last thing they needed was a murder inquiry.

"So what now?" Daphne asked. "It's too bad we can't toss him overboard like a burial at sea. But we cannot just dump him on the side of the road. Miles would have a fit."

"And it matters what Miles thinks?" Graydon wasn't teasing anymore, but Daphne ignored his lowered brow. He had no right to ask such a personal question, and she did not want to think about her answer.

"It matters if Miles finds Uncle Albert under a bush somewhere. Besides, it would be wrong. I mean, hiding him for a while is one thing; never getting him into the family plot is another. Oh, I wish we'd never got into this!"

"What about the wedding, then? I thought you believed your mother's happiness depended on delaying the baron's official demise."

Daphne swallowed her fears. "I did. I do."

Ohlman nodded approvingly and opened the icehouse door.

While Graydon and Ohlman struggled with the cask, his lordship went on: "Besides, you make it sound like we've sunk into a life of crime. You've been listening to Prosy Pomeroy too long, my girl. Buck up, I have a better idea."

Ohlman allowed as how Major Howell's strategy might work. Daphne thought Gray was so brilliant, he should be running the war effort instead of Wellington. She almost threw her arms around him in excitement and relief, but she caught herself before she embarrassed both of them. They were not on such familiar terms, not by half, and she had to keep it that way. He was doing this for his father's benefit, Daphne reminded herself. And he was still an unprincipled libertine. Uncle Albert secured to the back, Gray stole a quick kiss before he climbed into his curricle, proving her point. She wished him a sincere Godspeed anyway.

After the major left, Daphne waited for her mother to come down, feeling that she really had to discuss recent events with Mama. Lady Whilton ought to be informed about Uncle Albert and their plans for him—especially since the plans couldn't be changed now whether she approved or not. Otherwise Daphne was as guilty as Lord Hollister of going behind Mama's back, even if Lady Whilton had been flat on that same back in bed, in her laudanum-induced stupor.

When her mother did not come down, Daphne went up to her mother's room. They were going to be late for church soon, and then she'd have to wait for later to have a private conversation, after Miles had come and gone.

Before she reached Mama's room, she saw Lord Hollister coming out of that selfsame door, in a burgundy velvet robe and slippers. Daphne ducked quickly back to her own room before he spotted her, spotting him. No, she could never make her home with those two. At least Lord Hollister's presence in the family wing resolved one question: the wedding was on, the banns were going to be called, whether Mama was ready or not.

Daphne didn't suppose Mama was ready to discuss her unlamented and uninterred brother-in-law either.

"Ashes to ashes, dust to dust." Ah, Daphne thought, if the vicar only knew . . .

Miles came for lunch after church, as he usually did. Graydon's innuendos taking effect, Daphne started thinking how Miles most often appeared at mealtime. Yes, he was a trifle pouchy near the jowls, but he was fit, not flabby, although he did have to loosen a waistcoat button after a Cook's excellent vol-au-vents.

Miles was just a good trencherman, Daphne told

herself, and he was older than Gray. That made it harder to keep trim, she understood, no matter how active the man was. Furthermore, Miles was too busy for the idle exercises of the town bucks, boxing and such. She shook herself to stop making excuses for her country neighbor. Miles was an upstanding man, a conscientious landlord, a suitor to be proud of even if he was no Bond Street beau. And he was understanding, too. He'd better be, because she had to tell him about Uncle Albert so he'd call off the search.

# *Chapter Fifteen*

Sometimes a good meal can make bad news more palatable. Not this time. Daphne's confession that, not only had they recovered Uncle Albert without notifying the local magistrate, but they'd already removed the evidence, did not sit well atop mulligatawny soup, eels in aspic, fricassee of lamb, and custard pudding.

She had no trouble getting Miles alone after the meal, the two older ladies retiring for naps, and Mama and the earl retiring for heaven knew what. Mama was so distracted, she didn't even question her daughter's unchaperoned state. Of course, Daphne was no schoolroom miss, and Miles was too decent to take advantage; everyone knew that. Not even proper Ohlman blinked twice when Daphne suggested a walk in the gardens after nuncheon.

Daphne hated to do it, cut up this good man's peace in such a way, but she saw no alternative. He couldn't be permitted to waste his days searching haystacks for a needle that was safely found. Waiting to tell Miles until after Graydon was long gone seemed even worse, more devious than the act of moving Uncle Albert in the first place. At least she felt more guilty about using Miles in this shady way. It did not bode well for the open, trusting, mutually respectful relationship she craved. Instead it smacked of manipulation, of managing him for her own ends rather than considering his wishes.

Right now Miles was wishing for his usual midday nap. He was also wishing he'd never laid his eyes and his hopes on Miss Daphne Whilton. She was a fetching piece, all right, in peach muslin with trailing ribbons, and her dowry was considerable and her connections were impeccable. Married to a baron's daughter, b'gosh. He never thought to rise so high. And if this proposed wedding came off, he could be the next thing to son-in-law to an earl.

On the other hand, he might be caught up in a horrid scandal, forced to resign his cherished post as magistrate, humiliated before his friends and neighbors. His father would suffer a relapse; his mother would go into a decline. Miles looked at Daphne and saw, not the poised and polished lady who captivated half of London, but the hobbledehoy urchin who used to follow Graydon Howell around, falling into one scrape after another. Now she was dragging him into her mingle-mangles, too.

Miles prized his reputation and his position, especially since he lived in a neighborhood of wealthy aristocrats. Usually the office of justice of the peace went to the richest landlord, the highest title. The Earl of Hollister could have been magistrate for the asking, but he preferred city life and national politics. Daphne's father had in fact held the local laws in his capable hands before Miles's father the squire took over at his death. Thank heavens the recent baron had shown no interest in presiding at shire affairs.

Miles did, and he did the job well. His even-handedness was well known, his diligence was commended by peer and peasant alike. His precinct was almost devoid of crime until this recent spate of chickens missing from yards, hams pilfered from smokehouses—and dead bodies. Now his honor, his impartiality, was severely compromised.

He didn't see the glorious spring day or the budding flowers; he saw his consequence crumbling into dust.

"You have placed me in a deucedly awkward position, Miss Whilton."

"Yes, sir, I realize that, and I truly would not have had there been any choice. I felt that keeping you in the dark was somehow worse."

Sometimes the darkness was a comforting place. "Worse? What could be worse than obstructing justice? Don't you realize that all of you could be clapped in gaol for this ill-advised prank?"

"Prank? I assure you, sir, this was no prank. And I do not believe any crime was committed, whose solution could be obstructed." Daphne was getting annoyed now, that Miles was being so unrelentingly stiff. Uncle Albert wasn't this rigid. She marched back and forth in front of Miles, as if her agitation could make him understand. "We merely removed my uncle's remains to prepare them for burial."

"You purposely hid a dead body, for heaven's sake!" Miles found himself shouting. He could envision his hopeful future with Miss Whilton and her dowry going the way of his reputation, so he tried

*149*

to moderate his tones and his temper. "That is, you thought you were acting for the best, I'm sure."

Daphne stopped her pacing and sank down on a bench under a lilac bush. "No one was hurt, Miles, and it's done. Give over, do. You are not to blame; you knew nothing about it. And the only one who could possibly care is that weasel Terwent."

Miles was trying to let himself be convinced, he really was. He sat beside her on the bench, thinking. "I suppose a family does have the right to select a mortician. But London?"

"No one does cremations in the country."

He groaned. "And why the deuce did the baron have to be cremated if there was nothing to hide, like a bullet wound or a broken neck? The gossip-mongers will surely have a party over that one."

Daphne was well primed. "He was cremated because we were afraid of disease. My uncle was ailing, you know. The doctors were not certain of the cause. Cremation is the safest precaution in these cases."

"Fine, but why are you not telling anyone else, if this is all so aboveboard?"

"Because we don't want the boys to hear about their father's death secondhand," she replied promptly.

"The boys? Your cousins?" Miles was incredulous. "You're the only one who remembers that Albert was their father. I doubt they care one way or the other, if they even recognize him."

"Still, it's only proper they be notified first. Eldart will be baron now. That has to be monumental, and we do not wish him to be besieged by hangers-on until his guardianship is legalized."

Miles took time to wonder about that guardianship. A minor baron with vast resources ... and Daphne his closest relative if one discounted her mother, who'd be in London with the earl. "I suppose that might wash, excusing the delay, that is. When do you propose telling the heir?"

"As soon as the boys get here next week. They've already left school with their tutor, en route home for the wedding, you see, so we decided there was no rush. Cremation cannot be done overnight, you know."

He didn't. He didn't suppose cremating a body would take the two weeks until that wedding either, but somehow suspected it would, with Howell pulling the strings. "That's all well and good to tell the children, but what about Terwent? The fellow is dashed persistent."

"If he calls again, I'll direct him to London. I'm sure Uncle Albert is there by now."

"And when he doesn't find his employer there, he'll go straight to Bow Street. Those chaps aren't going to be nearly as easy to convince as I am."

Miles hadn't been easy at all. Daphne could feel a damp spot on the back of her gown. She turned to pick a stem of lilacs. She took a deep, calming breath of the fragrance. She hoped they'd last until the wedding. "Bow Street will understand that the baron's family did not see the need to consult a servant about the disposition of his body."

"But there wasn't any body," Miles persisted. "How are you going to explain how the baron got to London, Miss Whilton, and how come that jackanapes Howell delivered him to the mortician?"

Gray might be a jackanapes, but Daphne reserved the right to call him that for herself. "Graydon Howell has been a friend of the family forever, sir, and I'll beg you to remember that. If he heard rumors while he was in London on business that the baron had been taken ill somewhere, of course he would lend what assistance he could. As for how and when and where and why, that is no one's business." Daphne was proud. Cousin Harriet couldn't have done better in depressing pretensions. Of course, Miles was correct—he usually was, in his prosy way—there could be embarrassing questions. Gray had given his assurance that he'd take care of everything, so she could only pray he was right. He usually was, too, as in his pointing out that Miles was developing considerable *embonpoint*. Unless her starchy suitor was wearing two sets of clothes, he was gaining weight. "And isn't it time you stopped calling me Miss Whilton, Miles?"

Not when she stuck her nose in the air like a duchess, it wasn't. If Daphne wasn't happy with her suitor at this moment, he wasn't happy with her, either. "It wouldn't be proper," was all he said, as if they hadn't been having the most wildly improper and implausible discussion of his life. "I cannot sign the death certificate, you know, if I have not examined the body."

"Of course not, Miles. I would not ask you to." She ignored his sigh of relief to go on: "All I'm asking is that you not tell anyone that Uncle Albert is dead. You could just say you are investigating, which you are. After all, as you say, you've not seen him since you brought him here, and without proof . . ."

Miles was happy enough to jump on that suggestion. The whole thing was too smoky by half, and the least said, the better. Besides, no rational person would believe the story anyway, disappearing bodies and such. Which reminded him, "That still leaves the question of who removed the baron from the icehouse."

"But they brought him right back. Likely it was some of the servants—we've taken new ones on, you know, for the company—who thought it was a barrel of ale. They returned the barrel as soon as they realized the mistake. It wasn't your dire chicken thieves, Miles."

The chicken made a nice change from rabbit stew. Handy threw in a handful of the herbs and stuff he'd pulled from someone's kitchen garden. He and Sailor and Sal had visited a farmhouse last night after bringing back the body in the barrel. Sal got the chickens, Handy got the vegetables, and Sailor made away with a shovel and pitchfork, the only things he could find lying around.

The boys hadn't spotted anything that looked like a potato or an onion, not even in that farmer's own garden, only some green stuff. In disgust, Handy threw into the cooking pot another handful of leaves and stems from Mrs. Bagshott's herb patch, the ones she grew to keep her cat from getting fur balls.

At least the ensuing digestive upset gave Jake something else to think about besides his aches and pains, and how his nephews had let a dead body get away. The way he lit into Sailor and Handy with that cane would have made Uncle Albert proud, if Jake hadn't been so weak on his feet that every swing sent him reeling into one or another of the stone walls.

"You didn't even look for a wallet or rings or nothing! How could you be so dumb?" *Swish* went the cane through the air, *whap* as it connected with one of the hapless lads, then *thud* as Jake's head hit another wall. "Marks what carry canes like this allus have a watch or a lookin' glass on a chain, or a stickpin in their chokers. They got brass buttons and pockets full of change. Hell, they got gold in their teeth!"

No way were Sailor and Handy going to go back and pick the fillings out of a dead man's mouth, or pocket in this instance. But they still needed a stake. Jake didn't think he could hold the pistol steady enough to hold up another coach. Hell, he didn't think he could lift the pistol, much less aim it, and he didn't trust either of his nincompoop nevvies with it. They'd likely shoot each other. No, with his luck, they'd shoot him.

Instead he sent Handy into the village with the silver flask. He chose Handy because Sailor was too distinctive, being of inordinate size, with flaming red hair and freckles. The runt, contrariwise, was a frail-looking lad with pale silvery hair down to his shoulders and a high-pitched voice. No, not too distinctive at all.

So Handy took the flask and went from back door to back door, asking if anyone knew who owned the thing, because he found it on the road and wanted to return it to its rightful owner. "I juth want to do what'th wight," he lisped. The menfolks looked away, but the women cooed over him and handed him baskets of muffins and paper-wrapped sausages and jugs of cider. Such a nice boy.

Handy was far out of town with two pillow slips filled with booty before any of the housewives realized that while he had their attention in the kitchen, his accomplice was stealing their laundry off the clotheslines. "Good dog, Sal."

Now they had food on the table—or on the floor, since the table had long been consigned to the fire. And they had clean, respectable clothes to wear to look for jobs at that wedding. Of course, they'd both have to find some kind of disguise since the law would be looking for Handy and Sailor and Sal after today, but they'd do it. And they weren't going to hand any loot out the window to Jake neither. Let him do his own stealing for once. The boys meant to snabble what they could at that mansion, then run with it before Jake knew they were done. They were going to Portsmouth and buy passage to America, to start new, decent lives. Sailor was going to be a pirate, and Handsome was going to be a gigolo.

# Chapter Sixteen

Terwent the valet heard about the pilfering in the village with the silver flask as decoy. He decided against going to London, and went to Magistrate Pomeroy instead.

Even Miles had to agree that the man made a good case for foul play. The descriptions of the flasks matched, and Terwent swore his master never went anywhere without his "medicinal spirits." Miles could believe that, from his short exposure to the old tosspot.

So what happened? Had that here-and-thereian Howell ditched the body under a hedge for some vagabond to find and strip? Or had the whole tale been a Banbury story for his benefit and they really killed the old coot? Miles was so upset, he couldn't finish his dinner. He left some peas.

Here was a fine rowdydow indeed. Terwent was demanding they form a search party to comb the area for the baron's corpse. The townsfolk were insisting he call up the militia to rid them of the ring of vicious hoodlums. And Miss Whilton was asking him to keep his mouth shut. His worst problem was Miss Whilton.

Any female so lacking in delicacy as to suggest he suborn the law for her was capable of anything: lies, misdemeanors, murder. Her beauty, her bounty, and her blue blood couldn't change the fact that Miss Whilton would be the death of his career as justice of the peace, to say nothing of his peace of mind. And he'd have to marry her, b'gad, if she accepted his proposal! A gentleman couldn't renege on an offer. She was thinking on it, she'd said, begging him so sweetly to be patient. Pomeroy could have bitten his tongue out, to get back his honorable proposition. Deuce take it, he'd waited years for her to grow out of her hoydenish ways, then two more for her to forget that childish attachment to Rake Howell. Patient be damned. Why the devil couldn't he have been a bit more patient?

Daphne, meanwhile, wasn't thinking of Miles at all, his proposal or his predicament. Nor was she any more patient than he was, chewing on her pencil stub as she waited for Graydon to return. No matter what he'd said, she couldn't help worrying over what problems he'd face in London. What if his curricle turned over and Uncle Albert rolled out? There'd be hell to pay, and no mistake. But that was borrowing trouble. Gray would never put his carriage in the ditch. He was the most competent whip she knew, for all his other sins.

Just what had the infuriating man meant by inviting her on a picnic after dark, or blowing her a kiss as he pulled off this morning? Probably nothing. Gray simply couldn't help dallying with any female in the vicinity. And she couldn't help wishing it were otherwise.

Graydon was making quick work of his job in London, anxious to get back to Hampshire and Daphne. He didn't like leaving her alone to face that prig Pomeroy. He didn't like leaving her alone *with* that prig Pomeroy. Hell, he didn't like leaving her alone, period.

He stopped at a grave site at the edge of town and asked the sexton where to go for his special needs, congratulating himself on his cleverness. He couldn't see driving about the city all day asking directions, not with Uncle Albert's barrel in the boot.

Of course, the place he wanted was shut up on Sunday, but Death didn't wait for a weekday; the major saw no reason for himself to wait either. He banged on doors until he found someone who could direct him to the establishment's proprietor, who wasn't best pleased to be dragged from his Sunday dinner. Until he saw the color of Lord Howell's gold.

"And the family isn't in such a rush to get the thing done," Graydon explained, "so you can take your time. I just couldn't leave him lying around, you understand."

Jedediah Biggs didn't understand why the cove couldn't wait for a mortician and a regular funeral wagon, nary a bit. More gold joined the pile. Then Jed Biggs wiped his soot-stained fingers on his pants and said, "Time is all I've got, till you bring me a death certificate. No death certificate, nothing for me to put in my records. No records, and I could be transported for removing evidence of a crime. You could've kilt your old granfer for his gold and no one the wiser, iffen I don't keep records. Hell, he might be the husband of some sweet young thing you've got your eye on, randy-looking buck like you."

Graydon wasn't interested in hearing any more of the man's theories. He supposed the fellow was hinting that enough gold could eliminate the need for any records whatsoever, but the lawyers and such would have to be notified anyway. And he hadn't killed the old shabster. There was nothing to hide except his body for a bit.

So Graydon left to get a death certificate.

"Ain't you forgetting something?" Mr. Biggs jerked his permanently blackened jaw toward the barrel, now in the yard of his brick row house, right on his wife's primroses.

Graydon saw no need to encumber his search around town with such a traveling companion. The pyreman, as he liked to call himself, saw it differently. "There's no magistrate going to give you that piece of paper without seeing the body. You could say it's your aunt Tillie, what's leaving you her silver tea set, or a servant, instead of some bloke you killed in a duel. Magistrate's going to want some proof."

"Bloodthirsty chap, aren't you? I suppose you've seen it all in your days."

"That's neither here nor there. I gots to have that paper. The magistrate might even want to hold an inquest."

Graydon gave the notion some thought. "Interesting how the legal system works. How long do you think an inquest would take?"

Biggs scratched his head. "A day or two for them to send a sawbones out to examine the body to fix the cause of death, then maybe weeks before they hold the hearing, to let you hire a barrister, or leave the country."

Graydon could only suppose he looked guilty as hell, driving around with a corpse, the way this man's imagination was running. But weeks were too long a delay, and he'd have to be in town for the hearing. "No, that won't do. But I refuse to go tripping about town with a dead man as groom. He can't even get down to hold the horses, don't you know. I'll bring my godfather back if he insists."

Biggs spat on the ground. "Now, what good's some other swell going to do me?"

"Oh, didn't I say? My godfather's a magistrate. He's not the Lord High Magistrate of all of London, but I don't think this little matter is worth bothering Uncle Roderick, do you?"

Graydon's godfather didn't insist on seeing the body, naturally. "What, and ruin my appetite on a Sunday? It's that swine Whilton, you say? Good. Didn't kill him, did you, my boy? No? Good. See you at the wedding next week? Good. Your father's getting a fine wife. I dangled after Cleo Harracourt myself before she chose Whilton. Too bad the daughter's such a high stickler."

"Daphne? She's as game as a pebble!"

"Won't have a rake like you, I heard. Too bad."

When Graydon got back to the row house, Mrs. Biggs sent him off to the crematorium with a flea in his ear about care-for-naughts who didn't respect the Lord's day or His flowers.

Biggs apologized, once he had the certificate in his hand, all full of official stamps and seals. "And I can't do the job right away; the place is full of missionaries fresh off a boat what came from spreading God's words, and God knows what diseases. You wouldn't want your relation mixed in with that crowd."

"No, he might contaminate them. But take your time, as I said. Uncle Albert's in no hurry."

"May as well pick out an urn meantime; save you a trip back. M'brother runs the shop next door."

A trinket for Lady Whilton? Graydon wondered how she'd like a Grecian urn with handles, or maybe a brass one that looked like a spittoon. There were copper and silver ones, marble and jade, porcelain urns and plain earthenware crocks for ashes up the River Tick. One looked like a genie'd appear if you rubbed hard enough. Uncle Albert had already granted everyone's fondest wish by dying. It was a deuced hard choice. Graydon didn't want one with angels or flowers on the sides. Nehemiah Biggs didn't have any with a pair of dice on them.

The decision finally made, Graydon thought of returning to Hampshire that night, but his horses were tired and his father had given him a commission. All he had to do was wait for the shops to open Monday morning, so he passed the evening at his clubs, returning early to Howell House for a good night's sleep.

The gift for Lady Whilton was an easy selection, two ruby hearts joined by a diamond arrow. If that wasn't sincere, and expensive, nothing was. He couldn't properly give Daphne jewelry, although there were sapphires that almost begged to match her eyes. He reluctantly settled on a gold locket to replace the one he'd given her so long ago, another lifetime, it seemed, that she'd tromped on that fateful night. He'd offer it as a wedding gift, to celebrate the joining of the families. He told the clerk to hold the sapphires, too, in hopes of another joining.

To prove his constancy to Daffy, he picked out an extravagant diamond choker for Lady Seline Bowles. She'd know it for her *congé*, a parting gift. Unfortunately the clasp was faulty, and he didn't want to wait around to have it repaired.

"Oh, we can deliver it, my lord."

Yes, and bandy Seline's name and his all over Mayfair. "No, I have to return to town in a few days." He could deliver the necklace in person, which was the honorable thing to do anyway, while he fetched the urn. Seline's hysterics couldn't be any worse than toting around Albert's ashes.

If Jake were a cat, he'd be dead. Twice. As it was, he didn't know if he could survive another day of his nephews' company. He'd walk out on them, taking nothing but his dog and his cane, if he could walk. He couldn't, though; he needed a horse. A horse, his kinfolk for a horse. So he sent the boys out to steal him a mount, promising them one more try at the high toby.

Finding a field of hayburners was easy; catching one of them was a horse of a different color, gray, to be exact. Old Dan used to be chestnut, now he was just grizzled. The farmer only kept him around out of sentiment, and as a ride for his little grandchildren. All the other horses ran from the two thieves, who smelled of smoke, blood, and worse, but Old Dan didn't have a lot of run left in him. So he left with Sailor and Handy.

They hoisted Jake aboard and tied the dead

man's linen cravat around the horse's neck for Jake to hang on to, since there was no saddle, no reins. Then they led him back to that narrow stretch of roadway to wait for a carriage.

Jake was a real highwayman now. He had a horse, a pistol, a gang. He was proud. He was also delirious. The boys picked him up and put him back on Old Dan.

Unfortunately but not totally unexpectedly in the country, the next traveler wasn't a diamond-bedecked dowager in a fancy coach. It was a farmer. A pig farmer, to be exact, driving his herd from one place to another, right down the center of the highway. As Old Dan stepped aside without instruction, Jake called to the boys to watch out for little 'uns as might get lost. Sailor tried to lose one, but it squealed so loud, its mama chased him into the ditch at the side of the road. The farmer came and kicked Handy into the ditch, too, to make his point. The ditch being filled with muddy, stagnant water, and Jake for once not in it, he whistled in delight. Which was the sound the farmer made when he called the horses for supper.

Old Dan turned for home. Jake didn't. He didn't land in the ditch—hallelujah!—but he did land in the path of the prize sow, all three hundred mean, myopic pounds of her.

Sailor and Handy had to drag him home, through the ditch. Sal wouldn't come with them, they smelled so bad. When they got to the cottage, Jake was shaking so hard, he couldn't even hit the boys with his cane. "A fire," he croaked. "Light the fire."

But the fireplace smoked worse than before, so much that Jake couldn't breathe at all, not without moving his cracked ribs. He shoved his wet coat on the flames to douse the fire, which at least got him some steam. "Get up on the roof an' stick a branch down the chimbley," he gasped at his nephews. "Someat's stuck in there."

Jake waited until he heard a lot of noise above him before he raised his head to look up. First he saw sky through the holes in the roof. Then he saw Sailor's big foot. And Handy's little foot. Then *lots* more sky all of a sudden. "Oh, sh—"

Sailor carried him outside to a little clearing. Handy started him a fire out of the squirrel's nest they'd found, then tossed on parts of the roof as they cleared the debris out of the cottage.

When Jake was almost warm and dry, Sal returned from wherever she'd been, dripping water all over him again. But she also laid a fish in his lap. "My friend," Jake rasped as he impaled the fish on a stick with great effort and shakily held it to the fire. "My best friend." He hauled his bruised arm around the damp dog and buried his battered head in Sal's mangy fur while the fish cooked. "You're more like family than those two jackasses can ever be."

When it was ready, Jake split the fish and gave half to his best friend, his comfort and provider. Then he choked on a fish bone.

# Chapter Seventeen

"*I* got me a shovel!" Sailor bragged. "I knew it would come in handy, Handy."

They couldn't take Jake into the village to be laid to rest in the churchyard. They couldn't afford the burial, and they couldn't afford to be recognized. Besides, Jake had never stepped foot in a church that either Sailor or Handy ever recalled.

"And he was happy here."

Handy nodded. "Best days o' his life."

So they planted him in that little clearing, not far away from the tumbledown cottage in the Woodhill Manor home woods. While Sailor dug, Handy gathered leaves and twigs and pebbles to cover over the grave so no one would notice. They thought of making a cross out of the rotten roof lumber, but that would have been too obvious, so they stuck the cane in the ground as a marker.

"Too bad we got no way to write his name on it."

"Couldn't spell it anyways."

As a final act of mourning, Handy picked a bouquet of wild violets—and stuck them in his buttonhole. Sailor did the same. They were free! It was time to go make their fortunes.

They gathered all their belongings, Jake's belongings, and the dead man's belongings, and left the cottage without a backward glance. And without Sal.

But Jake had warned them they had to get prettified before they could get hired on at any fancy house, and they still did not have the wherewithal for such luxuries as soap. Sailor was all for trying the bridle lay again. They still had the pistol, and he liked the sound of "Your shaving kit or your life." Handy thought they'd do better waiting till dark and breaking into the emporium in the village. They stood in the roadway arguing until they heard carriage wheels. As luck would have it, the painted wagon that trundled by belonged to the first of a Gypsy caravan that was headed toward the other side of the village. A fair was going to be set up to honor the earl's wedding, and to make a profit off his wealthy guests.

Gypsies being prodigious traders who asked few questions and gave out less information, the boys soon bartered the silver flask and the brass-fitted satchel for soap, razors, scissors, boot polish, and a soft leather tunic for Sailor.

"Giorgio roms go courting, eh?" The old Gypsy mother nodded and put some colorful ribbons in with the bundle. "For your sweethearts." When Handy reached for the package she grabbed his wrist and turned his palm up. "For free. Yes, a pretty fair-haired girl is in your future." For

Sailor: "A golden female will be sharing your bed."

This was getting better and better. They hurried off to the pool by the icehouse. It wasn't any hotspring bath, but it was better than the ditchwater. And it was a good thing for Lady Whilton that it was springtime and not winter, or her ice would be black from their ablutions.

Clean, combed, and shaved (Sailor, at least), they each donned one of the clean shirts that had been in the baron's portmanteau. Sailor's just made it to his waist, Handy's fell to his bony knees. They put on the dead man's hose and surveyed the rest of the choices from Sal's clothesline foray. There was a pair of breeches from the blacksmith's laundry that almost fit Sailor. With his new tunic, no one would notice that the buttons didn't meet. But there was nothing that fit scrawny Handy without sliding down to his toes, except the blacksmith's daughter's skirts and petticoats. Sal was quick; she wasn't a genius.

Handy shrugged and donned the skirts, threading the Gypsy's ribbons through the long pale curls he hadn't cut off yet. "She said I'd have a fair-haired girl in my future."

"She didn't say you'd be one. Now if they take us on at that manor house, you'll have to sleep with the maids."

"Too bad, ain't it?"

The housekeeper at Woodhill Manor was in a dither. The guests were starting to arrive for the wedding, provisions were being delivered, and the house was not up to her standards. Lady Whilton was no help, with her head in the clouds all the time and the earl where he hadn't ought to be even so close to the wedding, in Mrs. Binder's considered opinion. Not that she'd whisper one word of disparagement about her mistress, but it didn't set a good example for Miss Daphne, nor for the silly maids who were giggling in corners so much they weren't getting half the work done. The footmen were worse, with their rolling eyes and knowing grins. At least the footmen were Ohlman's concern, for all the attention he was paying, what with spending half his time in the wine cellar and the icehouse. The guests weren't coming just to drink the cellars dry, for heaven's sake.

Not even Miss Daphne was up to her usual competent self, worried about that handsome devil staying in the guest wing, the housekeeper guessed. Now, if *that* rascal overstepped the line, Mrs. Binder'd have at him with her rolling pin, the same as she used to when he filched cookies from the kitchen. Meantime, Miss Daphne was losing her lists and changing her mind about the menus and room assignments, causing more work rather than less. Mrs. Binder would be sore glad when this marriage took place.

Thus it was that she was happy to see two clean, neat young persons apply for positions. She could use the help, if they proved worthy.

"We got references, ma'am," Sailor offered, handing over the forged letter.

Mrs. Binder read the glowing commendation, but frowned. "This here is for two brothers, Sailor and Handy."

The boys hadn't thought of that. "Well, he's Sailor, all right. And I'm ... I'm his sister Andy. T'other one stayed on at the last post."

Mrs. Binder wasn't happy. She peered at the pair in front of her. "You don't look like brother and sister."

"We don't look like brothers, neither," Handy muttered, but Sailor kicked him.

Mrs. Binder ignored both, her eyes narrowed. "I bet you're sweethearts, that's what. Well, I've got enough of that kind of nonsense already. If there's one thing I won't put up with, it's canoodling among my staff."

The boys swore they weren't, never did canoodle together, never would. Mrs. Binder didn't quite believe them, but she was desperate. She fixed Sailor with a steady glare. "One wink and you're out, understand?"

Sailor never had learned to wink, so he nodded.

Mrs. Binder went on: "I can't hire any footmen, that's Ohlman's province, but they're short at the stables, what with all the carriages they're expecting. Know anything about horses, boy?"

Sailor had just stolen one that week. He nodded.

"No matter, you're big enough to handle a shovel."

Sailor nodded again, grinning. He knew all about shovels.

"Good, go on with you and tell them I said you were to help. And you, girl," the housekeeper addressed Handy, "can you polish?"

He'd gotten that boot polish to darken Sailor's red hair all right, hadn't he? With visions of silver polish—and silver plates, silver candlesticks, and silver tea sets—floating in his mind, Handy swore he could polish with the best of them.

Mrs. Binder handed him an apron and some rags and escorted Handy to a narrow closet with row upon row of chamber pots. "Here, you're hired. Start polishing."

Relief, that's all it was, Daphne told herself, when Gray strode into the room, barely using his cane. He was returned safely and successfully, she gathered, from his wink in her direction and jaunty grin before he turned to greet her mother and the others. It could only be relief that made her spirits lift instantly and her heart start beating faster. She refused to entertain any other notion, although he was looking so devilishly handsome in his tight-fitting riding breeches with his dark curls all wind-tossed that her feet were itching to run her across the room and into his arms. Relief was a powerful emotion. Luckily she was serving tea.

Daphne was the first person Graydon saw when he entered the parlor. He thought she'd always be the first one he'd spot, no matter how many others were around, that his eyes would seek her out, instinctively knowing where she was. He winked so she'd know his mission was accomplished, then grinned when he saw how a cloud seemed to lift from her brow. She *was* happy he was back. Lud knew he was happy to be here.

His grin faded when he realized who else was there for tea. Of course. And he was sitting in her pocket, that dashed mushroom Miles. Graydon paid his respects to Lady Whilton and the other ladies, slipped a small package into his father's hands, and returned to take a seat on Daphne's other side.

"I say, Pomeroy, there's a curious noise out on the highway you might want to look into. Sounds like a wolf howling in the woods." It was a broad hint, but had merit.

"There are no more wolves in Hampshire. A lost dog or something."

"Well, I couldn't see anything from the road and couldn't leave my cattle, but I asked a field worker passing by to go see. In case the dog was in trouble, a trap or something, don't you know. Offered the fellow a coin, but he crossed himself and said it was a banshee, before he ran off."

Miles dabbed at his mouth with his handkerchief. "There are no banshees, either."

"Of course not. It's most likely just a lost dog, as you said, but the noise could frighten little children. Perhaps you should take a ride that way, if you have so much time on your hands." He stared pointedly at what else Miles had in his hands, a plate full of almond cake.

Miles resented being called to account by a Bond Street lounger, dressed to the nines and bang up to the mark, after a four- or five-hour curricle ride. He snapped, "I'm not the dogcatcher, by George."

Cousin Harriet grumbled, "You haven't caught a lot of anything else, either." She turned to the newcomer. "Howell, did you hear there's a gang of outlaws working the countryside, stealing anything not nailed down? Homer Riley says they even tried to get his pigs, right on the highway, in broad daylight."

And Graydon had driven along that same highway, his head in the clouds, with a fortune in a ruby brooch in his pocket. While Cousin Harriet nattered on about missing laundry, even before the Gypsies came to town, Graydon wondered when he could give Daffy the locket he had in his other pocket. He still wished it weren't such a trumpery bit, but she used to like the other one. She used to like him, too, he reminded himself.

She did seem pleased when, after Cousin Harriet went to fetch her needlework, he was able to recount his London adventure. Even Miles turned pleasant when the major told them how a London magistrate had signed an official death certificate. All was in order, he explained, right down to the blurred date of death.

"And there's no need to mention Albert's passing yet, since the ashes won't be back for days. The undertaker won't spread it around and neither will the magistrate, respecting the family's wishes."

"Then you don't think I should discuss it with Mama?" Daphne asked, looking toward her mother across the room.

Graydon's gaze followed hers to where the governor had his arm around Lady Whilton and was whispering in her ear while she giggled like a schoolgirl. The rubies had done the trick, then. "I'd hate to ruin their idyll. They seem so . . ." He couldn't think of the right words, but Daphne understood.

She nodded and smiled. "So . . ."

"So preposterous, if you ask me," Miles finished. "At their age! Dashed embarrassing, I'd say, and highly improper."

If Miles considered that a little cuddling was improper, Daphne thought, heaven help them if he found out about the earl's late night rambles. Perhaps Gray was right again and Miles was a trifle stiff-rumped. Well, he'd just have to learn to relax a little. He might start taking lessons from Graydon, who was grinning fondly at the older couple. No, then Miles might learn too many raffish ways. She'd rather have him this way, starch and all. She smiled at him and passed a box of chocolates.

Now that everything was all right and tight with the baron, Miss Whilton was looking better to Miles, downright appealing in fact, in a plain blue frock. Amazing what a crisis averted could do to a female's prospects. And if this leering son of an earl thought she was suitable to be a countess one day, Pomeroy supposed Daphne could learn to be an adequate squire's wife. With his mother's help and example, he could check her wilder starts. Get her breeding, he figured, that ought to do it. It calmed the mares down, anyway.

Lord Howell was contemplating similar notions as she smiled, but mares had no part in his musings. Damn, that jaconet muslin hugged a figure that any opera-dancer would envy. Those simple lines had to come from one of London's premier modistes, to be so demure yet so alluring at the same time. And the minx knew it, the way she was flirting with that maggot Miles, batting her eyes at him.

Those eyes *were* the color of sapphires, he mused, glad he'd had the jeweler put the set aside. He tried to picture Daffy in his sapphires, necklace, bracelet, and earbobs, and nothing else. The temperature in the room went up about ten degrees. Deuce take it, she was more luscious than a bonbon, half of which that pig Pomeroy was gobbling from the box Graydon had brought back from London.

# Chapter Eighteen

"Don't get in my way, old man. I demand to see the magistrate. It's my right as a citizen." Terwent shoved past Ohlman into the parlor.

The valet was only partly subdued by all the faces turned to stare at him. He made a hasty bow, but his agitation was so great that he ignored the presence of earls and officers, ladies and the two lackeys Ohlman sent for, to toss him out. He went right up to Miles and shouted in his face, "Now you've got to do your dooty."

Miles flushed and told the man, "Stop your caterwauling. You're in a gentleman's house."

"I'm in *my* gentleman's house and he might right now be a-lying dead. In the village they're saying there's a spirit loose, some boggart moaning in the woods 'cause he ain't had proper burial."

"It's a dog, by Jupiter!"

"Did you go see it for yourself, then, Mr. Magistrate?"

Before Miles could answer, Graydon spoke up: "Did you, Mr., ah, Terwent?"

"Why no, I . . . ah, I . . ."

"Waited for the official inquiry. Highly commendable, I'm sure. As is this loyalty, this dedication. But to Whilton? My word, it beggars the imagination." Graydon helped himself to a bonbon.

Terwent didn't even try to bluster through his employer's good points; the baron had none. "He owes me my salary. And if he's gone and stuck his spoon in the wall, I want the pension he promised."

"Ah, such altruism. It makes more sense, at least. So what say you, Pomeroy? Shall we go take a look at this, ah, boggart in the woods?"

"It's a dog, blast it!" Miles looked regretfully at the remains of the tea, but got to his feet. "I suppose I'll have to, to stop all the yammering about haunted woods."

Howell thought he'd ride along, just out of curiosity, although he'd been driving since early morning.

"If you'll wait a few minutes, I'll change into my habit," Daphne said, and got up to leave.

"What's that, Miss Whilton? Oh, no, you mustn't come along. Highly unsuitable."

Daphne paused at the doorway. "What's unsuitable about my going for a ride, Miles? The woods are on Whilton property, after all."

Miles persisted. "But there's no saying what we might find. It's not the place for a lady."

"Nonsense, especially if you're looking for the lady's uncle!" She knew they wouldn't find Uncle Albert, but that didn't satisfy her curiosity either. "I'm going."

"I for—" She was gone. Miles sat down again, shaking his head.

Graydon gave him a pat on the shoulder and a complacent grin. "Not yours to order around yet, old boy. No saying but that Daffy'd listen anyway. Stubborn female, Miss Whilton, don't you know?"

Miles hadn't known, actually.

"Oh yes, needs a light hand on the bridle, else she digs her feet in and won't budge. I should know." Graydon also knew how much Daffy would hate being likened to a fractious filly, but he couldn't help needling his rival. "But why don't you go on; I'll wait here to escort her."

Miles wouldn't budge, mulish female or not.

They followed the eerie keening toward the old woodsman's cottage in the home woods. Daphne hadn't been there in years, her father having declared it off-limits since the place was in such dangerous disrepair. She made a note to have it torn down before someone got hurt. The noise was loud enough now to send chills down her spine. Daphne automatically turned to Graydon, riding beside her, for reassurance. He winked. It was all right then.

As they'd all suspected, there was a dog in the clearing, head back and howling. It didn't seem hurt, so Daphne left the old blankets tied on her saddle. She dismounted and started toward the scruffy tan cur.

Miles had his pistol out. "Stand back, Miss Whilton. It might be rabid."

"Nonsense, it's a she and she's just frightened. What happened, girl, did you lose your way?"

Then Terwent, who was riding pillion behind Daphne's groom, jumped down and shouted, "I knew it! I knew it! There's his cane."

And indeed, there was Uncle Albert's unmistakable bone-headed cane, sticking out of the ground. Graydon kicked some leaves and clutter aside to reveal freshly turned earth.

Miles was livid. "If this is some kind of joke, if you've been lying to me all along, leading me on, expecting me to be bought off like one of your lackeys when the—"

"Stubble it," Graydon ordered in his officer's voice. "You still have no idea who is buried here. You'd do better to send for some lads with shovels than stand around and rant."

"I'm not ranting!" But he directed the groom to ride back to Woodhill for a work crew and a cart, with Daphne's permission.

Daphne was still petting the dog. She hissed at Graydon while Pomeroy's back was turned. "You don't suppose . . . ?"

Howell shrugged. "I never checked the barrel when I got to London. But if Albert is here"—he jerked his head toward where Miles was using the cane to sweep the debris away from the grave site—"then who the hell are we having cremated?"

The men came, with extra shovels. Miles looked to Graydon, who just grinned. "Not my job."

Terwent crossed his bony arms. "Never."

So Miles Pomeroy took up one of the shovels and began digging. No one paid any attention to the tall stable hand next to him, the one who was sweating so badly, the boot polish was running from his hair down to his chin. If anyone did notice, they assumed it was dirt, from the grave. Sailor pulled his hat down lower over his hair and kept digging, and sweating.

Daphne had untied one of the blankets and sat down, the dog beside her. "Was this a friend of yours? Are you lonely? Hungry?" She crumpled a roll she'd stuffed in her pocket at the last minute, and fed it to the yellowish mongrel. "I bet you don't even know how to find food. Don't worry, someone in the stables will feed you, I'm sure, and give you a warm place to sleep."

So the Gypsy was right again: Sailor'd be sharing his bed with a golden-haired female. He kept digging.

When the body was nearly unearthed and Daphne would have stepped closer, Graydon put his arms on her shoulders and gently turned her away. "There's no need. You stay here."

It wasn't the baron, whoever he was. And he wasn't pretty. "Stay there," Graydon told Daphne, and for once she listened, to Pomeroy's chagrin.

Terwent had gone white, but he shouted, "I know him! It's that cutpurse from the tavern!" He turned, long nose twitching. "And that's the bloody, thieving dog!"

Daphne took her hand back from the hound's head.

"It must have been a falling out among crooks," Miles said, "though I don't see any bullet holes or knife wounds."

Graydon had been exploring while the men were digging. "More like a falling roof than a falling out." He pointed to the piles of rotten timbers, the roofless cottage. "That would explain why he looks so . . . battered."

"Yes, yes, I would have come to the same conclusion if I hadn't been busy digging." Miles was hot and sweaty from being out of shape, and filthy, while Howell was neat as a pin and impressing Miss Whilton with solving the case. Damn. "Yes, it appears that there was no foul play, just a criminal getting his just deserts. Unfortunately now the parish will have to pay to rebury the thatchgallows. I suppose it's cheaper than a trial and a hanging, but—" He had to pause to lift one of the stable-hands-turned-digger out of the hole where he'd suddenly fallen in. Big fellow, even dirtier than Miles felt. Miles took out his handkerchief to wipe his face, hoping he did not look like such a fool in front of Miss Whilton.

"But it should end your crime wave, Pomeroy. The man's accomplices must be long gone by now. They've cleaned the place out and moved on, at any rate. They didn't leave anything but the dead man."

"And the dog," Daphne added, coming closer now that the body had been wrapped in a blanket and loaded onto the cart. "They left the dog out here and alone, the heartless savages."

"The dog is a thief, Miss Whilton. I had more complaints about this animal stealing chickens and laundry than about the highwaymen. They seem to have stolen nothing."

"Perhaps you ought to arrest the hound then," Graydon said, "to show the local citizenry how conscientious you are."

Before Miles could respond, in kind or with a handful of dirt, Terwent spoke up: "They did, too, heist something. They got the baron's cane, didn't they? So where is he?"

"Yes, Howell, where is the baron, and how did his cane come to be marking a felon's grave? I'd like to hear your explanation for that myself," Miles said.

"Obviously the gang held him up when he left the Manor." When they rolled Albert out of the icehouse, to be exact, but Graydon didn't say that. Daphne was nodding her agreement.

Terwent was clutching the cane, polishing it with his sleeve as his beady eyes darted from one to the other. "They killed him, I know it!"

"No, I don't think so. We'd have found the body by now. What I bet happened was that some traveler chancing by saw the baron in distress and came to his aid, then took him up with them."

Daphne elaborated: "If he was unconscious, the baron couldn't have given his address, so perhaps the good Samaritan took Uncle Albert to his own house."

"He always had his calling cards in his pocket, for when he was, ah, temporarily disoriented."

"Drunk as a wheelbarrow, more like." Miles grumbled his disapproval, for the baron's drinking habits and for this whole unsavory mess. Good Samaritan, in a pig's eye.

"If he did have identification, this unknown benefactor must have driven him straight on to London, where the poor bastard might be lying in pain, waiting for his loyal valet. It would be just like Whilton to change his will when you don't show up. Don't you think so, Daffy?"

Terwent was already headed out of the woods when Daphne softly asked, "But what if he died on the way? You know Uncle Albert was not a healthy man. The shock . . ."

Miles snorted, but Graydon stroked his chin. "That's always a possibility. And it's also possible the thieves stole his card case. You know what, Terwent, if the baron is not at home when you get to London, you better check the morgues. And Bow Street. And don't worry about your salary. I'm sure

*181*

Lady Whilton will take care of your expenses. Don't you think so, Daffy?"

"Of course, Terwent. You'd be doing a, um, service to the family if you find my uncle."

So the valet got into the cart for the ride back to the village where the baron's own coach and driver were waiting. He sat up by the driver, not in the rear with Jake.

Pomeroy mounted and turned to follow. He wasn't even sorry to leave Miss Whilton alone with that glib-tongued Howell. Why, he felt like Adam, caught between Eve and the serpent. Too bad her dowry, and that twenty thousand pounds, was such a tempting apple. He left with a curt farewell.

Graydon tossed Daphne up onto her horse, and waited while she arranged the brown velvet of her habit. "Don't worry," he told her when she seemed distracted, her eyes following her stocky suitor. "He'll get over it."

Daphne wasn't so certain. That complete honesty that made Miles so strong and sure demanded nothing less in return. Everything that Miles was, everything he stood for, had just been belittled.

"He's not the man for you anyway, Daff. He'll never make you happy in the long run."

She looked down at the handsome face from her dreams, that laughing mouth that lied so easily. No, Miles might not be perfect, but he would never play her false, he would never break her heart.

Sailor and Handy had a bare half hour after dinner to escape Mrs. Binder's eagle eye and compare notes while they restored Sailor's hair coloring.

"They're puttin' Jake in a pauper's grave, no marker."

"But he's gettin' to the churchyard after all."

"And we're gettin' nowhere."

Mrs. Binder hardly let Handy out of her sight, and the head stableman kept Sailor busy from before dawn to after dusk, when Sailor collapsed onto his straw pallet. Neither one of them was ever permitted near anything worth stealing, unless you needed some manure or a chamber pot. Worse, Handy found out that a footman was on duty all night in the house. He used to drowse some, the maids' gossip went, but with that earl switching bedchambers at all hours, he didn't dare. Mrs. Binder would have the girls' hides for gossiping about their betters, but she didn't sleep with them, three to a bed.

"Maybe we should leave?"

It was a very warm bed. "Not yet, Sailor."

"Fine for you, you get to share with the maids. I get Sal in the straw. And she's got fleas."

"The food's good."

"An' no one's beatin' us on the head with his cane."

So they decided they may as well stay until the wedding. With more guests coming, there were bound to be more opportunities . . . and more manure to manhandle, more commodes to clean.

# *Chapter Nineteen*

"*W*hat can I do to help?" With only ten days or so before the wedding, there had to be something Graydon could do to relieve those little lines of concentration from Daphne's brow. She was so busy with her lists and errands and consultations with the gardeners, the cook, and the housekeeper, he hardly saw her at all, and never alone. They'd scraped through the highwayman business well together, but how was he to build on that friendship if he never spoke to her except at dinner, where she continued to wear that abstracted frown? He could only hope she wasn't pining because her cabbage-head of a country courtier hadn't been coming round so often.

By sheer luck and a rainy day, he'd tracked her down in the estate office room this morning. The library was receiving a thorough dusting, the billiards room was under renovation by carpenters, the music room was in the hands of the piano tuner, and the morning room had been taken over by a squad of seamstresses. The small parlor was being used by the older ladies to put the finishing touches on the new altar cloth for the church service, and the drawing room, all the vast expanse of Aubusson carpet, gilded chairbacks, and chinoiserie, was off-limits. The earl and Lady Whilton were "making plans." More like making cakes of themselves, Graydon thought, but fondly. He wasn't worried over the servants' gossip, only about the governor's heart. At this rate . . .

Daphne was fretting along similar lines, chewing on her pencil stub, when Graydon entered the office, hoping to find a quiet place to read the newspapers.

She put the pencil down and gave him a tentative smile. "Can you help? Well, yes, I suppose you are the only one I can ask. With so many guests arriving soon, the room assignments are getting complicated. This is a trifle indelicate, but do you suppose it would be beyond the pale for me to move your father into the master bedroom? I mean, Uncle Albert won't be coming, and the room would just sit there empty while we are getting overcrowded."

He laughed. "A trifle indelicate? Daffy, that's coming on too brown. What you mean is, there's a connecting door and you wish to cut down on the wear and tear on the hall carpet!"

She laughed back. "I was thinking more of saving Mama the embarrassment of having the guests see the earl in his nightcap before breakfast."

"I don't think your mother cares, Daffy, so do it if it will make things easier for you."

"Even though Uncle Albert died there?"

"I don't think those two would be distracted if a hundred barons died there. And they don't know anyway, do they?"

"No, I couldn't spoil Mama's happiness." She made some notations on her list, mostly to hide her blushes at the tone of the conversation. "Good, now that's done."

"See how much assistance I can be? What else shall I do for you?"

"Why, there's nothing, but thank you. Surely you have business of your own. Howell Hall, your correspondence." She nodded toward the papers in his hand. "The war news. I'm sorry if you cannot find a quiet spot. I can—"

"Botheration, Daffy, I don't need to read about the latest parliamentary debate over the price of ammunition. I want to help you!"

She stared at him, at the vehemence in his voice. "Well, I'm sure I—"

He leaned against the edge of the desk, looking down at her. "Listen, Daffy, I'm not very good at this. But, well, do you remember that harum-scarum little girl you used to be?" He didn't give a chance for her indignation to rise. "She was pluck to the backbone, but she was a sad romp. And you're not that little girl anymore."

"Certainly not! But that doesn't mean I'm hen-hearted or anything."

"Of course not, goose. I'd rather have you at my back than half the men in my regiment, but that's not my point. I just meant that you've changed. And I've changed, too. I'm not that unbroken colt intent on kicking over the traces anymore." He put his hand over hers, on the desk. "I just want the chance to show you."

Daphne felt the tingle up to her shoulder, but she wasn't sure what she was hearing. "You want . . . ?"

"I want you not to rush into any bargain with the stodgy squire. I want . . . I suppose I want you to assign me some herculean task, to prove my worth." He withdrew his hand and ran it through his hair. "I want some time alone with you."

"That wouldn't be . . . that is, I don't think . . . Ah, but there is something you can help me with. The boys."

"The boys?"

"Yes, Eldart and Torrence, my cousins. They'll be home this afternoon, and I'm confused as to what to do with them."

He crossed his arms over his chest. If she wasn't offering cake, he'd accept the crumbs. "Well, if you put Dart in the master's suite, that'll be putting the cat among the pigeons for sure."

"No, no, they have their rooms in the nursery wing. I meant about telling them about their father. I'm not a good conspirator after all, I suppose, because I keep worrying that we've done something terrible, so disrespectful to Uncle Albert."

"Nonsense, the man was a rakeshame of the first order. He didn't deserve your respect."

"Yes, but what if Dart and Torry feel differently? I cannot lie to them, but I don't want them to feel guilty forever, or blame me, because we did not mourn their father properly."

"Then you'll just have to ask them what they want to do. Do you want me to go with you to ex-

187

plain? After all, I share whatever blame there might be."

Daphne eagerly accepted his assistance with this latest knotty problem, ignoring the new one he'd just given her. She'd think about the rest of his words later.

So they took the lads apart that afternoon after all the greetings had been made, the boys' new inches made much of, their school records praised or disregarded as befitted the marks.

Daphne explained how their father was sick, and without his medication. Graydon explained how anger and drink exacerbated his condition. "So he died."

The boys just stared, wide-eyed and openmouthed.

Daphne and Graydon skipped the part about the wine cellar and the icehouse and the body snatchers, and went right to London and the cremation, on account of the wedding and all the company, and their aunt Cleo's happiness.

"But we'll hold a proper funeral right after the wedding, I promise, with all the pomp and ceremony befitting a baron."

"Do we have to?" asked Dart.

And, "Can we go riding now, Daffy?" asked Torry. So much for guilt, blame, and their sense of loss.

Graydon smiled over their heads at Daphne, who smiled back and said, "Yes, if Lord Howell will accompany you. There have been outlaws in the neighborhood. I don't want you out by yourselves."

The boys ran off with a whoop to put on their riding clothes, and Graydon glared at Daphne. "You said you wanted to help," she innocently replied to his raised eyebrow. Then grinned.

Hercules had it easy, Graydon thought in the ensuing days. He didn't have to bear-lead two wild young cubs who'd been shut in a schoolroom for months. They needed a man's influence, Daffy had pleaded. Their tutor was a scholar, she insisted, and could only keep them occupied for an hour or two in the mornings. They'd be bored and underfoot otherwise, she cajoled, and hadn't he offered to help?

It wasn't that he minded the boys. They were likable enough lads, who listened well to the major's lessons on shooting and fishing and riding, all the activities he remembered from his own youth and still enjoyed. Torry and Dart caught on quickly, just the way their cousin Daffy had. But they weren't Daffy. Graydon was no nearer to her—and his goal—than he'd been before.

That's what he thought. No Greek hero could have won Daphne's admiration more easily than by befriending her beloved cousins. As she watched through the windows Daphne marveled at how quickly he won the boys' affection, how kind and caring he was to devote so much time to them. And what a wonderful father Gray would be to his own sons, she thought with an ache in her heart caused only partially by yearning to go join their croquet match instead of selecting music with the church organist.

A few days later, Graydon received two messages among his correspondence sent down from Howell House in London: The diamond necklace and the baron were both awaiting his lordship's pleasure. His lordship, however, was finding uncommon pleasure in the Hampshire countryside and didn't wish to make the journey to London. Even if the trip took a mere two days, they were two days lost in his campaign to win Daffy's regard. Further, he was determined to instill in Dart and Torry a love for the land that they would keep forever. If Dart was to be baron, Graydon wanted to make sure he was better than the last, committed to his property and people instead of his own profligacy. Dart should know every inch of his grounds, every one of his tenants, the way Graydon would want his son to know, if he had a son.

The major's own father's benign absentee landlordship wasn't good enough. Graydon resented that his ancestral estates were being overseen by bailiffs, inhabited by strangers. As soon as that lease with Mr. Foggarty was over, he intended to take up residence. On the other hand, if Howell Hall wasn't rented, he and his father would have had to stay there, far away from Lady Whilton and her precious daughter.

No, he did not want to leave. And that trip to London boded ill on two counts: Seline the Moon Goddess's tantrums, and Terwent. So Graydon took the easy way out: he sent a message. Most of the staff at the Grosvenor Square house was off on holiday until after his father's honeymoon in Scotland, Graydon having decided to take up bachelor lodgings again if he came to Town. Still, he thought, there should be someone competent enough to complete two simple missions. *Deliver the package at Rundell's jeweler's,* he scrawled, *to Lady Seline*

*Bowles with a note saying thank you, and bring the urn from the Biggs establishment to Hampshire as soon as possible.*

A very junior footman received the note. The butler was out of town, the underbutler was away for two days, and the note, as far as James could cipher it out, indicated the young master wanted the pieces of work done instantly. So he fetched the two parcels, showing Lord Howell's note as his *bona fides*, and laboriously penned a message to the master's light-o'-love: *Thank you, and please—* James did a bit of editorializing—*bring the urn from the Biggs establishment to Hampshire as soon as possible.*

Lady Seline was packed and ready to go before the ink was dry on the footman's note. The diamonds were lovely, of course, but the invitation to join dear Graydon for his father's wedding was better. It was as good as a declaration, in her opinion. And Lady Seline was nothing if not opinionated.

Seline believed, for instance, that darling Howell's message could have been more loverlike, rather than the courteously worded note making her his lackey. She meant to take the dear boy to task, when she had a firmer commitment, of course. Like the ring that went with the choker, which she knew for a fact had been in Rundell's window just last week. Perhaps she'd tease him a bit about his rag manners before accepting the proposal she knew was coming. A man didn't invite his mistress to his former fiancée's house without good and honorable reason.

She'd forgive him for the last-minute invitation, of course. He'd had to test the waters, to make sure Miss Whilton's family wouldn't be offended. Seline supposed his gallantry owed the little country chit that much. And he was gallant, if not eloquent, sending a magnificent gift so she wouldn't feel slighted.

The poor dear must be finding it awkward, Seline considered, forced into company with the forward miss. Well, the discomfort would be over as soon as Seline got to Hampshire, for she'd see the two were never in each other's company. That's what she was invited for, wasn't it? To be at dearest Graydon's side. And to bring his father's wedding gift, of course.

The tall alabaster vase was an odd choice, she thought. She'd opened the crate as soon as her carriage left the city and headed toward country roads, the driver ordered to spring the horses. With her maid asleep on the opposite seat, and the precious crate nestled at Seline's side, what else was she to do? Besides, the top wasn't nailed down, and the straw packing lifted quite easily.

The raven-haired widow decided the thing must be a rare antique, or Napoleon's own, or something to make it more valuable than it seemed at first glance, although she did admire the cloudy swirls of black and gold in the grayish alabaster. (Graydon had settled on something smoky as the best match to the baron's character.) Then she tried to lift it, to see if there was an inscription or a date. The vase weighed so much, there must be something special indeed inside, for the top was sealed with wax and string. Seline didn't dare open the lid. Well, she would have, had the journey not come to a halt so soon. She was in Hampshire the same day she'd received dear Graydon's note. Wouldn't he be surprised?

*Chapter Twenty*

Changed? The man swore he'd changed? The only thing that changed was Daphne's room assignments. And without notice. He forgot, was all the blackguard could mumble. Forgot? In a toad's toenail! How in Heaven's name could he forget he'd invited this elegant, sophisticated woman of the world? His world. His mistress, by all that was holy! No, he hadn't forgotten; he'd been afraid of telling Daphne lest it ruin his current, pass the time till something better comes along, flirtation. With her! The lying, cheating, conniving scoundrel!

Daphne was almost as angry at herself because she hadn't changed enough, either. She was still the gullible little fool, almost believing his tender promises, his gentle touches, his affectionate smiles. They hadn't meant one blasted thing, not to him, at any rate. Did the leopard change its spots? No, not even when it was made into a lap robe, which was about as flat and dead as she was wishing Major Lord Howell at this very moment. How dare he make a May game out of her until his paramour arrived?

And bearing gifts, by Jupiter!

It wasn't enough that Daphne had to greet the stunning widow and welcome her to Woodhill while Graydon was struck all aheap at the woman's incredible beauty. No, she had to explain the urn, too, while he stood mumchance after removing the woman's silver-fox stole to reveal a diaphanous confection of the palest gray, with silver ribands under her magnificent breasts. Daphne threw her own barely adequate chest back, in her simple muslin.

And how could he have trusted Uncle Albert's ashes to a woman who used rouge and eye blacking? Daphne hadn't told Cousin Harriet, but he'd blabbed to his bird of paradise! If Lady Bowles was like all the other she-cats of her ilk, interested in nothing but the latest *on-dit*, the news would be all over London, with half the guests wondering if they were to attend a wedding or a funeral. And they'd be wondering at Mama's lack of mourning, chiding her for disrespect and breaking society's rules. Oh, how could he?

As easily as he'd agreed his father should move to the baron's suite, the sly dog. Well, if Graydon thought Daphne was moving Lady Bowles into the newly vacated room next to his, let him think again. Daphne would rot in hell first, which she was most likely going to, anyway, for all the lies she was telling.

"The vase? Oh, that's a surprise Graydon and I devised for you, Mama. Gray ordered it when he was in London last week."

Lady Bowles had insisted the urn be carried in by one of her own footmen, in her silver and black livery. She hefted it from him by the handles, and made a show of presenting it to the bridal pair, with her best wishes from "Dear Graydon." Lord Hollister almost dropped the unexpected weight, then handed it back to the footman with a questioning look toward his son. Knowing the ruby brooch had been his son's wedding gift, the earl was almost as astonished as Graydon, but not quite. Graydon still didn't say anything, his face gone almost as gray as the smoky urn. Daphne didn't notice his coloring, only that he'd selected a container to match his mistress's signature colors. And her eyes.

Daphne's own eyes were spitting fire as her mother turned to Graydon in delight. "Oh, I love surprises, dear, but I hate waiting. Won't you tell us what's inside now?"

Some gurgling noise came from Graydon's throat, that was all. Daphne poured him a glass of sherry, and kicked him when she handed it over.

"It's, ah, something special," he managed to say. "For when you get back from Scotland. The, ah, surprise won't be quite ready until then, will it, Daffy?"

She trod on his toes again, for calling her that silly name in front of Lady Seline. Daphne would wager her month's allowance that no one ever called the Moon Goddess Sally. Right now Her Moonship was casting a very big shadow on Daphne's life.

Meanwhile her mama was kissing the major's cheek for his thoughtfulness. She ought to kiss him twice, Daphne fumed, the two-faced dastard. At least he'd had the sense to snatch the urn away from the footman and try to place it inconspicuously on the mantel. He even dismissed the servant before any more tittle-tattle hit the servants' grape-vine.

Lady Seline, of course, insisted the urn be given the place of honor among the other wedding gifts on display in the small parlor. She tucked her hand in Graydon's elbow and led him there, to exclaim over the Sevres bowls and ormolu clocks and silver platters that Lady Whilton and Lord Hollister needed about as much as they needed Uncle Albert's ashes. The widow cleared a space on the linen-draped table, right in the center.

"Now we can all take turns guessing at the secret contents," she cooed. "How utterly delicious." Lady Seline had not been happy to discover the vase was a joint venture between dearest Graydon and the country quiz. Nor was she happy when Lady Whilton suggested she might want to rest in her room this afternoon, or sit with the ladies at their sewing.

"Oh, goodness, no. You mustn't think I'm such a poor traveler." Or that much older than the fresh-faced Miss Whilton. She tapped Lord Howell's arm lightly with her long, manicured fingers. "I cannot wait to see the countryside now that I am here, and breathe the wholesome air. In fact, I was hoping you'd drive me out to see your own estate this afternoon, Graydon dear."

Graydon dear was watching his life pass before his eyes. He was drowning, and clutched at the only life ring he could think of. "It's leased," he gulped. "Can't barge in on the tenants."

"Oh, but I'm sure we can drive by. I so much want to view your childhood home." And measure it for alterations.

"Sorry, Lady Bowles. Hate to disappoint a lady

and all that, but I'm already engaged for the afternoon. My young cousins-to-be, you know. Down from school. I promised them a fishing trip today."

"Cousins?" Seline inquired. "I thought you had no close relations."

"He doesn't," Daphne replied, thinking the world was a better place without any more black-hearted Howells. "They are my cousins, and there is no reason for you not to escort Lady Bowles, Major. I can see to the boys for today." And from now on. She'd make sure the boys were never again exposed to such a shameless libertine. A male influence? Hah! She'd have done better taking them to watch the rams at work.

"No, no, a promise is a promise," Graydon insisted.

"Since when?" Daphne almost shouted, or cried.

Her mama stepped in and drew the widow aside. "No matter, Lady Bowles, you will get your chance to see Howell Hall this evening. We've been invited to dinner by Mr. Foggarty, the tenant. Perhaps you'd like to lie down after all. Daphne, do send off a note to the Hall that we'll be bringing an additional guest. No, no, Lady Bowles, I assure you Mr. Foggarty won't mind. He is everything gracious."

He might be the kindest man in the county, but his table was still going to be at sixes and sevens, like Daphne's room arrangements.

"I don't believe I know a Mr. Foggarty," Seline said.

"That's because he's not of the *ton*. He's just a retired merchant," Graydon commented, and noted Seline's pursed lips that she'd be asked to take her mutton with a Cit. "Perhaps you'd rather not attend, since the company is so plebeian."

Lady Bowles wasn't to be routed that easily. Their host could have been a coal-heaver and she'd go. "No, no, I'm assured country manners are more relaxed. When in Rome, and all that."

Both Daphne and Graydon were thinking that the Romans may have had a good idea, throwing their unwanted citizenry to the lions.

Lord Hollister was laughing. "That's the first time I've heard Full Pockets Foggarty called plebeian. Why, he's the richest man in four shires."

"I'm sure I'll be charmed."

"What do you mean, you didn't invite her?"

"Hush up, for goodness' sake. People are staring." They were at the rear of Howell Hall's music room, where the vicar's wife was performing at the pianoforte. Lady Bowles was seated next to their host, so Graydon could get away for his first words with Daphne since the widow's arrival, albeit they had to be quiet words.

Daphne pasted a polite smile on her face for Admiral Benbow, sitting nearby, and repeated, although in a lower tone of venom, "What do you mean, you didn't invite her? *I* didn't invite her. My mother didn't invite her. Your father didn't—"

"Blister it, Daffy, I know who *didn't* invite her. It was some curst footman at Howell House who did."

"A footman?" she squealed, and Graydon coughed to cover the noise.

"Will you lower your voice! We're in the briars as is, without ruining Foggarty's entertainment. And yes, a footman. I sent a message about bringing the ashes, with a separate note to be delivered to Lady Bowles about another matter entirely. The butler was on holiday, so some underling—if I ever find out which one, he'll be under six feet of dirt—handled the errands. He garbled the notes."

"You expect me to believe that some untrained servant took it upon himself to invite your mistress to your father's wedding?"

"More or less, yes. And she's not my mistress!"

Admiral Benbow's eyebrows shot up. He wasn't quite that deaf. Daphne whispered, "Now who's shouting? And if she's not your mistress, why was she hanging on your sleeve all day and all through dinner? Why were you sending her messages? And why, my lord Mistruth, was she wearing your diamonds?"

Seline had appeared downstairs before they were to leave for Foggarty's wearing another gray gown, this one of sheerest silk, with a décolletage that ended where the waist began. Filling in that vast, milk-white expanse between neck and neckline was a diamond necklace so exquisite that even Lord Hollister had to notice. He hadn't looked at anyone but Cleo Whilton in weeks, but now he had trouble keeping his eyes above Seline's chin. "Lovely, my dear, lovely," he enthused, until Lady Whilton rapped his arm with her fan.

"Thank you, my lord. Doesn't your son have excellent taste?"

Lady Whilton dragged her betrothed out to the carriages before he could comment on Graydon's taste, in gems or in women.

Seline was telling the others: "And I've hardly had a chance to thank him."

Daphne wondered how the woman meant to express her gratitude, if not by plastering herself to Graydon's side as she seemed to be doing. Daphne also noted how Seline fiddled with the necklace all evening, drawing attention to it and her bosom, after which she would announce to everyone that dear Graydon had given it to her.

Daphne felt the complete dowd in her muslin and pearls, with a ribbon through her hair. The widow wore a matching gray turban on her head, with one black ostrich plume that complemented the one long black curl permitted to fall down her smooth, white, half-naked back.

"Not your mistress, hah! Next you'll be telling me your horse recites Shakespeare."

"She's not my mistress any longer, dash it. I never saw her when I went to London. The necklace was to be a farewell gift, an indication that the affair was over."

"I should think a handshake would have done better. Your subtlety seems to have been lost on Lady Bowles."

"Nothing subtle about it at all. These things are understood."

"I wouldn't know."

"Thank heaven."

"And neither, it seems, does the . . . lady."

The vicar's wife finished her piece. They applauded politely. Then Lady Bowles was persuaded to honor them with a few selections on the harp. It needed only that. "Get rid of her," Daphne demanded.

"I haven't even had a chance to speak to her in private. I couldn't very well announce to her in front of the company that her invitation was an error, could I? Be reasonable, Daffy; how can I ask her to leave now that she's here?"

Daphne was fanning herself, intent on the music.

"I promise I'll talk to her tonight, tell her the affair is finished."

"The affair? Is that what you think she traipsed out of London during the Season for? Don't flatter yourself, *dear* Graydon. It's your title and fortune that harpy's after now, not your—" More polite applause drowned out whatever Daphne almost said, happily.

Unhappily, Graydon insisted, "I never mentioned marriage to the woman, I swear. I never had the slightest honorable intention toward her."

"Then tell her. That should do the trick of getting rid of the witch, unless you're nodcock enough to present her with a diamond ring at the same time."

Somehow Graydon didn't think this was the appropriate moment to give Daffy that little gold locket.

He tried to convince Seline to leave, he honestly did. He knew he'd never get anywhere with Daffy while his mistress—his ex-mistress—was in the house. He never got her alone at Foggarty's, though, and his aunt shared their carriage on the way home. Graydon didn't dare leave it till morning, however; Daffy'd be in such a taking by then, he'd need years to win back her trust, the little shrew. The adorable, *jealous* little shrew.

Cheered by that thought, he was smiling when he scratched on Seline's door late that night, after everyone had gone to bed. She was waiting for him, an answering smile on her face and her arms outstretched.

Seline's smile turned to pure rage and one outstretched arm grabbed up a china cat from a nearby table when he explained his mission.

*202*

He ducked. "Be reasonable," he seemed to be repeating all night. It worked as well now as with Daphne. A perfume bottle followed the statue into the wall. "You know we never once discussed marriage." He caught the pillow, and the hairbrush. "I wouldn't have asked you to be my errand boy, so there was only one explanation for the necklace. We have to discuss this like adults."

The book from her bedside hit him on the side of his face, but it didn't hurt as much as her next words: "I'm not leaving."

He loosened his neckcloth. "Please, Seline, you are making this deuced awkward."

She folded her arms over her magnificent chest, still adorned with the necklace. "You invited me, sirrah, and I told that to all my friends when I made excuses not to attend their parties and such. I could never go back now without becoming a laughingstock."

"How would you like to go to Brighton then? I would stand the expenses, of course."

"With you?"

"No, dash it, that's the whole point."

"No, *chéri*, the whole point is Miss Daphne Whilton, isn't it? If you think I am going to simply step aside so you can have your bucolic belle, your attics are to let. Besides, a girl has to look out for her own interests."

"If it's the matching ring and earbobs you want . . ."

"Dear Graydon, you always were so generous. I'm sorry, darling, but now that I've set my sights on a higher target, nothing but a wedding ring will do. No, I'm not leaving. Mr. Foggarty seemed taken with me, didn't you think?"

Oh lud. How the hell was he going to explain this to Daffy?

Seline walked him to the door. "I'm truly sorry, dear boy; we would have suited, I think. But don't worry. Miss Whilton looks good in green." She planted a kiss where she'd hit him with the book and showed him out. "Good night, *mon cher* Major."

And that was the way Daphne saw him, in the hallway outside the black widow's door where she'd come to see what the commotion was about. Graydon's clothes were all mussed, he wore a dazed expression on his face and lip rouge on his cheek, and he smelled of the widow's scent.

"She's not leaving," he said.

So Daphne hauled off and hit him. It was no ladylike slap, but the full-fisted blow he'd taught her in case she ever had to defend her honor. Graydon supposed he was lucky she didn't employ the other defensive maneuver he'd taught her. He also supposed this wasn't a good time to give her the locket, either.

# Chapter Twenty-one

*N*ot only wouldn't Daphne believe the major's explanations, she wouldn't even listen to them. Nor did she feel the slightest remorse when he appeared downstairs the following day sporting a large black-and-blue mark on his jaw. Good. The black matched his heart, and the blue . . . well, the blue matched Daphne's spirits.

She threw herself with renewed vigor into the wedding plans. That way she wouldn't have to think about Graydon's perfidy or watch him drool down the demirep's dress, the way every other male was doing, from Lord Hollister to the lowest footman with an excuse to hold a door for her. Even Ohlman's breath came a little quicker when he poured the wine, from over Lady Seline's shoulder. To be fair-minded, Daphne admitted Graydon paid the Moon Goddess no more attention than the others did—but no less, either.

A rose on her pillow melted some of the ice wall around her heart, especially when she read the accompaning note: *She's not my mistress*. The message didn't say she never was, which would have made Miss Whilton happier, except that she'd know it for a lie. Daphne no longer expected abstemious morality from her childhood friend—she'd stopped believing in the White Knight and Father Christmas, too. At least Graydon hadn't thought she was that much of a gull.

"Did you get my message?" he asked hopefully when she passed in the hall, her nose in the air as though he'd brought the scent of the stable in with him, or the widow's, again.

"Don't waste the roses," was all she said. "We need them for the wedding."

That night there was a bouquet of violets, wild ones, from the woods. *She's not my mistress* appeared again. In fact, Daphne had to admit, he'd done his best to keep out of the widow's company.

Gray left the house before Seline was down in the morning, and at lunch he spoke to his father about handling his accounts while the earl was in Scotland. Then he rode out again with the boys, this time looking over properties for Mr. Foggarty to purchase, so the lease for Howell Hall could be terminated early. After tea he disappeared to discuss plans for a drainage problem at the Hall with Woodhill's bailiff, and later permitted Mr. Foggarty to take Seline into dinner. Afterward, at cards, he made sure to partner his aunt in a game with the vicar and his wife.

So if he wasn't Lady Seline's lover—Daphne stayed awake listening for sounds in the corridors; there were none—and wasn't her beloved either, what was the woman still doing here?

The answer had to be Mr. Foggarty. The poor man.

Then Miles started coming around again in his usual pattern of mealtime visits. Woodhill really had a superior kitchen, and his parents were nagging at him to make a match with Daphne and her dowry. Besides, he could puff off his letter of commendation from Bow Street. That villain they'd unearthed was a known felon on Bow Street's list of nuisance criminals, if not a hardened murderer. Now Miles had to warn the Woodhill staff to be on the lookout for the man's youthful accomplices, a tall redhead and a diminutive blond lad.

"And make sure you keep an eye on the dog. That's what clinched the identification," he told Daphne proudly as she walked with him into the parlor where the rest of the company was already at tea. "That animal is ... a Diamond of the first water."

"That scruffy mongrel?" No, Miles had caught his first glimpse of the Moon Goddess, in gossamer silver tonight, with sequined stars sewn to her skirts. Miles stared, struck speechless.

"Gets 'em all that way, the first time," Cousin Harriet snickered. "The blood all rushes from the brains to between their legs. Can't talk, can't think, can't see the hoity-toity miss gives off as much warmth as the moon she poses as."

Daphne made the introductions, and Miles made a cake over himself, to the point of ignoring the tea cakes. Daphne turned away in disgust, to see Graydon's gloating smile. "She's not my mistress," he silently mouthed in her direction.

And she'd never leave now, not with another handsome man to beguile. Of course, Pomeroy was no match for Mr. Foggarty for wealth, but he was younger, better-looking in a virile, rustic way, and came from decent family. She could polish him up nicely before parading him around London to prove her respectability at last. Only the highest sticklers would refuse her entry then. Now the lower sticklers were beginning to look askance on her affairs, her gaming, and her unpaid bills.

On the other hand, Foggarty could leave her a wealthier widow, sooner. And who was to say he couldn't use some of that fortune to buy himself a title for paying off Prinny's debts? Then she could have it all, her place in Society and the wherewithal to enjoy it. But squires needed wives, while rich old men mostly wanted bed-warmers. And Pomeroy was Miss Whilton's beau, which made him even more attractive. No, Seline wasn't budging.

And the wedding was getting closer. With the arrival of more guests, the earl's kinfolk, Mama's old schoolmates, Graydon's godparents, Lady Seline was not so conspicuous. Oh, she would always stick out as the brightest star in the night sky, but not so obviously as Graydon's mistress. He treated her with the same respect he gave his ancient relatives, and Seline flirted with him, Daphne noted, only when there were no other men around for her to practice her wiles upon. Or when Daphne was watching, the cat. If she hoped to make Miss Whilton jealous, she was meowing up the wrong tree.

Daphne was beginning to believe Gray's protestations of innocence. Not because flowers kept appearing in her bedroom, and not even because he seemed so indifferent to the widow and to her attentions to other men. No, what convinced Daphne that he might truly have ended the affair and its complications was how assiduously Lady Bowles was working at attaching another gentleman. If Seline had the least chance with Gray, with his looks, title, wealth, and charm, she'd never glance at Miles or Mr. Foggarty. No woman in her right mind would.

Cousin Harriet's gown needed last-minute alterations, Dart broke out in a rash from the starched collar on his new shirt. Torry skinned his knee, and the lobsters arrived lethargic. One of the guests' maids was thought to be increasing, the gardener cut off the tip of his finger instead of a bloom, and that dog swiped a whole haunch of venison to share with the stable hands. Two carriages collided on the way to the village, the vicar was developing a sore throat, and there were clouds. Lord Hollister had too much to drink the night before and couldn't remember where he'd put the wedding ring for safe-keeping, and Mama was having spasms that Uncle Albert would arrive to ruin everything. Daphne had a headache. Ohlman had another glass of sherry.

It was a lovely wedding.

The village church was filled, every seat taken with family and guests, with servants and local people standing in the back and outside waving branches of orange blossoms. There were flowers everywhere, inside and out, woven into garlands up the aisle, draped over the doorways, in massed arrangements of red, white, and pink roses.

The earl and his son stood by the vicar, next to the intricately wrought new altar cloth, waiting for the rest of the bridal party. Lord Hollister was elegant in black swallowtails and white satin breeches, with a red rose in his lapel. Graydon was the proud picture of British manhood in his scarlet regimentals, for the last time, he insisted. His papers would be processed by the end of the month. Torry escorted Cousin Harriet to her front-row seat at one side of the aisle; Dart walked with the earl's sister to the other side. The boys hated their white velvet coats and short pants, but wore them with resignation, Daphne having threatened them with a quick return to school if they protested once more.

Then Daphne walked down the aisle by herself, as maid of honor. She was radiant in soft pink, with a circlet of roses in her hair and ribbons trailing down her back. More than one of the congregants was heard to whisper that Miss Whilton looked like a bride herself, beautiful and beaming on everyone she passed. Daphne was so delighted this day was finally coming to pass, she could have cried.

Ohlman the butler *was* crying as he led Lady Whilton down the aisle. He'd argued against such a heresy, but Lady Whilton would not hear of his protests.

"Perhaps it wouldn't do in London where they are all such snobs, but here in Hampshire where we know everyone? There is no one else I would rather have, no one else who has looked after me so long or so loyally. I cannot very well ask my brother-in-law, can I?"

She certainly couldn't, so Ohlman accepted the honor, and wept with pride as he handed his mistress into the keeping of her new husband. Lady Whilton went gracefully, elegant in her rose-colored satin with the double-heart brooch pinned at the center of the neckline. Luckily they were rubies and matched her color scheme, all selected not to clash with Graydon's regimental jacket.

The vicar cleared his sore, scratchy throat. "Dearly beloved," he began.

Daphne let go a deep sigh. The roses had bloomed on time, the organist hadn't missed a note, the vicar's voice would last through the service if he cut the sermon short. The church smelled of flowers, and the boys had no mice, frogs, or snakes in their pockets.

It was such a lovely wedding that Ohlman wept throughout the entire ceremony. Cousin Harriet had to hand him her handkerchief.

All of the servants wanted to watch their mistress get married and their own Ohlman take his part in the ceremony. The kitchen staff had to stay behind, with the wedding breakfast to be held immediately after the service, but most of the other indoor servants were being permitted to attend. Not the newly hired, temporary staff, of course, for what did they care anyway? And someone had to stay behind.

In the stables, every driver and groom had been assigned to getting the company sorted into and out of their carriages to and from the church, holding horses during the ceremony, bearing the servants off in wagons, carting the massive floral tributes around. Again, only the newest hand was left behind to mind the remaining riding horses.

Opportunity was knocking, if not on the front door where one footman was left on duty, then on the rear parlor window, which Handy had open in a flash. Sailor was waiting on the other side with the wheelbarrow he used to cart the manure. Jake's gang was going to Heaven in a handcart, with Lady Whilton's wedding presents.

Handy had all of his possessions and two pillow slips hidden under his skirts. He hadn't dared approach the guest bedrooms above where jewel boxes waited on every vanity and bureau; too many of the visiting valets and maids were also waiting there to refurbish their employees between the service and the reception. The dining room with all its silverware was too near the kitchens, and the hired musicians were tuning up in the grand parlor.

The smaller room was empty of everything except a king's ransom in gifts, just as Handy's roommates had described it. The circumstances couldn't have been better if Jake had planned it. The only problem for Handy was deciding what to take.

Small and valuable, Jake always told them. Easy to hide and easy to sell. Gold letter openers, gold picture frames, gold candlesticks went into the first sack. Silver platters, silver bowls, silver candlesticks followed. Lots of silver candlesticks. Pearl-handled knives, gem-inlaid candy dishes, ivory inkstands, all got packed and handed out the window to Sailor, along with two dishes of sweetmeats left on tables nearby for when the company returned, and three cut-glass decanters from the mantel.

The last items were so Sailor and Handy could have a celebration of their own, since they'd be missing the servants' party later that night. Sailor had wanted to stay for the food and drink and a chance to dance with those little maids Handy kept crowing about, but they didn't dare make the heist, hide the plunder, and come back. The last time they buried something, Sal dug him up.

Sailor started on one of the decanters while Handy went back with the other pillowcase. There were the statues and vases: jade, porcelain, and crystal, all worth small fortunes to a boy raised in London streets. All went into the bag. A music box, a globe, three paperweights, and a marvelous egg that opened up to reveal a tiny bride and groom. Sailor wrapped that up special in his nightshirt, the same flannel nightshirt that had been the baron's, then Jake's. He stuffed in some more silver candlesticks, then spread the gifts remaining on the table around better, filling in empty spots, so no one would notice the theft too soon. It fair broke Handy's heart to leave so much, but they just couldn't carry those huge centerpieces or the tea services or the sets of rare books.

Jewelry sure would have been nice, Handy thought, a watch or a necklace or a gent's stickpin he could pop into his pocket, but these swells didn't give good stuff like that as wedding presents, it seemed. A bunch of the nipcheese ones just wrote letters, it looked like, for there was a pile of rolled-up parchments in an enameled bowl. Handy dumped the papers out and packed the bowl. Stock certificates, consols, acres in Jamaica, and a bill of sale for a thoroughbred mare rolled off the table. "Cheapskates," Handy muttered as he gathered them up again onto the table so the room still looked neat.

Church bells started to ring. Handy quickly handed the second bag of booty out to his brother, who tossed it onto the wheelbarrow. So much for the porcelain and the crystal. And now they had to leave in a hurry in case someone heard the sound of shattering giftware.

Handy gave one more look, and grabbed up the alabaster urn that was smack in the middle of the table. The maids said it was something special, with everyone guessing what was inside. God knew it was heavy enough to hold a pirate's horde. The nobs'd be sure to notice it was gone, though, so Handy snatched a vase of flowers that was about the same size off the mantel and put that in the urn's place. It didn't look right, so he took the flowers out. And took them along with the urn when he jumped out of the window. They'd look nice on Jake's new grave.

# *Chapter Twenty-two*

*W*heelbarrows don't work so well in the woods. And maybe Jake would have figured a better plan for the getaway, rather than going back to that old fallen-in cottage. But they couldn't go trundling down the highway in broad daylight, and the loot had to be reapportioned before the broken crystal cut through the muslin pillowcase, and they had to do something about changing their disguises. And Handy demanded a bit of celebration, to catch up with his brother.

So they left the barrow at the icehouse and carried the plunder through the stands of oak and evergreen, Sailor complaining the whole way of the weight of that blasted urn Handy was making him carry as gentle as an infant.

"Jake allus said small and light. You have to go an' prig a bloomin' marble flowerpot with handles."

"Well, you went an' tossed the glass gewgaws. I had to find us somethin' else, didn't I? 'Sides, the maids was all in a swivet over the thing. Must be an antique or somethin'. Shut up and pass the bottle."

They arrived at their former hideaway thinking it was too bad Jake had been dug up, or they could have put the flowers on his grave right there, so he could join in the party.

Sailor wet his whistle, and then his hair to get rid of the blacking. They used the boot polish this time on Handy's new coif, once they hacked off his long blond hair. He was back in boy's clothes, too, with an improbable mustache drawn over his lip in an attempt to add to his manliness.

Sailor was not going to look like anything but a big carrot-topped sprout who kept pulling his cap down over his ears. He smelled so badly of manure, though, they figured no one would get close enough to recognize the footpad of his description.

Since they had to wait until dark to use the road, neither having enough confidence to attempt byways and deer tracks, they unpacked. It might have been wiser to get on their way, put as much distance as possible between themselves and the scene of the crime, but if they were wiser, Sailor mightn't smell of horse dung and Handy mightn't look like an underage pimp. If they were wiser still, they might have stolen some food to put in their stomachs, beneath the potent whiskey in the decanters. Then again, if wishes were horses, these two would likely wish for theirs well done.

Handy emptied one of the sacks of stolen goods out onto the bare dirt floor. If any of the rare Sevres or Dynasty ware had survived, they were potsherds now, tossed aside for some future Lord Elgin to weep over.

The ornately embellished egg didn't make the

journey, either. Handy took a few minutes to scrape the gold filigree and seed pearls off the shell, which had taken some poor, underpaid artisan a month to decorate. Disappointed, Handy tipped the other bag open. The silver and gold had taken a few nicks and dents, that was all. It was still sellable, still worth more money than either of the thieves had ever seen. They were on easy street, as soon as they could find it.

A few candies and brandies later, Sailor wanted to open the urn. "Why lug that ugly thing around if the good stuff is inside?" he asked.

Handy wanted to wait, to bring the whole package to Fred the Fence.

"Then you gots to carry it," his brother ordered, which was the deciding vote. Handy used one of the pearl-handled knives to slice through the wax that sealed on the lid, then pried the top off with a small gold pickle fork. He tipped the urn over, right there onto the dirt floor of the abandoned cottage.

Sailor stuck a finger in the gritty pile, licked it, shook his head, and sneezed. "Ashes."

Handy poked through the dark mound of finely ground rubble with the pickle fork. "Must be somethin' in here that needed special packing, like a diamond mine."

"No, you clunch, it's ashes."

"Why the hell give a jar of ashes for a weddin' present?" Handy wanted to know, as if his brother were a font of information.

Sailor shrugged and sneezed again. "Rich folks is different, that's all." Still, he kept sifting through the ashes, letting the stuff trickle through his thick fingers, until something didn't trickle. Something that looked a whole lot like a finger. Sailor jumped up, which scattered more of the ashes. "It's him!" he screamed. "The bloke what died! The one in the barrel. Now they got him in a flowerpot!"

Handy was halfway out the door. "Oh Lord, he's come back to haunt us. We're never goin' to be shut of the blighter!"

"Why's he after us? We wasn't the ones what had a thing against coffins. We would've got Jake a nice one, if the dibs was in tune."

"He's mad at us, is all. Maybe he wanted to stay in that icehouse, like a clause in his will or somethin', and we disturbed him. Spirits like their rest, they do." Handy looked around, saw the ashes all over the place. "He's going to be a whole lot madder now."

"Quick, get him back in the jar!"

So they scrabbled around trying to sweep up the ashes without a broom. They used the broken pottery shards to gather the piles together, and unavoidably gathered a lot of dirt from the cottage floor, too. And slivers of glass, chips of porcelain, crumbs from the broken eggshell, and a few chicken bones from their last meal here.

"What if we ain't got all of him? He'll come back to haunt us like one of them phantoms. You know, with a cape where his head was s'posed to be and only red gleams from what was eyes."

Handy's manly lip was trembling, fake mustache and all. "How're we going to get more of him? You went and sneezed on the poor bastard, scattered him from one corner of the place to t'other."

The drink was talking now in Sailor, and it was scared, too: "What if . . . what if it was his ballocks or somethin' that we lost? He'd be so mad, he'd come get ours."

"No way!"

"I swear he would. Wouldn't you, some fool tips your rocks on the ground?"

Handy was already feeling the cold hand of doom squeezing at his privates. So he ran outside and found two round stones, almost of a size and shape. "Here, maybe he won't notice." He stuffed some fish bones down the urn's mouth, too, in case the ghoul lost a toe or something. Sailor sacrificed his lucky marble, in case it was an eye he sneezed into the next county. Handy threw in those little seed pearls for teeth, unaware the baron's had been just as false. "There, good as new."

They crammed the top back on the urn as though that would keep the demon inside. But it wasn't going to work. The dead man's ghost already had them in its clutches and was giving them a good shake.

"We got to bring him back," Handy said, his voice even more high-pitched than ever.

"I ain't touchin' him." Sailor's hands were shaking so violently, they couldn't have touched his own poker to make sure it was still there.

"Well, I ain't."

"You took him."

"You sneezed on him."

"Maybe we could just put him in the ground with Jake?"

Handy gave the matter his full consideration, from across the room. "No, he must want to be with his loving fambly. They wouldn't've put him in the center of the table that way otherwise. We got to get him back. You're bigger. You can—"

"Not me. I ain't—"

\* \* \*

Ohlman still had tears in his eyes halfway through the wedding reception at the Manor. He cleared his throat to catch Daphne's attention while she was organizing her cousins and some of the local children into teams for races on the lawn. Their elders sat on chairs under the canopies erected to shield delicate complexions from the sun, or they strolled around the gardens, relaxing after the lavishly abundant wedding breakfast, which, of course, did not start until after noon. It was a magnificent sight, Daphne thought, like a painting. All the ladies' pastel gowns dotted the landscape like flowers—except for Lady Seline's silver tulle, of course. And the men's more somber garb added contrast—except for Graydon's scarlet uniform, which made him the focal point of the composition wherever he happened to wander. Of course, he would have captured the imagination anyway, being so tall and athletically built and devastatingly handsome.

He was capturing Daphne's attention a lot more than she wished that afternoon as, almost against her will, she kept darting glances in his direction to see if he was worshiping at the Temple of the Moon like half the other men present. More often than not, he was circulating among the guests, greeting old friends, introducing the London visitors to the locals, playing host, making everyone comfortable and welcome. Ah, but she never denied he had charm.

Right now he was at Ohlman's side, waiting for her to finish with the children. Ohlman was weepy, and Graydon looked grim as he took her arm and led her a distance away from any of the clusters of guests.

"Trouble," he said, "but try to smile."

Ohlman was wringing his hands. "Nothing like this has ever happened in all my years of butling. And today of all days, when Lady Whilton, Lady Hollister, that is, put such faith in me."

Daphne had no problem smiling. "Are you still in a fidge over that? I've had nothing but compliments over the ceremony, and Mama is so happy." She looked around to find her mother in a circle of her bosom bows, laughing and giggling like a debutante.

"She won't be happy when she finds half her wedding gifts have been stolen!" It was a good thing Graydon had his arm under hers to catch her when she tripped.

"Ohlman?"

"I'm afraid so, Miss Daphne. While we were at the church, it seems. Mrs. Binder is beside herself, because two of the servants are missing also, the last two she hired as temporary help. They didn't go into the village with the rest."

"No, they stayed and robbed us blind!"

"Not quite, miss. Mrs. Binder is in the parlor right now, comparing the remaining gifts with the lists you've been keeping for the acknowledgments. I took the liberty of locking the door behind her, so no one wanders in and notices their present is not on display."

"Clever man. What would we do without you? Do you think most of the gifts are still there?"

"All of the important ones, from what I recall, Miss Daphne, and the written ones. Most of what seems to be missing are small knickknacks, tableware, candlesticks, and the like."

"Then there is nothing to worry about. Mama

didn't need any of those things anyway, so she won't notice that stuff gone. We won't have to tell her and ruin her wonderful day. We can thank the givers and they never need to know their silver jam jar or china creamer has done a flit either. See? Now, relax and tell Mrs. Binder she is not to blame. We can all make character misjudgments." She turned to Graydon, smiling. "Can't we?"

He didn't laugh at her teasing. "It gets worse."

"Worse? What could be worse than thieves stealing the presents on the day of the wedding with all these people in the house?"

"They stole the urn."

"The urn? *That* urn?"

Miles wasn't concerned with the theft of the gifts. He was more concerned that Mr. Foggarty was making headway with Lady Bowles whilst he was dragged aside by Daphne. "You should have posted a guard," was all he told her, his eyes on the widow.

"I did post a footman, and he made sure no one entered the house. One of the thieves was already inside, though. We think they were a brother and sister; at least that's what they told Mrs. Binder when she hired them. He was tall and dark, she was small and blond."

Miles wasn't listening. Foggarty was kissing Lady Seline's fingers, the lecher.

"So what are you going to do about it?"

"I'd plant him a facer if I thought it would— Oh, about the robbery? Nothing I can do now. The culprits are long gone. What, did you think they were going to sit around waiting to be arrested? Your cracksmen are too smart for that, if they planned this robbery so far in advance to get hired on as servants. They're halfway to London by now to sell the goods. You can give me a list of the stolen properties tomorrow and I'll send it on to Bow Street, who'll keep an eye on the known fences."

"That's all? You're not even going to look for clues or call out dogs to follow their trail?"

"Now?" he squawked in agony as Foggarty led the widow off toward the maze. When they were out of sight he recalled himself enough to say, "Uh, that is, you were the one who didn't want to disturb your mother's wedding." Miles looked over his shoulders to make sure no one overheard. "Your uncle and all."

"They took him, too."

Miles looked so pitiful then, thinking of what a fool he'd appear in front of the dashing widow, chasing after the remains of a man not officially dead, that Daphne almost forgave him for his wavering affections. Almost. Miles Pomeroy was supposed to be waiting—anxiously—for her answer to his proposal. He was supposed to act like he cared. He was also supposed to put duty above pleasure and go searching for Uncle Albert. Was there no such thing as a man with a constant heart?

# *Chapter Twenty-three*

$\mathscr{I}$t was the finest wedding the county had seen in years, so everyone agreed after the bridal couple left for Scotland amid shouts and cheers, ribald jokes, and rose petals. Then most of the local guests departed, the vicar to go rest his voice on Daphne's urging, because she was going to need his services in the not too distant future, she hoped. The vicar hoped she meant another wedding, to young Howell after all and not that fickle Pomeroy, who was busy making sheep eyes at a woman no better than she ought to be. He didn't say anything, of course; his voice was too weak.

The house guests were having their carriages brought round, too, in order to make London by nightfall, or the first stage of their journeys to some other country residence or fashionable retreat. The earl's sister was one of those leaving, setting off on a tour of the New World, now that her brother finally had someone to look after him.

Daphne and Graydon stood side by side at Woodhill's front door, accepting congratulations and wishing Godspeed as Ohlman and his minions handed over canes and hats and oversaw the loading of baggage. Pomeroy and Foggarty were among the last to leave, each trying to outstay the other. Daphne finally had to hint Miles away, saying, "I am sure you must be *yearn*ing to be on your way. *Earn*ing our regard with your devotion to duty. We'll be interested in *learn*ing the results of your investigation tomorrow."

Reluctantly Miles left to go beat the bushes in a halfhearted manner. The other half of his heart belonged to the most beautiful woman he'd ever seen, who unfortunately was not the woman whom he'd asked to wed. Pomeroy was a troubled man, so troubled that he never noticed the wheelbarrow by the icehouse or the tracks leading into the woods. He found nothing but a guilty conscience.

Foggarty took his leave with a wink and a leer— for Graydon. "Two beauties, eh? Lucky dog."

Then Daphne turned to Lady Bowles, who'd parked herself in the hallway as though she were family. "Should I have one of the grooms send for your carriage, my lady?"

Seline brushed aside the hint. "Oh, I sent my coach back when I arrived, sure that dear Graydon would escort me home. But don't worry, my dear, I won't rush off on you in your hour of need."

"Need? What need is that?" Daphne's tone was sour, as she was sure that Graydon had taken the widow into his confidence again.

"Your need for a chaperone, of course. Graydon's aunt is gone, and it would be highly improper for you two to be alone in the house."

"My cousin Harriet is here as my companion. I

assure you there is no need to put off your own plans. And if Gray has to accompany you . . ." She'd murder him, that's what.

Seline waved one graceful hand in the air. "But your cousin took to her rooms hours ago. Too much champagne, I believe. No, you need me to lend countenance, even though you are almost brother and sister now."

Daphne fumed but Graydon choked. A man didn't want to carry his sister upstairs and make mad, passionate love to her. Perhaps they needed a chaperone after all. But Seline Bowles playing propriety? When pigs grew wings. "Your new respect for the conventions mightn't have anything to do with a certain nabob, would it?"

"Don't be tiresome, dear boy, and I shan't be either." With that she floated up the stairs to plan her wardrobe for the coming days.

As one, Graydon and Daphne hurried to the small parlor. There was a neat inventory of missing items, with *Urn, alabaster, gift of Miss Daphne and Major Howell*, heading the list. Daphne sank onto a sofa and kicked her slippers off. "Uncle Albert is really gone again. Lud, how can we hold his funeral without him?"

Graydon poured them each a glass of wine from the solitary decanter remaining on the mantel. He handed one to Daphne and sat beside her. "A toast."

"Not to Uncle Albert, I hope."

"To the thieves. Can you imagine the poor cawkers' surprise when they realize what they've got?"

Daphne pretended to read from the list: "Ten candlesticks, silver; two figurines, jade; one baron, incinerated. Oh dear." She sipped at her wine, wondering why the man's presence made her forget to panic at the hobble they were in now. Gray was sitting so relaxed, with his coat unbuttoned and his carefully arranged curls falling onto his forehead. He always could make her feel safe and secure. When they were children he used to tell her not to be afraid of the thunder and lightning, that he'd protect her. She used to believe him, too. Daphne sighed.

The major heard her and said, "Don't worry, sweetheart, we'll come about."

There, he was doing it again, keeping the storm at bay.

Graydon reached into his pocket and pulled out a small box wrapped in tissue. He held it out to her. "Here, I've been wanting to give this to you for ages, but the time never seemed right. It's to celebrate our parents' wedding."

She unwrapped the package to reveal a gold heart on a chain, similar to the one she used to have. She swallowed the lump in her throat. "It's lovely, Gray. Thank you."

"It's just a token. I wish it could be fancier."

"Like Lady Seline's diamond necklace?"

"Brat," he replied with affection. "If I got you diamonds, your name would be a byword in the neighborhood, and well you know it. You deserve something better than this, though, for being such a trooper about this whole coil, and making the wedding such a success."

"No, the locket is perfect." She started to open the sections.

"A portrait inside would have been too egotistical, even for me. What was in the other one, anyway?"

"A lock of your hair your mother once gave me." Daphne fussed with the catch so he couldn't see her face. When she finally got the locket open, a tiny scrap of folded paper fell out. "What . . . ?" The message read: *She's not my mistress.* "You gudgeon."

"That not what I wanted to say, either, Daffy, but the time was always wrong."

Daphne's heart was hammering so loudly, she was surprised he didn't hear it. "What did you want to say?"

"I—"

The time was still wrong. Ohlman cleared his throat from the doorway. Daphne tucked her toes under her skirts so the butler wouldn't see she was barefoot.

"Pardon, Miss Daphne, but that Terwent person has returned. He insists on seeing you or Major Howell. I explained that you were resting after the wedding and all, but he is determined to wait on the doorstep until he sees you."

Graydon sighed. "You may as well show him in, Ohlman. The deuced chap is as hard to dislodge as a tick."

"And we don't want him feeding the gossip mills in the village either," Daphne agreed.

The valet hadn't improved in the days he was gone. He was still pinch-faced and prune-lipped, long-nosed and livid that he was being done out of his rightful share of whatever villainy was going on.

He'd been to Bow Street, it seemed, and all the morgues. Everyone knew of Awful Albert Whilton, but no one knew where he was. In desperation, Terwent had called on the magistrate, who allowed as how some soldier had kindly brought the baron's body to London some days back, with his identification on him. The family had been informed.

"Is it true?" Terwent demanded. "He was already cold when you sent me haring around town?"

The baron had been cold, all right, from the icehouse. Graydon reflected on the peripatetic barrel and truthfully admitted, "We were as confused as you about the whole matter. Of course, we weren't surprised to learn of his death, considering the baron's state when he left."

"And we did notify his man of business, who must have missed you in London." Daphne was careful not to say when they'd sent the letter. "So now we are merely awaiting the return of the ashes until we proceed."

"Ashes? You're not burying the bas—the baron?"

"No, the condition of the body, don't you know, and the amount of time gone by." Graydon studied his fingertips.

Terwent's nose was twitching; he was smelling a rat. No body, no funeral. No funeral, no reading of the will. And no reading of the will meant no pension for Terwent. He wasn't sure why these toffs were so determined to keep him from his due, but if they weren't up to something crooked, his name wasn't Sam Fink, which, in fact, it was. Close as inkle-weavers, these two, with her shoes under the sofa. They had more than their heads together, unless he missed his guess.

"Them ashes better be getting here in a hurry or I'll be knowing the reason why. I'll go straight to the magistrate, I will. And not that local bumbler who sits in your pocket"—with a glare toward Daphne—"but his nibs in London. He'll get to the bottom of this; see if he don't."

Lord Rivington should be back in town from the wedding by then, but Graydon saw no reason to have this unpleasant little leech disturb his godfather's rest. "The ashes will be here tomorrow, without fail." He tossed the valet some coins. "Why don't you put up at the Golden Crown again, and we'll send for you as soon as we know more details."

Daphne didn't want this man snooping around the house any more than Graydon did. "We'd offer you a room, but the Manor is still at sixes and sevens, with the guests and their servants."

Terwent left, still muttering about those ashes being there tomorrow or else. The moment the door was shut behind him, Daphne ran, without bothering to put on her shoes, over to the long table where the remaining gifts were displayed. She was studying the selection when Graydon reached over her shoulders and picked up a silver Russian samovar.

"This one, I think. It has a lid and handles."

"But it's got a spigot!"

"So the baron will think he's in a taproom and feel right at home."

The Wedgewood was too pretty, and the Ming too valuable. Daphne nodded and followed him to the fireplace, where they tried to fill the coffee urn with the ashes from the grate. Without a broom and dustpan, they had as much trouble as Sailor and Handy, at last resorting to tearing pages from the gift list book to serve as sweepers. Not enough volume, Graydon decided, and threw another log on the fire. Not enough weight, Daphne judged, and tossed her slippers into the flames. They were ruined anyway, and Uncle Albert had always been as tough as shoe leather.

By the time they were finished and the urn was back on the table, Graydon felt like a chimney sweep, but Daphne looked like Cinderella to him, all warm and rosy, with streaks of soot down her face, and dirty toes showing beneath her bedraggled skirts. Was there ever a prettier sight? He took out his handkerchief to wipe her flushed cheeks, stepping nearer to do a better job. And nearer, until there was hardly any space between them, and her cheeks were even pinker, and her blue, blue eyes were staring up at him.

"Ahem," said Ohlman from the doorway.

Graydon stepped back. "No, I can't find the speck in your eye, Daffy."

"Pardon, Miss Daphne, but Master Torrence is ailing. The nursemaid fears he had too much punch, but thought you should be called since the lad is feverish."

Torrence wasn't the only male with fevered brow, Ohlman reflected with satisfaction as Miss Daphne swept from the room with a hurried good night to the major. Her presence wasn't required in the nursery whatsoever. The boy's tutor was with him, and they'd already administered a sleeping draught, but Ohlman wasn't going to fail in his duty again, not twice in one day. Bare feet indeed!

Except for Ohlman and Mrs. Binder, who were consoling each other with the private stock in the housekeeper's apartment, the servants were all finished with their celebration and had gone to bed.

Tomorrow was the big cleaning day and they'd be up early, with headaches.

When the last candles were finally extinguished, Sailor and Handy crept out of the woods and slinked toward the house. They met Sal, who was patrolling the grounds for leftovers. She didn't bark at them, naturally. They were old friends, and her mouth was full.

Slowly, silently, like shadows at Stonehenge, the two bandits made their way to the colonnaded porch of Woodhill Manor. They inched their way up the marble stairs, each holding one handle of the urn. Since Handy was so much smaller than Sailor, the urn bumped a few times, chipping the alabaster and making enough noise to waken the dead. Luckily Uncle Albert was a heavy sleeper.

At last they were at the massive front door. The boys lowered the urn to the ground, banged on the knocker, then ran as if all the hounds in hell were at their heels.

It was only Sal, with half a roast duck to share.

# Chapter Twenty-four

*It is back.* Such was the message in Ohlman's hand both Graydon and Daphne received with their morning hot water. They met at the top of the stairs and together hurried in search of the butler. He couldn't explain, other than that the container had been left on their doorstep last night, like an infant at the church gates. Now it was locked in the butler's pantry. Ohlman wasn't taking any more chances. They all went to look.

The alabaster was chipped and the lid was unsealed and the contents rattled.

"What's that noise? It never used to make noise." Graydon tried to look inside, but the neck was too narrow.

"My word, I wonder what they did, the thieves who took it."

"We'll never know. Maybe it's better that way. There are some peculiar people in the world."

"But what if it's not . . . ?"

"For all we know, Mr. Biggs could have sent us

one of the missionaries who were his previous clients. Don't think about it. Just be happy we have *someone* to show Terwent."

Ohlman nodded, then added, "It also feels lighter than it did." So they added some of the ashes from the samovar, shoe leather and all, and glued the lid on with sealing wax. They all watched as Ohlman locked the door behind them.

Then it was time to notify the vicar, tell the boys to put on their black armbands, and inform the rest of the household.

"Good." Cousin Harriet wasn't precisely grief-stricken. She refused to put on mourning for the dirty dish. "He wouldn't for me." Daphne couldn't argue with that.

Lady Bowles, on the other hand, wore perpetual mourning, so she was prepared.

"We'll understand if you choose to leave now," Daphne hinted. "With a funeral and mourning, this won't be a very lively house party, I'm afraid. We won't be entertaining, of course." She pointed to where the servants were draping hatchments over the doors and hanging crepe from the mirrors.

"Oh, but I couldn't desert you now. Furthermore, Mr. Foggarty is planning a lovely dinner. It would be a shame if we all had to cancel. Why, he'd have no company whatsoever. But don't worry, I'll make your excuses."

The few remaining guests hurried their departures when Daphne explained the situation. They didn't want to add to her burden, they said. They didn't want to perjure their souls by pretending to be sorry the old curmudgeon was dead, more like.

Daphne sent messengers round to all the houses in the neighborhood, the village, and the tenant farms. Not many chose to come to pay their respects to a man they didn't. What, give up a day's planting for that bastard what tried to raise the rent on them? Not likely.

So it was a small group that returned to the village chapel for the service. Miles may have come out of duty; Mr. Foggarty definitely came to see Seline, for Daphne could hear them chatting in the back row. A few locals did attend, mostly the grandmothers with nothing better to do. Two old men who remembered Uncle Albert as a nasty little boy came to gloat that they'd lived longer than the nasty piece of goods he'd turned out to be. Ohlman and Mrs. Binder were there representing the Woodhill staff. Terwent sat alone, weepers tied to his hat. And Mr. Rosten from the London solicitors' firm took a seat as the vicar opened his prayer book.

Daphne tried to pay attention, seated as she was in the front pew, and to set an example for Dart and Torry next to her. Her mind kept wandering, though, from the vicar's raspy voice to the man seated at the end of her pew, on Torry's other side.

How good he was, she thought, and not of Uncle Albert, whose urn was on the new altar cloth. Graydon had carried it there himself, to guarantee its arrival. Not many other men would go to such efforts for a wretch who wasn't even related, or work so hard to ease the boys' apprehensions. He wasn't wearing his uniform, but the midnight superfine stretched across his broad shoulders looked just as handsome. With the gleaming white stock and black brocaded waistcoat, he was a nonpareil, and Daphne felt even more blue-deviled at her own appearance.

She looked a frump. Her blacks were two years out of style, hot and heavy, and she looked ready for the coffin herself in the dreary ensemble, topped with an old black ruched bonnet of Mama's that hid every curl of hair. One week, that's all she'd give Uncle Albert of deep mourning. One week was seven days more than he deserved, and about how long it would take the village seamstress to stitch up some light muslins in gray or lavender. No, just lavender. Let the Moon Goddess keep her grays and silvers. Heaven forbid anyone think Daphne was trying to compete with the dashing widow.

Daphne's attention was recalled to the service when the vicar cut short the eulogy because his voice was reduced to a croak—and because he was reduced to lies, trying to find something good to say about the baron.

Finally they all trooped out to the graveyard and the family crypt. The boys pointed out the grave of the highwayman along the way. The newly dug plot had a bouquet on it, which curiously resembled the arrangement of flowers Daphne had done for the wedding reception. She shrugged and watched as the urn was placed on a shelf in the Whilton mausoleum. The vicar said a few last words, his voice miraculously restored, and they all gave heartfelt amens.

Graydon took Daphne's hand to lead her over the rough path back through the graveyard. "Do you think he'll stay put this time?" she asked.

"Definitely. I tipped the sexton to come back and nail the door shut."

* * *

Crime begets crime. That was Miles Pomeroy's favorite axiom, and it was true. Give malfeasance an inch, it would take a mile—of highway. The news around the darker side of London, mostly thanks to Terwent's panic-driven probes, was that there were easy pickings in Hampshire. Pigeons were just waiting to be plucked. So the hawks moved in.

There were five thugs waiting on the road Sailor and Handy had to take to get to London. Jake's boys had decided to stop first at the Gypsy camp to trade a candlestick or two for a pair of horses. Why should they walk the whole way when they were rich? The fact that they still couldn't ride a horse didn't bother them. Sailor was an expert on the species now, from cleaning their stalls.

But the Gypsies were gone, having heard that the magistrate was looking into current robberies. The caravan left before the blame, as it inevitably did, fell their way. Miles found the empty grounds, and the empty woodsman's hovel with its broken pottery and glassware. He was right, the bandits had come and gone. He could search the countryside from here till kingdom come—or till Lady Bowles ran off with Full Pockets Foggarty— without finding the culprits. They were halfway to London by now.

He was wrong. Sailor and Handy were no more than a mile from Woodhill when they were set upon by the London Mohocks. Now here was a gang Jake could have been proud of. Pop Bullitt's boys had guns, knives, and horses, and no morals to interfere with their chosen line of work. In no time at all they also had the two sacks of stolen goods from Sailor and Handy.

That wasn't enough. They wanted what was in the young men's pockets. Handy protested. What he actually said, in his high, girlish voice, was: "I'll sic my dog on you iffen you don't leave us alone."

The highwaymen laughed, and two of them dismounted to have at the runt who dared challenge them. One-eared Roger growled, "Thinks 'e's up to our weight, 'e does, the little bugger."

And Black Harry stomped toward Handy, huge fists dangling almost to the ground. "Seems top-heavy to me, anyways. I says we turn 'im upside down an' see what falls out."

Handy shrieked and Sailor jumped to his side. "He ain't heavy, he's my brother!" Fists started flying, so many that the mounted outlaws couldn't get off clean shots. Two more got off their horses and entered the fray.

Not even Sailor could withstand four antagonists with only Handy's screams to back him up. They were losing, and losing badly, when Sal came tearing up the road, barking and snarling, growling and slavering. She went right for the heels—of the horses. Pop Bullitt, the only gallows-bait still mounted, was having trouble staying on his pitching, rearing horse. There was no way he could hold any of the other terrified beasts.

"C'mon, the horses is boltin'. These two nancies ain't worth it."

The bullies ran down the road after their nags, Sal getting in a few last bites. Sailor and Handy dragged themselves off the road, under the hedges and into the woods.

They wouldn't have to worry about disguises for

a while. Not even their own mother would recognize them now, even if it hadn't been eight years since she'd left. Bruised and bloody, noses broken and one eye of each already swelling shut, the two once rich robbers huddled under some trees.

"Crime don't pay," Handy eventually sniveled.

"It sure as hell don't pay as good as shoveling horse dung." Sailor was removing his shoe and counting the pitiful horde of coins hidden there, tossed to him by gentlemen whose horses' stalls he'd cleaned.

"Think they'd take us back?"

"Yeah, when Jake writes us another reference."

Handy was emptying his pockets: a gold pickle fork, one pearl-handled knife, the tiny china bride and groom from inside the egg, some ribbons he'd saved from his feminine pose, the last bonbon, and the shilling every employee had been handed the morning of Lady Whilton's wedding. They hadn't stayed long enough to receive their pay.

"You almost got us kilt over that?" Sailor was so furious he blackened Handy's other eye. He would have done more damage, but Sal growled. The hound was carrying a silver candlestick that the highwaymen had dropped in their mad dash after their horses. She laid it at Sailor's feet.

"Good dog, Sal." He handed her that last bonbon. Handy didn't even protest.

They sat there, too tired, hurt, and discouraged to move, wondering if they were better off or worse from when they left London.

"At least we ain't got Jake beatin' us with a stick."

Handy's swollen-shut eyes couldn't see the improvement.

"An' they didn't take Sal." So they could start a flea circus.

"An' the weather's nice, so we don't got to worry about sleepin' outside.

It started to rain.

Mr. Rosten was ready to begin the reading of the will in the library. He looked over his spectacles to view the small audience, like an actor counting the house. It was almost a private performance.

Daphne was there, of course, in one of the comfortable leather armchairs, with Graydon standing behind. They had decided the boys didn't need to attend; even though they were most directly involved in the will's contents, they were too young to make any decisions, and Torry was still looking peaked. Miles was there in his capacity as justice of the peace, anxious to see this whole matter put to rest. Seline was there in her capacity as snoop. She refused to accept Daphne's polite hints to leave, thriving on the drama and Mr. Pomeroy's attention. Head-to-toe in black, Terwent hovered in the background like the vulture he was.

Mr. Rosten straightened his papers again. Then he adjusted his spectacles again. "Yes. Let me preface the reading of the will by saying that Lord Whilton had no interest in writing such a document."

"Most likely refused to believe he'd die," Graydon whispered in Daphne's ear. Mr. Rosten frowned.

"As the family's solicitors and financial consultants, however, the firm of Rosten and Turlow insisted that the baron express his wishes regarding the disposition of his estate and the guardianship of his minor sons. Lord Whilton finally agreed. His behests were conveyed herein." Mr. Rosten held up a torn sheet of paper with a few lines scrawled across it. "Which the firm of Rosten and Turlow dutifully transcribed into proper form." He held up a document of at least twenty pages. The major groaned.

"Quite. Now, this document"—he tapped the will—"is entirely legal, signed, witnessed, notarized, and filed with the proper authorities. This one"—the scrap of paper "—is not. Which shall I read, Miss Whilton?"

Daphne didn't need Graydon's hand squeezing on her shoulder to convince her to go for the shorter version. "The note, please, Mr. Rosten."

The solicitor fixed his spectacles more firmly in place. Then he looked up. "I shall, of course, leave a copy of the official will behind for your perusal."

Daphne nodded. Mr. Rosten cleared his throat. " 'Everything entailed,' " he read, " 'goes to the older boy. Everything not, to the younger. Make Daphne's husband guardian. Whoever the peagoose chooses, he's bound to be dull as ditchwater, but honest. Meantime, Rosten, you do the job.' My apologies, Miss Whilton, but those were your uncle's words."

Graydon was chuckling behind her, but her reply was drowned out by Terwent's voice: "What about my pension? Where's it say about my retirement he promised me?"

The valet had rushed forward to snatch up the legal papers, but Mr. Rosten put his hand atop them. "Your name was not mentioned, Mr. Terwent. Not verbally, not in his note. I believe your salary was owing, however. As guardian of the estate, I took the liberty of withdrawing such funds, and a month's bonus." He handed the valet a small pouch. "The firm shall write a reference, if you require."

"A reference? I wasn't going to have to work again! The old rotter promised! Why else do you think I stayed on with the miserable bastard?"

Mr. Rosten was ignoring the valet's tirade. He told Daphne, "I have seen that the London town house has been padlocked. It is customary to take such precautions when a death is announced and the residence is left empty." He did give a pointed glance to Terwent, who'd already removed a few items from the baron's rooms as soon as he heard the makebait was truly dead.

"Thank you, Mr. Rosten," Daphne was saying. "But about Torrence's portion . . ."

"I'm afraid the baron was a trifle optimistic. There doesn't seem to be any unentailed property left. In fact, the baron's personal debts will have to be paid out of the estate itself. Most improper, as I told him many times. Even if he had specified an amount for his servant, the funds would not have been available. Of course, as guardian, I shall set up a fund for Master Torrence, a percentage of the future income, shall we say. Unless you have my replacement already, ah, selected?"

Her cheeks going scarlet, Daphne stammered, "No, no, whatever you decide. I'm sure you'll do what's right. Thank you, Mr. Rosten. Would you like some wine?"

No one noticed when Terwent stormed out of the room. Ohlman and a footman did make sure he got in his hired rig and down the drive before shutting the door behind him.

\* \* \*

No pension! Neither that stiff-rumped solicitor nor that blue-blooded bitch had suggested making good on the old whoreson's promise out of the estate, or out of their own pockets, for all Terwent cared. Blast, the French had the right idea! Get rid of all the aristos, so no poor bastard like himself had to spend the rest of his days powdering their butts. What, was he going to have to change his name again to find some doddering old fool willing to change his will? Damn and blast!

Terwent was so angry, he almost ran over two boys playing ball in the carriageway. Two boys that bitch cared about. Two boys who were getting *his* pension money! Terwent backed the hired gig around. He pulled out the pistol he'd taken from the baron's luggage. "Get in or I'll shoot."

# Chapter Twenty-five

"Thank God that's over." Daphne may have said the words, but others shared the sentiment. Daphne was happy they'd squeaked through the wedding and the funeral without causing dear Mama a moment's grief.

Still chuckling over the baron's words, Graydon was pleased they hadn't misplaced Albert again. "Dull as ditchwater" indeed. The old rip must have thought she'd marry portly Pomeroy. Not a chance in hell, Howell mentally told him, addressing his comments to the right direction. The major took Mr. Rosten aside to discuss a few improvements that could be made in Woodhill's farming methods.

Lady Seline Bowles was delighted the reading had gone so quickly. Now she could spend the afternoon getting ready for her dinner with dear Fogey. Foggarty, she meant. And what delicious tidbits she'd have to share about the Woodhill will. Seline felt no remorse over gossiping about her hostess's family, not when Graydon still preferred that quiz in black bombazine to her own elegant self.

Miles was most relieved of all. No one had questioned the date of death, the cause of death, or the place of death. His career as magistrate was safe. His self-esteem as an honorable, law-abiding man was restored. So was his affection for Miss Whilton. That bit about ditchwater hadn't registered with Miles at all, only the fact of Daphne's husband getting to control this vast estate for years, until young Eldart came of age. They could even live here, so Miles wouldn't have the expense of setting up another household, for his mama wouldn't like those young boy cousins of Daphne's underfoot at holidays. Miles had also been relieved to see that, for all her faults, Miss Daphne had donned proper mourning. His mama would like that.

His mama had not approved of Lady Bowles. Fast, she'd declared, even for a widow. Wasn't she right now preparing for a dinner *à deux* with Foggarty? Miles felt his position demanded a wife above reproach, much less outright suspicion. Besides, he couldn't compete with the nabob. No, by light of day the Moon Goddess looked a little tawdry.

"Miss Whilton, a moment of your time, if I may?"

"Of course, Mr. Pomeroy. I'll just ring for the tea things, shall I, then we can have our chat." Daphne had noticed how his eyes followed Seline's every move. Who could blame him, as perfect as she looked? It was time and past Daphne put the poor man out of his misery and set him free to pursue the widow. Not that she thought he had much chance, not against Mr. Foggarty's purse, but it wasn't fair to keep Miles dangling.

When she told him of her decision, thanking him for the great honor of asking her to be his wife, but declining, Miles lost his appetite for once.

"It's not because I made a cake of myself over Lady Seline, is it?" Miles wanted to know.

She tried to convince him that she had decided they wouldn't suit, the widow notwithstanding.

"I know you set great store by such things, Miss Daphne. I admire you for it, I do. And I meant nothing but admiration for the lady. Deuced attractive female."

"Every man seems to find her so." Thinking of her as Graydon's mistress, in his arms, in his bed, made Daphne push her own cucumber sandwich aside.

Echoing her thoughts, Miles mused, "Don't suppose she's the type of female a man takes to be his wife, though."

"No, not a man like you, Miles. You deserve someone better, someone who would be happy in the country, raising dogs and children and roses. I don't think Lady Seline is cut out for such a life. She prefers London, the gossip and gambling and grand social events."

"Dashed expensive female, I guess."

Daphne pictured those diamonds around the widow's graceful neck. "Very."

Miles managed to take a bite of his buttered bread. "I don't suppose you'll reconsider? I mean, there's no reason to rush into a decision."

Daphne shook her head. "No, I shan't change my mind."

He saw how her eyes slid away, following Howell's movements. "So that's the way the wind blows, eh? Not surprised; Mama told me that's the way it's always been. I'd hoped . . . But there, enough said." He finished that piece of bread and reached for another, thinking of Admiral Benbow's unmarried niece. "Well, here's a piece of advice for you, then, my dear. Go ahead and take him. We're none of us perfect."

"No, no, you mistake the matter. We're just friends. How Major Howell chooses to live his life has nothing to do with me anymore, thank goodness."

Miles simply snorted and took his plate, now heavily laden since his future was once again clear, to the other side of the room to discuss a point of law with Mr. Rosten.

Graydon took Pomeroy's place at Daphne's side. "Deuce take it," he said as he accepted a cup of tea from her, "I can't take my eyes off you for ten minutes without you getting into a scrape."

"I don't know what you're talking about. Miles and I parted on the best of terms. There was no scrape."

"No? Then how come mealymouthed Miles left your side while there were still lemon tarts, hm? What, did he propose marriage again now that you are tied to another fortune?"

"That's none of your business, Graydon Howell!" But her blush gave her away. And Miles hadn't exactly brought the matter up this afternoon, she had.

He reached for a lemon tart and grinned. "Devil a bit, brat. Of course it's my business. We're partners in crime, don't you know."

"Yes, and I never thanked you properly for all you did."

"Fustian. You know you can count on me, don't

you, Daffy?" His face had gone serious, intent, his eyes trying to read her innermost emotions. She wasn't ready to let him see them, not sure of his feelings.

"Still, I don't know what I would have done without you."

"Likely married that prig Pomeroy."

He was right, she might have wed Miles if Graydon hadn't returned to remind her what it meant to love someone so deeply that you were almost—almost—ready to chance being hurt again and again, rather than let him walk out of your life another time. But he hadn't mentioned staying, now that the wedding and funeral were over. He hadn't mentioned anything but friendship.

Lest he see the moisture in her eyes, she stared out the window. "Oh dear, it's coming on to rain. I was afraid of that when the boys went out. Torry was still pale this morning, and it wouldn't do for him to catch a chill. I better go fetch them back."

But they weren't outside. They weren't inside either. They weren't anywhere that Daphne looked. Miles grumbled about ill-bred brats, playing ball while their father was fresh in the grave, or the urn as the case may be. "Besides, you spoil them." Daphne was well pleased she'd turned down his proposal.

"Breeding has nothing to do with it," Cousin Harriet insisted when she was consulted. "It's males. Always thinking of themselves and their own pleasure, not giving a rap for anyone else's fretting."

"They're only boys, Cousin. It's not like they've gone out on the town and forgotten the time. Most likely they decided to go visiting and they're taking

shelter with one of the tenants until the rain ends."
She tried not to let her worry show. They weren't
infants, but there had been criminals in the neighborhood, and she'd made them promise not to leave
the grounds.

Graydon patted her shoulder. "I'll give the
scamps an hour, then I'll go look for them. And I'll
give them a piece of my mind, too."

Lady Seline drifted past on her way to the carriage Mr. Foggarty had sent for her. She agreed to
ask the coachman to keep his eyes peeled for the
boys. "That's what comes of letting the beastly
creatures away from their tutors and nannies," she
said on her way out. "That's why they invented
boarding schools."

The hour went by and still Torry and Dart did not
come home. Daphne was thinking of giving the
wretches more than a piece of her mind when she
got her hands on them. Why did they have to disappear today of all days, with Mr. Rosten here? What
if he thought they weren't well supervised? He had
the authority to take them away entirely.

She wanted to ride out with Graydon, but he convinced her she'd do better waiting at home.
"There's no need for both of us to get wet when
they'll be straggling in any minute, needing dry
clothes and hot tea."

Miles went out, too, but with poor grace. "There's
no need to get in a fidge. Boys are always getting
up to mischief." He never had, but he wasn't one of
these wild Whiltons.

Miles and Graydon returned some time later,
cold and wet, and without the boys. "We'll change
horses and ride out again," Graydon told Daphne.
"And send the stable hands out with lanterns."

Darkness was falling. Torry and Dart should have been home ages ago, raining or not.

"Something's happened. I know it."

Gray didn't try to make light of her worries, he just put his arms around her, damp clothes and all. "We'll find them."

Then a window shattered. Amid the broken glass was a rock, with a note tied around it, a ransom note.

"Confound it," Miles swore. "Those Gypsies took them! I knew I should have run them off when I had the chance. Don't worry, Miss Daphne, I'll track them down. They can't have gone far with those slow wagons. Are you coming, Howell?"

Graydon was studying the note, which demanded the ransom money be placed near a crossroads halfway to London. "No, I believe not. I'll head in another direction, I think."

"Toward a warm fire, I suppose," Miles said with a sneer. He hadn't missed that cozy embrace. "I'll rouse up the sheriff and his men, miss. We'll get your cousins back before you have to lay out a shilling."

After he left, Daphne told Gray, "I'm going with you."

"And where is it we are going, my love?"

This wasn't the time to relish endearments. "After Terwent, of course. Gypsies don't steal children."

The major agreed. "Certainly not adolescent boys. They're more trouble than they are worth. No, it has to be Terwent. He was angry enough to pull a fool stunt like this, and he knows you'd do anything to get the boys back."

"Do you think he's taken them to London, then? They'll be hard to find."

"I think that if he were on his way to London, we'd have received this note by messenger or post, tomorrow or later. No, I think he must be right in the neighborhood, close enough to throw the rock himself."

"The old woodsman's cottage? He was with us when they dug up that body there. Do you think he'd be able to find his way back?"

There was only one way to find out, so they set off on horseback, with the pistols Ohlman had primed and ready.

Terwent had no intention of staying anywhere near Woodhill, not with his precious cargo. But he only had an open carriage, and two trussed boys were a bit of a giveaway on the open road. And it was raining. Even worse, one of the boys, the younger, was turning green and threatening to cast up his accounts. Terwent revised his plans.

That old tumbledown cottage was deep enough in the woods to be safe for one night. Once he'd sent his message, Terwent had only to wait until daylight, then head to the delivery place by himself. Unencumbered, he could pick up the ransom money and disappear into London's back alleys without any plaguey brats to watch over. Yes, this was a better plan.

Terwent decided he'd wait a day before sending a note telling the miserly solicitor where to find the devil's spawn. Maybe two. If the brats had an uncomfortable time of it before someone thought to look for them, well, Terwent had suffered enough in their father's service.

He made the older boy get down and lead the horse into the woods. A pistol to his brother's head bought Dart's compliance. "And I know the way, so don't be getting up to any tricks like your double-dealing father would pull."

At the cottage Terwent tied the boys' hands and feet with strips of torn shirts from his—the baron's—luggage. He could buy new ones tomorrow. Then he secured the boys to piles of fallen roof beams. They weren't going anywhere. The valet hefted a good-sized rock. He was.

# Chapter Twenty-six

$\mathscr{I}$t was raining and they were hurt. Like whipped dogs, Sailor and Handy crawled back to the only shelter they'd known, that old hut in the woods. By the time they got close, after a few false turns, they were scratched from sticker bushes, sopping from falling into streams, and hungry.

And it was dark.

An eerie sound was coming from the area they knew the cottage to be, a moaning, crying sound.

"It's the wind in the trees." There wasn't any wind.

"It's water running off the rocks." There were no nearby brooks.

"It's him!" they both screamed at once, jumping into each other's arms.

"It's him," Handy squeaked, "come back to haunt us for gettin' his ashes all arsy-tarsy."

Sailor pushed him away. "What if it ain't that deader after all? What if it's Jake, come back to rail at us a'cause we lost the loot?"

"I told you not to step on his grave, you lummox!"

"Well, I ain't goin' in there."

"*I* ain't goin' in there neither."

Sal went in. She pushed past the brothers and bounded through the cottage's gaping door, then barked excitedly. Sailor and Handy heard someone say, "Good dog! Have you brought a search party? We'll get you a steak if you go for help."

Steak? Sailor and Handy went in. They saw two boys, not much younger than themselves, tied to beams. What Dart and Torry saw was much more frightening: two bloody, swollen-faced trolls come to make a meal of them. Dart screamed. Torry blubbered. Sal barked.

Sailor and Handy looked at each other and grinned. Someone was afraid of them! They started to untie the boys, using the pearl-handled knife to cut some of the knots, and asked what happened to them.

Reassured, Dart started to explain about a valet gone amok. If there was anything in this world Sailor and Handy understood, it was muck. Then the Whilton brothers wanted to know what had happened to their rescuers, to leave them in such conditions. Sailor didn't mention the wedding gifts, only the bridle culls on the road, all fifteen of them. They all agreed the world was a dangerous place.

The heirs to Woodhill Manor and the bastards from London's back alleys were soon fast friends. They had a lot in common: they were all orphans, and they were all hungry.

"I'm sure Daphne'll give you a reward for helping us get back home," Dart offered. "She's a great gun."

Sailor wasn't keen on going back to the Manor.

Even looking like a cart had rolled over them, he and Handy were too identifiable.

Torry was thinking. "I'll bet she'd pay you double if you help us catch Terwent. Otherwise he might just snabble us again for the ransom money."

That made sense to Sailor and Handy. Double was worth the risk. And the more grateful this Miss Daphne might be, the less likely she'd be to ask questions. So they were going to catch Terwent. No problem. There were four of them, weren't there?

But he had the gun. While the four youngsters were arguing how to plot the perfect ambush, there not being a lot of hiding places in a one-room, roofless cottage, Terwent snuck up on them and cocked his pistol.

"Which of you bastards wants to be first?"

Neither of the bastards volunteered, nor the sprigs of nobility either. No one moved while Terwent tried to decide what to do with this latest complication. No one was going to ransom these dregs of society, that was for sure. Just when he was figuring the easiest way of disposing of their bodies, Sal got tired of waiting for her steak. She went for his arm. Terwent went down. Sailor started bashing him with the silver candlestick, and Handy used the gold pickle fork on Terwent's flailing legs. Torry and Dart dove into the battle. The gun went off, hitting one of the few remaining rafters, which collapsed around them.

That's when Graydon and Daphne rushed into the cottage, pistols drawn, breath coming in gasps.

"What the devil is going on?" The major handed Daphne his pistol and started pulling beams away. He hauled Torry up, then Dart. Both seemed all

255

right. Sailor was next. Graydon thought he recognized the heavyset youth from the stables under the blood and grime; Daphne was sure she recognized the candlestick. Handy crawled out from under a board, looking like the whole house had landed on him, not just one rotten log. "Who the hell . . . ?"

"They saved us, Daffy!" Both of her cousins were jumping up and down, shouting. "And we promised them a reward. You'll pay, won't you, Daff? We swore, word of a Whilton. Maybe we could find them jobs."

"I think they've already had jobs with us."

Graydon had finally uncovered Terwent, unconscious and like to remain so for a while. He started to tie up the valet with strips of linen Sailor handed him. One whiff of the lad convinced Graydon this was indeed the stableboy.

Handy was backing out the door, sure the jig was up. Daphne aimed one of the pistols at him.

"But Terwent would have killed us if it weren't for Sailor and Handy!" Torry claimed. "He said so!"

Daphne lowered the gun. What were a few candlesticks to her cousins' lives?

Graydon put both pistols in the pocket of his greatcoat and studied the heroic twosome. "I think your brave friends deserve more than jobs. And somehow I don't think they'd hold on to any reward money for long. No, a hot bath and a good meal, for sure, but then perhaps a change of scenery might suit them."

"Gorblimey, you ain't goin' to send us to gaol, is you?"

Torry and Dart and Daphne all protested, Daphne loudest of all, the waifs looked so pitiful.

"No, I was thinking more of finding you places on one of my family's shipping ventures. A little hard work, and then a new life in the New World. How does that sound?"

Sailor was thrilled. "I always wanted to go to sea!"

Handy wasn't. "I always wanted to marry a rich woman," he confessed.

Daphne couldn't see anything to appeal to anyone under those hideous bruises, but she wasn't going to spoil the boy's dreams. "Anything is possible in the colonies, I hear."

"Meantime you might like being a cabin boy. You'll have months to decide," Graydon told him.

Months when they couldn't get into any trouble that affected him, thank goodness.

When they got back to the house, Dart and Torry were taken off by their tutor and Cousin Harriet, and Sailor and Handy were taken in tow by Ohlman and Mrs. Binder, after a lecture on ethics of which the brothers understood two words out of five. Once they were clean and fed and bandaged, Mr. Rosten would see to their futures, far away from Woodhill Manor.

Miles appeared shortly after, ecstatic with his success. He hadn't found the boys—"I said they'd get home all right, didn't I?"—but he had managed to foil a highway robbery, and recover Lady Whilton's stolen wedding gifts. That should put an end once and for all to those London thugs' disrespect for country justice.

He and the sheriff and every able-bodied man in the village had set off after the Gypsies. Instead, they came upon Pop Bullitt's gang, which was in the process of holding up Foggarty's coach, which was bringing Lady Bowles home. Mr. Foggarty was keeping the widow company inside the carriage, such good company that they were not aware of either the holdup or the rescue. The first they knew of danger, in fact, was when Miles threw open the carriage door and shouted, "You are safe, Lady Bowles."

Her skirts up, his breeches down, they'd never doubted it for a moment. And Admiral Benbow's niece was looking prettier by the minute to Miles, even if she did have a squint.

His minions took the red-handed rapscallions into the local gaol, and Miles came along to return the stolen goods. He was delighted to take Terwent in custody once he'd heard the whole, except for the parts about Sailor and Handy and the candlestick and the pickle fork and the ghosts. Daphne saw no reason to muddle the case, when Miles was so satisfied. Why, his corner of the county was so lawabiding now, Miles was claiming, he might take time for a jaunt to London, give the fellows there some pointers. Graydon agreed that might be a good idea.

Lady Bowles sailed in, and out again as soon as her bags were packed. Dear Foggarty was taking her to look at some property in Suffolk he was thinking of purchasing. He wanted her opinion, and la, they all knew what that meant. Daphne naively suggested it meant he wanted her opinion, but Graydon privately thought it meant Foggarty wanted a cozy armful for the weekend. He wished them both good luck, and good riddance.

They were all gone, every last one of the distractions, interruptions, and inconveniences. There were no weddings, funerals, robberies, or kidnappings to stop Graydon Howell from saying what he'd been waiting two years to say. There was only a lump in his throat the size of Gibraltar.

He poured himself a glass of wine, but put it down. He needed a clear head if he wasn't going to make a mull of the thing this time, not Dutch courage. "Daffy, I—"

"You were magnificent!"

She was sitting on the sofa, wearing a look he hadn't seen on her face since she was seventeen, when he'd rescued her kitten from a tree. Of course, he didn't deserve her admiration tonight. "Gammon, the youngsters had already saved themselves. I didn't do anything."

"Oh, I don't mean that, although you did look quite the hero, windblown hair, pistol at the ready. Scott could write a poem about you. What I meant was so magnificent, though, was how you didn't quibble about taking me along, how you handed me a gun, and how you let me decide how much to tell Miles. You didn't come the toplofty nobleman or the commanding officer even once."

"Pomeroy would have had seven kinds of fits, wouldn't he?"

"Eight. He'd never show me the respect of treating me like an equal."

"Is that what I did, treat you like one of the boys? Lud, Daffy, that's the last thing I wanted to do!"

And then, without so much as a by-your-leave, Graydon showed her what he *did* want to do, what he had been waiting all these months to do. He took her in his arms and kissed her till her knees turned to water and her blood turned to fire and her brain turned to mush from his touch—and lack of air.

Graydon forced his arms away. "No, I am going to do this right, which I suppose means that I cannot demand you marry me, or insist you have to after that, ah, demonstration of affection. You do love me, Daffy, don't you?"

"I thought we were just friends," she said, enjoying herself hugely now.

"Friends! You don't go around kissing your friends that way, brat. No, you love me," he said with assurance she could resent, but couldn't deny. "That kiss only proved it. You always have, but I wasn't worth it. And I never even knew how much it meant until you stopped."

"I never stopped, silly."

"But I didn't deserve your love, or you, Daffy. You were the best thing in my life, the only thing, and I didn't know it till it was too late. Then I tried to make you proud of me, tried to become someone you could admire. If I live to be a hundred, Daffy, I'll keep trying, but don't make me wait that long, sweetheart, please?"

"Please . . . ?"

He dropped to the floor at her feet. "One knee doesn't bend all that well." Then he took both her hands in his and stared up at her. "Please, Daffy, please say you'll marry me and truly make me the happiest of men."

Oh, how she wanted to say yes. But. "But what about the other women? I just couldn't bear it, Gray, if I had to share you."

"No other woman meant anything to me, sweetheart, and there will never be another one. I can't swear that my eyes will never wander—even if a fellow owns the finest Thoroughbred, he can't help admiring a fancy piece of blood and bone—but my body will never follow because my heart won't let it. I swear. And you don't have to be dull as ditchwater to be honest. Here."

Graydon reached into his pocket and retrieved a flat box. He opened it to show a necklace of perfect sapphires, with a diamond heart pendant in the middle.

"Good grief, that's even finer than Lady Seline's diamonds! It's a gift for a mistress, Gray!"

"I know." He lifted the necklace and handed her a folded paper. On the paper was written *You are my mistress. The mistress of my heart.*

Graydon raised the necklace and put it around her neck, where it looked absurd on the high-collared black gown, so he solemnly undid the collar, button by button. "The sapphires match your eyes, only they're not as beautiful."

There were tears in those eyes. "Oh, Gray, I have waited so long."

"Too long." He reached into another pocket and withdrew an official-looking document. "I ordered a special license when I sent for the necklace. Say you'll marry me, Daffy, and we can get the vicar here tomorrow."

"What, marry without Mama? I couldn't do that!"

"She said she'd be thrilled. I asked before they left. And I asked my father, too, in case you're thinking he's head of your household. He said it was about time. I'll ask Dart tomorrow if you want, since he's Baron Woodhill now, but he can't refuse my request, not if he wants to learn to drive my chestnuts."

Daphne pretended to frown, though her heart was smiling. "That's getting very autocratic of you.

You're not going to be dictatorial and overbearing like your father, are you?"

He kissed her nose. "You're not going to be high-strung and temperamental like your mother, are you?"

"No, I mean to keep my pistol loaded."

"We can do better than that, sweetheart. Let me show you." And he did, in a way that erased the last doubts Daphne ever had. Neither one of them might be perfect, but they'd have a perfect life together.

"Hmm," he purred some indecent time later. "Remember when you said you wouldn't marry me if I were the last man on earth?"

"I lied. But you are, for me. The first, last, and always."

"I love you, Daffy."

"And I love you. Just don't call me Daffy."

He unbuttoned another button.

Ohlman shut the door.

# Love and romance from
# Barbara Metzger

 Available in bookstores everywhere.
Published by Fawcett Books.